The Merchant's Daughter

A Jayne Sinclair Genealogical Mystery

M. J. Lee

About M. J. Lee

Martin Lee is the author of contemporary and historical crime novels. *The Merchant's Daughter* is the seventh book featuring genealogical investigator, Jayne Sinclair.

The Jayne Sinclair Series

The Irish Inheritance

The Somme Legacy

The American Candidate

The Vanished Child

The Lost Christmas

The Sinclair Betrayal

The Inspector Danilov Series

Death in Shanghai

City of Shadows

The Murder Game

The Killing Time

The Inspector Thomas Ridpath thrillers

Where the Truth Lies

Where the Dead Fall

Where the Silence Calls

Other Fiction

Samuel Pepys and the Stolen Diary

The Fall

CHAPTER ONE

July 05, 1842
Wickham Hall, Cheshire

Last night, Emily Roylance dreamt she was in Barbados again. The waving palms, the songs of the slaves as they cut the sugar cane, the breeze fresh off the ocean, the tang of the sea floating in the air. It was as if she was there, back on the estate, sleeping in the arms of her nanny.

And then she woke up.

At first she was disoriented, still unsure whether she was dreaming or awake, but the creaking of the old timbers reminded her all too quickly that she was still in the house she hated from the bottom of her soul.

On the landing, the clock sounded the hours. She counted each strike to make sure she had the right time. Four o'clock in the morning.

Outside her window the first rays of dawn were fighting to creep over the trees that lined the drive.

She rose quickly, listening to the house.

There was no movement.

She crossed over to her desk and pulled out the notebook she had secreted in the back of one of the mahogany drawers, buried beneath her cotton nightdresses.

She opened the first page. The paper was virgin white, not touched by pen or human hand. She dipped her pen in the ink and wrote as elegantly as she could the first words.

An Account of the Life of Emily Roylance

The words lay on the page, frightening in their simplicity. Should she continue, or should she cease immediately before her brother and his wife discovered what she was doing?

She sat there for a moment in the early morning light, transfixed with indecision.

Was this the right course to take?

She had made the decision to write the story of her life in one of those rare moments of lucidity when the influence of the laudanum was no longer clouding her brain.

For the last week, she had been pouring the medicine prepared by Dr Lansdowne into the flower beds outside her window. She hoped the hollyhock would survive its daily dose of the soporific.

Now she felt clear enough to begin writing. A narrative that she would work on in the early hours of the morning, when the house was still and before the servants rose to light the fires and prepare breakfast.

In this account of her life, she had no intention to shock or discomfit whoever might, by some misfortune, discover this book. On the contrary, she hoped that nobody would ever read the unfortunate events that had blighted her life and placed her in the position she now found herself; a prisoner in a gilded cage.

The passing of Mrs Harriet Wilson, the author of the celebrated memoirs of her life as a courtesan, in the spring of the previous year, reminded her that time's wing'd chariot was for ever hurrying near. There was one thing of which she was sure: death would come to her soon. It was not an event that saddened her, rather, she welcomed it with open arms.

So it was with no small trepidation that she seized the moment to write her history. A moment when the usual fog of her existence cleared for a brief time and she could see what had happened and why it took place as it did.

If her brother discovered the words written here, no reader would ever contemplate her predicament or her downfall.

He would not appreciate the truths written in these pages, obsessed as he was in creating those stout, high walls that served to obscure their family origins and defend their name.

She understood and accepted that possibility, for these words were not written to be read but to provide insight to herself. It was as if, by describing all that had happened to her, she could somehow make sense of it, give it a wholeness that was so obviously lacking at the time the events took place. A life that should have been blessed with eternal sunshine, given the advantages of both her class and her fortune.

But a life that was shadowed from the beginning by a secret so devastating that, should it be revealed, would destroy her family in the eyes of polite society. A society that had become even more polite since the accession of the young queen to the throne and the arrival of her consort Albert from Germany.

The riotous and carefree days of the Prince Regent in the year she was born had given way to the more formal and hypocritical society of today. A modern society given to the worship of money and things material to the detriment of a basic civility and tolerance.

She picked up the pen and began to write.

My name is Emily Roylance and I was born on March 4, 1806; the daughter of Jeremiah Roylance, merchant, and Dolores Sharpe, spinster, on the Perseverance Estate on the island of Barbados. My brother Henry and I lived in the big house surrounded by fields of cane and were indulged by the servants and the slaves that my father possessed in abundance. It was an idyllic childhood where my every whim was encouraged and satisfied, with the word 'no' never passing my mother's lips.

My father was rarely seen. He was either working with the estate overseers, at his office in Bridgetown, or on one of his many trips back to Liverpool to settle his business affairs and sell the rum, sugar, molasses and other goods we produced on the estate in such abundance.

Mother, on the other hand, was a gay presence, always laughing and happy except when Father was at home, and then she became as quiet as the cane on a still day - passive and powerless, meek, charming, and submissive.

This heaven on earth, this Eden, was shattered one day in 1816 when I was but ten years old...

Outside her room, she heard a noise. The pen froze in its position above the paper, a drop of ink slowly falling from the sharpened nib.

Was somebody there?

Was somebody spying on her?

Then, the soft voices of the maids calling to each other down the corridor, followed by the padding of feet as other servants carried nightsoil from the rooms to the privies.

She dried the ink with a quick dusting of powder and closed the book. She would write more tomorrow night, but now it was time to stop and return to her bed to pretend to be asleep.

Placing the book back in its secret place, she crept back to the bed and crawled beneath the covers.

She had so much to recount, she hoped her brother would not discover the book before she finished her tale.

CHAPTER TWO

Wednesday, August 14, 2019
Harboro Television Studios, Manchester

The TV host, Danielle Hurst, held up a golden envelope. 'I have your *Where Do You Come From?* DNA results here in my hand. Are you excited, Rachel?'

'Can't wait to hear about them. Am I Anglo-Saxon? Welsh? Do I have a little bit of Viking in me?'

'We'd all like a little bit of Viking in us.' The host gurned towards the camera as the audience laughed at the risqué joke.

'But we're not going to reveal the results yet…'

The audience groaned as she dramatically hid the envelope behind her back.

'Let's talk a little about you first, shall we? Rachel Marlowe — you're famous for playing costume roles?'

'I do seem to have spent my life laced up tightly in a corset. It's the price an actress must pay to play the part.'

A quiet laugh from the audience at her self-deprecating humour.

'Lady Anne in *To Have and Have Not*. Catherine de Braganza in *Charles II…*'

'Dealing with his many mistresses…'

'And the fabulously aristocratic Diana Manners, in *The Coterie*, the BAFTA Award-winning production of British upper-class life in the years between the wars.'

'It was a wonderful part and she was an amazing woman to play.'

'Her life is not dissimilar to yours, is it not?'

'I don't think so. She was much posher than I am.'

'Didn't you grow up on a family estate in Cheshire, Wickham Hall?' A picture of an elegant Georgian building flashed up on the screen behind Rachel's head.

'I was very lucky. It was a wonderful childhood, full of activity, horses, dressing up and messing around. Daddy worked hard but Mummy was always there for myself and my brother.'

'You then went to Cheltenham Ladies' College. Very posh.' Again, a raised eyebrow directed at the camera and the millions watching on television from the comfort of their homes.

Rachel brushed back the dark fringe that covered one eye. 'It was a bit posh, but good fun and I loved my friends at school. Didn't learn much, though, I was one of those who wasn't terribly academic.'

'When did you first discover you wanted to have a career as an actress?'

'I've always known, ever since I was a child. My brother and I—'

'See, coming from a council estate in Southwark, I would have said "me and me bruvver"…'

The audience laughed again.

'We've both come a long way, haven't we?'

The audience laughed and a black studio manager waved his hands to encourage them to clap.

'Anyway,' continued Rachel after the applause had died down, 'as I was saying, my brother and I used to dress up and put on shows together for an audience of two - Mother and the cook. Cook was always complaining that she had to attend so many shows there was no time to make lunch.'

'And then RADA?'

A picture of a fresh-faced young ingénue surrounded by other equally enthusiastic students appeared on the screen.

Rachel looked up at it. 'No tight Gucci dresses for me then. The Royal Academy for Dramatic Arts was wonderful. It opened my eyes to the possibilities of acting. How to replicate another person, become them rather than remaining oneself. To hide your own personality in a part.'

'And you've never looked back?'

'I was lucky in my second year to audition for a part in the *Casanova* film and even luckier to get it.'

'Who can forget that outrageous dress?' An image of a beautiful woman spilling out of her dress appeared on the screen behind them. Danielle Hurst winked at the camera. 'Old Casanova didn't stand a chance, did he?'

'Not much, no,' Rachel said, self-deprecatingly. 'It was a bit revealing.'

'Revealing? I could see the freckles on your tummy through the material.'

'It was a wee bit tight. You know, I had to wriggle into it each day before the shoot.'

'No underwear then?'

'There was no room…'

Loud laughter from the audience.

'I mean, there wasn't even space for me to eat.'

'The sacrifices an actress has to make for her art.'

More laughter from the audience.

The host pulled the golden envelope back out from behind her back. 'But enough of your dresses, it's time for your results.'

A collective intake of breath from the audience.

'And we will get to them when *Where Do You Come From?* returns after the break.'

The audience applauded and cheered as the title card for the show appeared on the screen behind them. The floor manager stepped forward. 'And we're out. Relax, everybody. We'll start filming again in three.'

A make-up artist rushed forward to Danielle Hurst's side. As the woman dabbed the sweat off the host's brow and added a fresh coat of powder, the host leant forward and touched Rachel Marlowe's arm. 'Sorry about the breaks, but we like to have the feel of a live show even though everything is recorded. We'll splice in the film of you walking through your estate and in the local pub in editing.'

'How do you think it's going?'

'It's going great, the joke we rehearsed worked rather well, didn't it?'

'You think so? I'm so glad. I'm always so nervous on these chat shows. I was on Graham Norton last week, promoting *To Have and Have Not*, and I was so scared I wasn't going to be funny like all his other guests. Luckily, Tom Hanks was on the couch too. Now he is a true gentleman.'

'It's nerve wracking, isn't it? But don't worry, the audience here loves you. And I think you'll be surprised by the DNA results. They are *very* interesting…'

'Really? Sounds wonderful.'

The floor manager stepped in front of them. 'Taping again in thirty seconds, Danielle.'

The make-up artist rushed off the podium. Danielle Hurst checked her face in the monitor. Rachel Marlowe pulled her dress down over her knees and casually wiped the tips of her Louboutins, ensuring her legs were gracefully stretched out in front of her so they could be picked up by the camera.

'Three - two - one.' The floor manager counted down, folding down a finger with each number.

A broad smile instantly leapt on to Danielle's face and her voice was charged with enthusiasm. 'Welcome back to *Where Do You Come From?* – the celebrity chat show with a difference. We talk with the stars, look at their lives; where they were born and brought up, and how they live today. But we also perform a DNA test to show the real person behind the celebrity. Who were their ancestors and where did they come from? Maybe we'll even find some long-lost cousins they never knew existed. Tonight we have with us the gorgeous, beautiful and talented Rachel Marlowe, star of stage and screen.'

The audience erupted in a chorus of cheers and hollering, egged on by the floor manager.

Rachel smiled and waved at the audience.

Danielle held up the golden envelope. 'Excited, Rachel?'

'I can't wait.'

The audience went quiet. A soft drum roll was played off stage. The lights dimmed and a spotlight shone on Danielle and her guest.

'Feels like the Oscars, doesn't it?'

'I can hope…' said Rachel.

The audience laughed dutifully.

'This is the bit I like best,' said Danielle, ripping the envelope violently open. From inside, she took out a single sheet of paper.

On the monitor, the camera cut from a close-up of Rachel's face waiting expectantly, to a close-up of the sheet of paper, to a tight shot of Danielle reading the results, and finally back to Rachel, biting her bottom lip and curling her thick, dark hair around her finger.

'Rachel Marlowe, I can reveal the results of your DNA test are…' The drum roll increased in intensity, the audience was stilled. 'That you are 56% Anglo-Saxon, 28% Irish, 10% Viking – there's that little bit of Viking you wanted inside you – and finally, and most interestingly, you are 6% African, specifically the area around present-day Ghana.'

CHAPTER THREE

Wednesday, August 14, 2019
Harboro Television Studios, Manchester

'What?' Rachel Marlowe's mouth opened wide. 'What did you say? Ghana? You mean from Africa? African?'

'Well, according to our results you have an ancestor born in the area we now know as Ghana. How do you feel?'

'I'm shocked… I mean, pleasantly shocked.' Rachel quickly recovered and went into actress mode. 'I always thought I was so classically English. You know – upturned nose, peaches and cream complexion. And now to suddenly find out part of me is from Africa. I'm… shocked. Pleased, of course, because it adds another level to my own history. But I never expected that part of me comes from Africa.'

'You even have a long-lost cousin in our crew.'

'Really?' Rachel's eyes shone with excitement.

'It's Mike, and he's your cousin six times removed.'

The camera quickly panned round to the floor manager, who smiled shyly and gave a little wave.

'Mike, where were you born?' asked Danielle.

'In Manchester, but my dad is from Ghana.'

Rachel Marlowe pointed at the floor manager. 'He's my cousin?'

'Sixth cousin to be more precise. So that means he's related to your great-great-great-great-grandfather.' Danielle counted off her fingers as she spoke the words.

'Really?' Emily's mouth opened wide, but the actress within her quickly recovered her poise. 'That's amazing. Hi, cousin.' She waved to the floor manager.

'Here's our resident guru, Professor Syrus Jacobs, to explain the results to you.'

On the screen behind them, a man wearing a bright green cravat and a Panama hat appeared. His nose and cheeks were irrigated by faint red veins, like a satellite picture of a river delta. His voice was rich and musical as he began speaking.

'These are fascinating results, Rachel, most interesting. As I have said many times, the DNA results for the Anglo-Saxon and Irish heritages are not peculiar given that your family comes from the north-west of England and the waves of migration that have flowed through the region in the past. Viking, or Scandinavian, is less common in that area. You find it more often in Cumbria, around the Lake District, Yorkshire and towards Newcastle. And obviously, it's even more common the further north one travels, with the Outer Hebrides showing people with a very high percentage of Viking heritage.'

He took a breath. 'Again, a function of the centuries' of invasion by the Vikings before their eventual assimilation into Anglo-Saxon society by the tenth century.' Here, he paused a moment and scratched the end of his large nose. 'What is fascinating is the African DNA result…'

'Yes, Professor, but what does it mean?' The TV host overacted her sigh and gurned towards the camera, producing a dutiful laugh from the audience.

'It means that one of Miss Marlowe's ancestors in the not-too-distant past was an African from the Gold Coast, in particular, the area of present-day Ghana. From the result, we can postulate that one of her ancestors was a member of the Ashanti tribe. Interestingly, the Ashantis are one of the few ethnic groups where lineage is traced through the mother and the maternal ancestors...'

'And so they should. Thank you, Professor Jacobs.' Danielle Hurst cut him off just as he was about to explain the complexities of matrilineal ancestry. She turned towards her guest. 'How do you feel about this news, Rachel?'

The actress had recovered from her shock by now. 'It's amazing, isn't it? Somewhere I could have African relations that I know nothing about.'

'What are you going to do next?'

Rachel Marlowe smiled at the camera. 'I'm going to find out all about them.'

CHAPTER FOUR

Friday, August 16, 2019
Didsbury, Manchester

Jayne Sinclair was tired. It had been a long day driving to Buxton to see her father and stepmother, fighting constantly with the traffic on the A6. At one point, she had been so frustrated at an old driver dawdling along at 20 mph in a 40 mph zone, she had banged on her horn twice, urging him to hurry up.

Immediately she had realised the ridiculousness and rudeness of her behaviour. Quietly whispering a word of apology to the driver in front, she signalled left and pulled in to the kerb. Why was she so stressed? Was it the heat? Manchester was built to withstand long days of cold and drizzle, not temperatures of more than 30 degrees. Her house at night was stifling. Even Mr Smith had decided to seek shade away from his usual sleeping place beside the window in the hall.

Or perhaps it was because she had been working too hard recently. Maybe it was time for a rest. Since she had come back from her cruise with Robert and Vera at the beginning of the year, it had been non-stop, one case after another. Had the investigation into her biological father and her grandmother taken too much out of her? She thought perhaps it had. Without realising it, the stress had simply built up and she was now beeping her horn at some old bloke in a beaten-down car.

Time for a holiday. Paris? Rome? Or somewhere cooler. Iceland? She had never been to the north. Her ex-husband, Paul, had always preferred the city, or lively beaches like Ibiza for holidays, and she had always gone along. Since their separation, it was now time for her to go somewhere she wanted.

It looked like Iceland could be it.

She took three deep breaths.

Relax. You've been working too hard. Just be patient.

But patience was never a strong suit. Even when she was with the police, she was never happy on a stake-out. Sitting outside a suspect's house waiting for something to happen used to annoy the hell out of her. Even worse was sitting in a cold car with another detective grumbling about his sex life, his home life or his kids, the stench of stale coffee and even staler sandwiches accompanying every moan.

She realised this lack of patience was a major character flaw and had worked to make it better, but knew she still had a long way to go.

She took three more deep breaths and put the BMW in gear, signalling right to pull out into the traffic heading down the A6 into Stockport.

Twenty minutes later she was parking outside her home among the tree-lined streets of Didsbury. She loved this house, bought with her ex-husband as soon as they had married. And despite the marriage having gone south – more her fault than his, she felt – it was still her house, her home.

She levered her tired body out of the car's bucket seat, gathered her papers on her latest cases and walked slowly to the front door, feeling every bone in her body creak with age. A glass of wine and a good night's sleep should soon make her feel right as rain. She had only just opened the door when Mr Smith ran out from his place in the kitchen to greet her, his tail and body rubbing up against her leg.

'I know, I know, you're hungry.'

Three letters were lying in wait for her on the hall carpet. She picked them up and walked into the kitchen, followed by the cat mewing loudly.

Jayne switched on her computer to check her mail. The cat, meanwhile, continued to whine with all the insistence of somebody protesting at this cruel and heartless treatment of having no food in his bowl. How dare she not attend to his needs immediately?

She opened the fridge door and took out one of his gourmet dinners. Rabbit in a luscious sauce. 'You eat better than I do,' she said out loud to the attentive cat.

She had been talking to Mr Smith more often now. Perhaps it was the silence of living alone? Or the desire to hear the sound of a human voice, even if it was her own? Or perhaps it was simply because he seemed to understand her far more than most other human beings.

Probably the latter, she decided.

She filled his bowl to the brim and topped up his water from the sink.

Mr Smith approached the bowl cautiously, sniffing constantly, before settling down to lap up the meat and its juicy gravy.

Jayne grabbed a glass from the countertop and went back to the fridge for a nice cold New Zealand sauvignon blanc. It was one of those times when she had to be revived and resuscitated with the tart, grassy flavours of gooseberry and passion fruit that only a Marlborough wine contained.

She opened the Cloudy Bay and poured herself an extra big glass. One sip later and she was in heaven, enjoying the fruity wine as it tripped across her tongue.

Perhaps she would take a day off tomorrow. Not drive to Buxton, just stay at home with Mr Smith, reading or checking out a box set from Netflix.

She thought back to her own childhood, something she had been doing a lot over the last six months, memories flooding back at the strangest moments. The discovery that her father had, in fact, still been alive and was in prison had shaken her to her bones.

When he had died shortly after their meeting – the first since she was five years old – she had been left bereft for a long time. It was as if there was a hollow emptiness inside her. Something was missing.

She wanted to ask him so many questions. Did he remember his mother? What was growing up in Hereford like? Did he know anything about his family? Why had he married her mother? Did he love her?

Too many questions, and now, no chance of any answers. That was the problem with death; all the person's memories died with them. That's why she counselled all her clients to talk to their parents before they passed away.

She had solved the feeling of emptiness by throwing herself into work.

Too much work.

As she sat down, feeling the tartness of the sauvignon blanc circulating around her veins, she decided it *was* time for a holiday.

'So, Iceland it is then,' she said out loud. The cat looked up briefly before returning to his juicy rabbit.

She took another sip of wine. You should stop raking over the past, Jayne, it doesn't do you any good. You can't ask questions of a man who is no longer alive. The past has to remain dead and buried.

She smiled to herself. This was a ridiculous statement to make, given that her whole job was to rake over the past of her clients and discover the truth. There were still aspects of her family history she hadn't investigated. Where did the Sinclairs come from? And what about her mother's Irish family? She would do the research one day.

But not yet.

Not yet.

She picked up the wine again, noticing the letters next to the computer. All three looked official. She opened the first; it was an electricity bill. Her jaw dropped at the amount they were demanding. How had she spent so much on bloody electricity? There was only her and the cat in the house. Had Mr Smith been switching on her electric blanket to keep himself warm during the day? She wouldn't put it past him.

She picked up the second letter. A parking fine for overstaying ten minutes in some car park, demanding £65 on pain of death. She checked the dates. She *had* parked in that car park and come back late one day. They even had a picture of the rear of the BMW with a time stamp next to it.

Another bill to pay. Damn.

The third letter was still sitting next to the computer. Should she open it? After all, bad luck does come in threes.

She reached out and pulled it towards her. The front stamped with the name 'Threlkeld and Son, Solicitors', with an address in the centre of Manchester.

What had she done wrong now?

The paper stock was very fine and had that lovely smell that belonged to all good writing paper. She pulled out the document inside, seeing the headline immediately, typed in big, bold, black letters.

PETITION FOR DIVORCE

Jayne read the document carefully. Paul was asking for a divorce based on the irretrievable breakdown of their marriage.

Well, she couldn't argue with that. After he had been promoted to the job in Brussels, he had asked her to go with him but she had refused.

How could she leave a father with early-onset Alzheimer's disease in a nursing home in Buxton all on his own?

How could she leave her genealogy business? A company she had spent a long time setting up after she had left the police, and one which was just gaining a reputation for completing difficult genealogical investigations?

But she knew deep inside that if she really still loved Paul, she would have found a way to resolve those issues. The truth was, she didn't love him any more. He was a good man, but somehow, somewhere, they had drifted apart.

The document felt heavy in her hands even though it couldn't have weighed more than a few grams. The word 'divorce' stared back at her. She never thought of herself as a *divorcee*. What an old-fashioned word.

Did Paul want to be free now? Had he met somebody else? Or did he just want to move on with his life, creating something new without her?

Despite everything, there was still a tinge of sadness that it had come to this. But Paul was always the more pragmatic of the two of them. It was no surprise that he was making the first move. They had no children – Jayne had never felt grown-up enough to bring up a child – so the divorce should be relatively easy and uncomplicated.

She glanced at the document one more time. One sentence in particular caught her attention. 'It is hoped that an amenable and equitable distribution of the marital assets should be achieved by fair negotiation.'

What did that mean? What marital assets?

And then it struck her.

The house. The only thing of value they owned was the house. Did he want her to sell it and divide the money between them? Where would she live? Where would Mr Smith live?

The cat raised his head from his food for a moment, as if he knew she was thinking about him, then lowered it back down to begin devouring the meat once more.

Why hadn't Paul called her or at least sent her an email before applying for a divorce? She realised they hadn't spoken in more than a month. She had been so busy with her research she hadn't noticed the passing of time.

Why hadn't he called her?

Her mobile rang, rattling on the countertop as if encouraging her to answer.

This must be Paul now, ringing her to explain.

She picked it up. 'I would have thought you might call me to talk about the divorce first rather than just sending me a solicitor's letter.'

'I'm sorry. Is this Jayne Sinclair?'

A woman's voice. A well-educated woman's voice.

'Speaking. Sorry, I thought you were somebody else... I was expecting another call...' Jayne felt the end of the sentence trail into nothingness.

'I gathered that.' The voice had a smile in it. This woman was laughing at her.

'How can I help you?' Jayne said curtly.

'I believe you carry out genealogical investigations?'

'Yes, where did you hear that?'

'From my agent. She knows somebody you helped, Lord Radley. He confirmed your credentials. You made sure his line didn't die out.'

'A relative, transported to Australia. Not a difficult investigation.'

'But done under difficult circumstances, wasn't it?'

'All investigations throw up obstacles.'

'I also heard about the Hughes case. Another one of yours, I believe.'

Jayne was reminded of one of her first cases. 'Mr Hughes was adopted by an American family. He asked me to find his Irish roots.'

'Which you did, of course. Mr Hughes was very impressed.'

'How do you know him?'

'I don't, but my father does. They do business together.'

Jayne placed the divorce letter back on the counter. 'You said you had an agent?'

'I'm an actress. Rachel Marlowe. You may have heard of me. I was in *The Pallisers* and *Charles II*.'

'I'm afraid I don't watch much television. No time.'

'Oh.' The actress sounded disappointed. 'Well, I'm at the Exchange Theatre in a couple of months, *Love's Labour's Lost*, you must come and see me.'

Love's Labour's Lost. Sounds like her and Paul. 'I must. How can I help you, Miss Marlowe?'

'Please call me Rachel, or Rach if you prefer. Everybody else does.'

'How can I help you, Rachel?'

'It's rather a long story and I couldn't possibly be able to tell you over the phone. Could we meet tomorrow?'

Jayne thought about the day off she had promised herself and Mr Smith. 'I'm very busy at the moment, I don't know if I have—'

Before Jayne could finish the sentence, the woman said, 'I'll make it worth your while. Five thousand pounds if you can solve the case within the next week.'

'Why the rush, Rachel?'

'I just want to know the truth and I can't wait any longer.'

Impatient. Perhaps this woman and Jayne had something in common. 'I don't know...'

'It won't be a long meeting, and if you decide to take the case I can give you the money immediately. Plus another five thousand if you can find out the truth.'

Jayne stared at the bills on the countertop, finally fixing on the open letter from the solicitor petitioning for a divorce. She would have to hire a solicitor herself now, and that would cost money. 'I don't know. Sometimes in family history you don't discover the truth, just hit a brick wall. And besides, I don't know anything about your case. There may be no truth to discover.'

'I think there is, and if you come to San Remo tomorrow at, say, noon, I can reveal all the details.'

San Remo was a chic, expensive Italian restaurant in King Street, favoured by footballers and actresses. For some reason, the two always seemed to go arm in arm.

'You're being very mysterious, Miss Marlowe.'

'It's Rachel, and will I see you tomorrow at noon?'

Jayne stared at the bills in front of her. At least she could enjoy some good Italian food for lunch. 'See you there. How will I know who you are?'

'Oh, just tell Enrico you're meeting me. I eat there all the time.'

'See you tomorrow, Miss Marlowe.'

But the phone had already gone dead.

Rachel Marlowe *was* an impatient woman.

CHAPTER FIVE

July 05, 1842
Wickham Hall, Cheshire

Emily poured the glass of milk laced with laudanum the maid had placed on her bedside table out of the bedroom window. She was supposed to drink it before she went to sleep, but if she did, she would not wake up until late the following morning.

She took the lamp from beside her bed and put it on her writing table before searching out her hidden notebook.

She listened for a second. The house was quiet. Outside her window a nightjar chirped monotonously and, off in the distance, an owl hooted.

She took up her pen and began to write.

1816 – Perseverance Estate, Barbados

Of course, the trouble had been brewing for a long time but, obsessed as I was with my own childish amusements, I never saw it coming.

I was lying in bed after a long day, with my personal maid, Rita, lying at my feet gently snoring, but I was still awake. It being Easter Sunday, we had been to church that morning. I was wearing my new bonnet, specially bought for the occasion. Mother wasn't with us, she had decided to visit relatives in Bridgetown for the week, but I wore the pretty bonnet anyway.

Sunday School with Reverend White followed. That good man spent a long time explaining to us the inequities of the Papist celebration of Easter. I must admit I found myself yawning as he went into great detail, as I do find the Reverend's voice makes me sleepy. He speaks softly, as if the devil were hiding in the corner listening to his words.

Afterwards roast lamb was placed on the table by Cook and, of course, hot cross buns had been baked for the occasion. Mr Howard and two of the junior overseers, also from Ireland, joined us for the repast, a rare event. I tried to talk to him but I find the man sadly lacking in conversation. In particular, I found it very difficult to avoid staring at the oily juices of the lamb that seeped from his mouth and covered his whiskers.

After dinner the men remained in the dining room to drink and smoke. I was sent to bed despite my protestations that I would prefer to sit up and listen to their conversation. Father said he had never heard such insolence. As if young girls would attempt to elevate themselves to the position of listening to the thoughts of their male elders! My brother was allowed to remain, though. Obviously, hearing them was not going to damage his mind at all.

It was three hours later, around ten o'clock, and I was on the edge of falling asleep, when I heard a commotion at the front of the house. I quickly dressed in my nightgown and rushed out in my bare feet to the balcony.

A rider was on the driveway, his horse whinnying and prancing. It was Mr Davies, the overseer from the Bailey Estate, a lantern in one hand, the other desperately trying to control the excited horse. 'The blacks, they've risen up. Torched the sugar and the house.'

My father rushed out from his study where he had been going over the accounts with the housekeeper, Mrs Turner. It was a job he reserved for himself. 'Your mother hasn't a head for figures and I don't trust Turner not to cheat her.'

I always thought Father should leave such jobs to the estate manager, Mr Howard, but he would insist on doing this one himself, once a week. Usually when mother was in Bridgetown or away from the estate.

'Calm down, man,' he said to Mr Davies. 'What are you blithering about?'

The horse pranced around, sweat bubbling and frothing on its neck, Mr Davies pulling hard on the bridle. 'They've finally risen, Jeremiah, burning the Bailey Estate and killing people. Folks say the Simmons Estate and Utopia have risen too.'

I knew both places well. Sometimes I went over to play with the children at the Simmons Estate, but not often because Mother wasn't allowed to come, what with Mrs Harris not approving of her.

My brother came running out from the house, joining my father on the porch. The horse still pranced and whinnied in front of them like something from a circus.

Father thought for a moment. 'Saint Philip County is twenty miles away. Have the militia been roused?'

'Colonel Codd is collecting them and the army as we speak. The slaves are led by a ranger called Bussa. They must have been planning this for months.'

'Those fools and stupid idiots in Parliament getting their hopes up with stupid talk of emancipation and freedom, and the bloody Imperial Registry Bill.' Father spat on the ground. 'Henry,' he called out to my brother, 'take your sister inside the house and prepare yourself to ride. It's about time we made a man of you.'

'Yes, Father.' I heard a slight quiver in my brother's voice.

'Mr Howard, send a rider to Bridgetown and ask Mrs Roylance to return immediately.'

The scrawny Irishman stepped forward. 'Yes, sir. Can I ride with you, Mr Roylance? I'm right lookin' forward to some killin'.'

'No, Mr Howard, you will stay here and guard my family. Make sure no harm comes to them.'

The Irishman looked positively upset.

'Jacob... Jacob!' My father shouted the name louder as the huge black man approached, taking off his hat to reveal a domed forehead glistening with sweat.

Father stared at Jacob as the man looked down at the ground and fingered the brim of his hat nervously. Jacob was my favourite of all the slaves on the estate. He would often go down on all fours and let me climb upon his back, pretending to be a horse, whinnying, shaking his head and laughing as I rode him around the lawn.

He wasn't laughing now.

'Jacob,' my father said, staring at him, 'there is to be no tomfoolery on the estate while I am gone. Nothing is to happen to my wife or my Emily.'

Jacob glanced quickly up at me, before lowering his eyes to the ground again.

'No tomfoolery, Mr Roylance.'

'I will make an example of you and your family if anything...' My father paused for a moment, searching for the word. 'If anything untoward happens. Do you understand?'

For a moment Jacob looked up, the whites of his eyes stark against the blackness of his skin. Then he stared down at a fixed point on the ground again. 'Nothing will happen here, Mr Roylance.'

Father nodded once, then swiftly turned to my brother. 'What are you standing here for, Henry? I told you to prepare yourself to ride. Come, Mr Davies, take some food and ale with me. We must fortify ourselves before we set out to crush this rebellion. A glass with you, sir.'

The man dismounted clumsily from his excited horse.

'Mr Howard, make sure the overseers are armed, if you please.'

'Yes, sir.' Howard ran off towards the kitchen block.

I felt an arm on my shoulder. 'Come on inside, Emily.' It was my brother speaking.

'But I want to stay here and watch.'

'It's not seemly.'

'But I want to stay.'

'Father will punish me...' Henry didn't finish his sentence – he didn't have to. We both knew the consequences of disobeying Father.

Reluctantly, I turned and went inside the house.

I didn't know it then, but this was the start of the famous Bussa's rebellion. An event that shocked Barbados and polite society everywhere. It was to change my life, perhaps for the better, perhaps for the worse. I make no concessions to either, but leave it to you, reader, if you are there, to decide.

CHAPTER SIX

July 05, 1842
Wickham Hall, Cheshire

Emily lay down the pen and rubbed her eyes. Writing by oil lamp was tiring and she was no longer as strong as she used to be.

She listened to the house. Nothing stirred.

Dipping the pen in the ink again, she resumed writing, the memories of those days when she was young and innocent flooding back.

1816 – Perseverance Estate, Barbados

It was two weeks later, on April 28th, that he arrived at the estate. I had been playing with Rita, my maid, at the bottom of the lawn where the hibiscus and the wild jasmine grew and the stream flowed.

The air was still, without a breath of wind to disturb the heat. Over everything, the sweet, bitter smell of smoke still lingered from the burning of the cane fields by the rebel slaves. The fires had been put out long ago, but the aroma shrouded the land, a memory of what had happened.

Father and Henry were still away with the militia. The rebels had been defeated by Colonel Codd and his good men with great slaughter – over 200 rebels killed, or so I was told by my mother. It was in the same breath that she said, 'Don't think about these events, child. Young girls like yourself should never allow their minds to dwell on the more sordid aspects of men's work.'

Anyway, I was playing hide and seek with Rita. She was the seeker and I had decided to hide in one of the sheds on the other side of the stream. I knew I shouldn't have gone there, Mother had expressly forbade it. But Rita was very good at finding my usual hiding places and I wanted to finally beat her in the game.

I stepped through the rough grass, careful not to stain my shoes. The shed door was closed. Father occasionally used it to store tools that were used to repair the house. It also contained the trunk where he kept the whips and chains when he felt the need to chastise our slaves. But he rarely used those instruments of punishment now, preferring to leave the correction of the slaves to Mr Howard.

Father had shown me the chest once, though, saying, 'If you disobey me, Emily, I shall be forced to use this on your back.' He had been holding up a short leather handle, from which sprouted entwined ropes of cured leather, each one ending with a tip of pointed iron. He shook the whip and I jumped back with a start at the sound of the points rattling together. Then his mouth creased into a large smile and I knew he was joking, just trying to frighten me.

He placed his hand on my shoulder. 'Don't worry, Emily, nobody will ever use this on you. You are a lady, not a common slave. And one day, God willing, you will have the good fortune to marry a rich man and live in a large house. Would you like that?'

I was still staring at the whip as it rattled in his hand.

'Would you like that?' he repeated.

'Y-y-yes, Father,' I stammered as he put the whip away and closed the lid of the chest.

All these memories were playing inside my head as I approached the shed. Then there was a sound, a snuffle, from inside. Had a pig escaped and was hiding in there? Or was a wild animal trapped, unable to get out?

I thought about running back to Rita and telling her what I had heard, but she would tell Mother I had crossed the stream and then I would be in trouble.

There was another snuffle from inside the shed, louder this time, followed by the sound of something being dragged across the wooden floor. I reached for the latch and pulled the door open. The hinges creaked loudly from lack of oil. I half expected a wild pig or fox to rush past me, out into the forest and on to freedom.

Instead, in the sharp rays of light from the open door, a black man lay on the floor, a pool of blood beneath his right leg. He lifted his head towards me, resignation written all over his face. It was a look I had seen often on the faces of the field slaves of the estate; a submission to their fate, whatever it was to be.

'Are you hurt?' I asked.

His face grimaced in pain. 'A little,' he said through gritted teeth.

'I'll go and fetch Mother, she will know what to do.'

He held up his hand before I could run off. 'No, please don't. Not yet.'

I stood there watching him.

His black face was surrounded by a white beard which continued past his ears and formed a circle around his bald head. The hand he held up was cracked and deeply fissured, the skin like tanned leather. I stood there for a few moments, wondering what to do. The sun streamed down through the branches of the trees on the banks of the stream. In the distance, I could hear Rita calling my name. In front of me, the man groaned again, reaching for his leg but stopping before he touched the wound.

'What's your name?' he said.

'Emily Roylance. I'm ten years old and my father owns this estate. What's your name?'

As I spoke, I thought I saw some flash of recognition in his eyes, but then it vanished as another wave of pain washed over his face. He seemed to focus on

37

my question and answered me slowly. 'My name is King Wiltshire and I come from the Bailey Estate.'

'Are you a real King? Do you own the estate?'

I don't know why I asked that question. No black man owned land in Barbados, they just worked on it.

He shook his head, laughing and groaning at the same time. 'Not me. It's just my name, given by my massa. He thought I had a noble face.' He twisted his head to the left and right proudly, groaning as he did, and then took three deep breaths to calm himself. 'I'm a driver. I drives around to Bridgetown and all over the island. What's the name of this estate?'

'Perseverance. We have sixty-seven field slaves, twelve house slaves and three overseers. We grow cane and make rum.' I remembered my father's description of our land. 'We are the fourth biggest estate in Barbados,' I said proudly, just as my father did.

The man nodded and seemed to think over my words. 'I have been here in the past. Do you know a Mr Jacob?'

'Yes, he lives here with his wife, Ruth, and their daughters Sarah and Mary. I play with them sometimes, but my father says I shouldn't become too friendly.'

The man called King Wiltshire laughed again. Or at least I thought he laughed, but there were tears in his eyes. 'Could you ask Mr Jacob to come here?'

'I... I don't... know,' I said reluctantly.

'It would help me,' he said. 'As you can see, I'm hurt real bad.'

'How did you get hurt?'

He was silent for a moment. 'A man, he shot me.'

'Did you do something wrong?'

Again, he was silent and his eyes closed. I thought he was falling asleep when he answered again. 'No, I didn't do nothing wrong, but people won't give up what they have without a fight. Can you fetch Mr Jacob?'

'Are you a rebel?' I asked, the truth finally dawning on me.

A large drop of sweat ran from his bald head, past his nose and on to his soiled shirt. 'I just wanted my freedom. We all just wanted to be free.'

I stood there not knowing whether to scream or to run. I looked over my shoulder. Nobody was nearby. If I screamed, would Rita hear me?

'Please help me. Get Jacob...'

Those were his last words as his body slumped down on to the floor of the shed, his head hitting the wood with a thump. I could see his chest rising and falling slowly, see the blood slowly drip from the wound in his leg to the pool on the floor.

I stood there for a moment before running to the bridge across the stream, hearing my shoes thump on the wooden planks. Up the far bank and stopping at the edge of the lawn, I could see Mother walking around in the drawing room, but I went left instead, along the drive to the slave quarters.

A few of the younger children were sitting out on the bare ground, tossing wooden balls carved by their fathers to each other, chanting in a strange language. I rushed to Jacob's hut. It was empty, neither he nor his family were to be seen. But that wasn't unusual; Ruth and the children would be working in the fields in the afternoon.

I ran to the smithy, Jacob was bound to be there. Past the old slave house and out on to the main road, the smithy was the last building on the right where the smoke from its chimney wouldn't drift across to our house.

Jacob was out front, naked to the waist, hammering a red-hot piece of iron into shape on his anvil.

When he saw me, he stopped, his hammer raised level with his shoulder. 'What is it, Missy Emily?' he asked.

Between gulps of air, I managed to splutter, 'A man... in the shed.'

He put the hammer down and quenched the metal he had been working on in a bucket of water, releasing a stream of steam.

'A man in the shed, you say?'

'He wants to talk to you. An old man,' I added, by way of description as if Jacob would know what I meant.

He picked up an iron bar that was leaning against the door. 'Can you show me where he is?'

I ran ahead with Jacob following me, past the big slave house and along the lawn, across the bridge and up the bank to the shed. Jacob stayed close all the time.

When we got to the shed, the door was still open as I had left it. The old man was still lying on the floor, but now his eyes were open and he was looking straight at both of us. 'Hello, Jacob,' he said.

'Hello, Father.' Jacob put down the iron bar and knelt close to him on the floor. 'Well, you sure look like you have got yourself into a whole heap of trouble this time.'

Jacob looked down at the leg, wiping away the blood to reveal a small round hole in the centre of the thigh. He bent over to look at the back of the leg and, in the light streaming in through the door, I could see an even larger hole at the back.

'Yes, sir, you got yourself a whole heap of trouble.'

'Help me, Jacob, help me.'

Jacob looked over his shoulder at me. 'You should go now, Missy Emily. Don't tell nobody about this.'

'Not even Mother?'

'Not even your mother. It's best if she doesn't know.'

I nodded. 'Are you going to get the doctor?'

Jacob shook his head. 'Can't do that. Not for this man. You should leave now.'

I looked past Jacob at the old man lying on the wooden boards. He lifted his head slightly off the floor, the white curls covered in sweat and dirt. 'Thank you,' he said slowly, before letting his head fall back on the wood.

I turned to go, taking one last look over my shoulder as I walked away. Jacob had his powerful arms wrapped around the old man and was lifting him up to a sitting position, whispering all the time in a strange tongue. The language was the same as Rita spoke under her breath when she was angry with Mother.

Jacob had cradled the man in his powerful arms and was lifting him up. I caught the look in his eyes and I hurried down the bank and across the bridge, back to the house and my mother, to be chastised for getting my dress and shoes dirty.

The next morning I overheard Mr Howard talking to Mother.

'Jacob and his family vanished from the estate last night. I've set a search party with the dogs to look for them.'

'Why did he leave? I thought he was happy here.'

Mr Howard shrugged his shoulders. 'You can never tell with those people, sometimes they just ups and goes.'

I never saw or spoke to Jacob, or the old man, or Ruth, Sarah and Mary again. Well, that's only partially true. I did see them once more.

Mother and I had gone into Bridgetown after hearing that a new shipment of cloth from England had arrived on one of the ships. Jacob, the old man, Ruth and the children were hanging on gibbets on the road into town. Each of them had a placard round their neck with just one word written on it:

Rebel

Mother hurried me past, trying to put her body between my eyes and the corpses hanging there.

I looked anyway. Jacob's feet were bare and his body swayed in the light breeze off the harbour. The children were next to him, still wearing the ragged clothes they always wore.

I missed playing with them.

CHAPTER SEVEN

Saturday, August 17, 2019
Central Manchester, UK

Jayne was greeted at the entrance to San Remo by a beautifully coiffeured man wearing a blue suit, brown shoes and no socks. ''Ow can I help you?' His Italian accent was strong but welcoming.

She immediately flashed back to a restaurant in Umbria where she had enjoyed remarkable food delivered with style and panache. One of the happier days of her marriage to Paul.

'I'm here to meet a Miss Rachel Marlowe.'

'Rachel, she at 'er table, come with me.'

He took a menu from beneath his desk and led Jayne to a young woman sitting alone at a table staring into her phone.

Not the person Jayne was expecting at all. This woman had long dark hair, a fresh complexion, beautiful eyes, and could easily be described as petite.

As Jayne approached, the woman looked up and a broad smile crossed her face. 'Jayne Sinclair, I presume,' she said, standing up and holding out her hand.

'Rachel? Rachel Marlowe?'

'You look surprised?'

The maître d' pulled out a chair and gestured for Jayne to sit. He then placed a menu next to her table setting and retreated back to his place at the entrance to the restaurant.

Jayne recovered quickly. 'It was just that I was expecting somebody older... Your voice...'

'You mean this? *Good evening, my name is Rachel Marlowe.*' She mimicked an older, more mature woman.

'Exactly. That's how you sounded last night.'

'Sorry, my telephone voice. Years at RADA trained me to adjust my voice to match my character. On the phone, the more "mature" lady pops out. You're not the first to be surprised. As for the pictures, you'll be amazed by the miracles they can work with make-up.'

'I should know better. My years in the police trained me never to force my expectations or preconceptions on any suspect.'

'So I'm a "suspect" now, am I?' Rachel laughed.

'You know what I mean. We so often have preconceptions about the people we meet. It's important not to be influenced by them.'

'Like all actresses and models are ditzy airheads?'

'Exactly. And all policewomen are dour, humourless drudges.'

'I played a dour, humourless drudge once. It wasn't much fun.'

'On TV?'

'On stage. One of Elizabeth Gaskell's books turned into a play. Won't do that again. Shall we order?' Rachel put the menu down.

'You're not eating?'

'Oh, they know what I want. Unfortunately, a pound of fat around my tummy looks like ten tons on telly. I'm permanently on a diet – not much fun, I'm afraid. But you eat what you want. I like watching other people eat. A vicarious pleasure.'

Jayne stared at the menu and decided to indulge herself. The daily special of nduja and chestnut ravioli to start, followed by grilled branzino and a rocket salad.

As if hearing she was ready to order, the waiter came across. She gave him her order while Rachel just said, 'The usual.'

'And maybe a glass of pinot grigio?'

Jayne shook her head.

'Please have one,' Rachel urged. 'I'm going to.'

Jayne shook her head again. Work was work.

The waiter took their menus away. There was a moment's silence between them before Jayne spoke. 'Much as I am enjoying this restaurant, Rachel, you didn't ask me to come here simply for the pleasure of watching me eat.'

'You don't take many prisoners, do you, Jayne?'

'It's not one of my most likeable traits, but at least we won't spend hours beating around the bush. I'm a genealogical investigator, so I'm guessing you want me to research your family.'

Rachel smiled. 'Got it in one. In particular, I want you to research me.'

'You?'

'Let me tell you about myself...'

'You were born on July twenty-third, 1992, in the Countess of Chester Hospital. Your father is Sir Harold Marlowe, a noted financier and philanthropist. Your mother passed away when you were ten years old and you have one elder brother, David. You were educated at Cheltenham Ladies' College and won a place to study history at Trinity College Cambridge but, to the consternation of your father and brother, decided to go to the Royal Academy of Dramatic Art, graduating third in your year. Whilst at college you began acting in film and on stage, and almost immediately won the part of

Lady Hermione in the television soap opera, *To Have and Have Not.* Your pictures make you look a lot older than you do in real life, I'm afraid. Another reason I was surprised when I met you.'

Rachel grimaced. 'That's television for you, ages everybody. Did you know Ant and Dec are only twelve years old?'

'Now that doesn't surprise me one bit.' They both laughed and then Jayne continued. 'Your address is currently given as Wickham Hall near Chester, but my bet is you probably live somewhere else. I can find the address out if you like.'

Rachel smiled, this time revealing a cat-like pleasure in Jayne's answer. 'I do know where I live, thank you. But a word of warning – don't call it a soap opera. Sir Anthony Blanche, who writes the bloody thing, thinks he's creating art.'

Jayne laughed. 'I'm sorry to say I've never watched it.'

'Don't worry, it's classic upstairs-downstairs drama that sells particularly well in America for some obscure reason.' The lightness in her voice tailed away. 'You *have* researched me?'

Jayne shrugged her shoulders. 'Not really. Just a quick check with Google this morning. I like to know the people who might become my clients.'

'So you are wondering why I wanted to meet you?'

'The thought had crossed my mind. You seem to come from a wealthy, well-established family.'

'That's just it. My brother, David, would be mortified if he knew I was meeting a genealogist.'

'Why?'

'He thinks he's researched the family history all the way back to 1066.'

'William the Conqueror's time?'

Rachel nodded. 'Apparently, we are related to one of William's liege lords from Normandy who was given land in Cheshire after the Battle of Hastings.'

'But you don't think he's correct?'

'It's not that. I'm sure he's right, he's frightfully clever.'

'That's why he's standing as a Conservative candidate in the next election?'

'You *have* researched my family,' Rachel laughed. 'It's a safe seat with the incumbent retiring to the Lords. He's one of the up-and-coming young men, is my brother.'

'So what's the issue?'

Before Rachel could answer, the waiter reappeared with a salad for her and the ravioli for Jayne.

'Let's get started. I'm starving as usual. Rabbit food may help to stave off the pangs of hunger for at least seven minutes. Your pasta looks delicious.'

Jayne tucked in to the ravioli. The pasta was smooth and thin, while the chestnut filling with its spicy sausage and a hint of rosemary was to die for. She was tempted to ask for a glass of chianti to go with it.

After a few mouthfuls of salad, Rachel continued speaking. 'There's a new programme going to be broadcast next Friday. It's called *Where Do You Come From?*'

'I've heard about it. A sort of *Graham Norton Show* with DNA.'

'That's the perfect way to describe it,' Rachel said between mouthfuls of rocket. 'I'm going to be the first guest featured. My agent convinced me to do it, said it was going to be "great publicity, advance your career, take you on to a new level". You know, the usual stuff they say when they want you to do something, making it out to be the most important thing on earth. I don't know why I listen to her. We've been shooting for the last week in London, in Cheshire, on the set and at rehearsals for my new play. The final interview was shot in front of a studio audience last Wednesday.'

She paused for a moment, putting her fork full of salad leaves down on the plate. 'The results were a bit of a shock.'

Jayne stopped, her own fork laden with ravioli., just about to enter her mouth. 'What do you mean?'

Rachel reached into the Hermès Birkin sitting next to her on the banquette, pulling out a folder. 'Well, apparently I am 56% Anglo-Saxon, 22% Irish, 10% Scandinavian and 6% African from from the area around Ghana.'

Jayne shrugged her shoulders. 'I don't know how accurate those percentages are. As far as I remember they are averages from a range, not a specific number. Frankly, your results are not surprising, there are many people of mixed heritage in the UK. We are a nation of immigrants, always have been. Not as much as America, but our history has waves of immigration and settlement that are reflected in our DNA.'

'But Ghanaian? My family is part of the Cheshire hunting, shooting and fishing set. How have I got Ghanaian blood?'

'It could be an error. DNA samples are occasionally compromised.'

'The television consultant said they checked the samples. There was no error.'

'So what's the problem?'

Rachel laughed out loud, so loud the couple on the next table turned to look at them. 'You don't get it.'

Jayne frowned. 'I don't get what, Miss Marlowe?'

Rachel leaned in close. 'I want to celebrate my African background if it's there. To hold it up for the whole world to see.'

She held up two fingers. 'Two reasons. First, so I can finally escape the shackles of all these Victorian upper-class damsel-in-distress roles. I never want to see another bloody corset till the day I die.'

She leaned in closer. 'I want to play real women, Jayne – modern women with modern problems, not caricatures of the past.'

'And the second?'

She sat back on the banquette. 'A bit more selfish. I would like to see the look on the faces of my brother and his snobbish friends when they realise we actually have Ghanaian ancestry.'

CHAPTER EIGHT

July 07, 1842
Wickham Hall, Cheshire

Emily took three deep breaths to calm herself.

Her brother had just been spying on her in the library. She didn't hear him enter through the door, nor as he tiptoed silently to stand over her.

He crept in so silently as to be a ghost. A ghost come to haunt her once more. Luckily, she had already finished writing for the day and was reading the story of Mr Dickens in *Bentley's Miscellany*.

'Sister, I think we should pay a visit to Dr Lansdowne again. I notice your stocks of medicine have been depleted considerably.'

Inwardly, she prayed that none of the servants or gardeners had noticed she had been pouring the noxious concoctions into the jardinière under the library window. Dr Lansdowne was a vile man; only his supposed cures were more vile.

'Really, brother, is that necessary? I have been feeling tolerably well of late.' She affected an unconcerned manner but inside her heart was beating fit to burst.

He made that little coughing sound that always indicated he disagreed with something she had said. 'You have been spending far too much time in the library, Emily, you should get out more. I am going riding with Clara this afternoon, would you care to join us?'

Clara was his wife, a misshapen shrew of a woman, her wit as barren as her womb. Emily had thought of her as a friend when they were at school together but since her marriage to Henry, she had changed.

'No thank you, brother, I would prefer to stay indoors today.' She indicated the magazine in her hand. 'I have so much reading I need to do.'

'Too much reading will make you go blind. It is a well-known fact. I have it on the word of Dr Lansdowne himself.'

'If it is true that Dr Lansdowne does not read, brother, he must find it difficult to keep up with the latest advances in medicine.' She smiled to lessen the blow of her words.

Her brother frowned and then his face softened and he leant towards her slightly. 'You do understand I only care for your health and happiness, don't you, Emily? Dr Lansdowne is one of the most trusted medical practitioners in Liverpool.'

'Dr Lansdowne is a charlatan,' she snapped, 'a man who bleeds his patients dry of their money as he bleeds them for their humours. I have more medical knowledge in my little finger than Dr Lansdowne has in his whole body.'

Her brother looked like he had been slapped across the face by one of the whips their father had once used on their slaves. His jaw tightened and she could see him struggling to control his anger.

'Nonetheless, you will be visiting Dr Lansdowne next week,' he said. 'By your words today it is obvious that you need some more, some stronger medicine, to control your feminine outbursts. A consequence of your sex, which is understandable but not excusable.' He ended the sentence with a smile. The smile of a hyena about to prey on a wounded animal.

She couldn't bear his intolerable smugness any more, but she stayed silent, hoping he would leave her in peace.

'Clara and I will depart for London at ten a.m. on Friday and will spend three or four days there. On our return, we will ask the good doctor to visit us again to assess your condition. I bid you good day, sister.'

With that, he turned and marched out the door as if a ramrod had been surgically attached to his spine, his time with the Cheshire Yeomanry obviously serving him well. She heard his feet stomp down the corridor with all the rhythm of one of his snare drums.

Next week.

She had till next week to finish the book of her life. After that, the servants would be tasked with administering new medicine prescribed by Dr Lansdowne and her whole being would vanish in a haze of dreams and faint memories. She didn't know what was in his vile concoctions, but it affected her disastrously. Even worse, she always seemed to desire more and more and more.

It had taken her much effort and the help of Rosie, her old maid, to wean herself off the effects of the last doses. But Rosie was no longer in her employ. Sacked without a reference by her father long ago.

She had to finish her story. Because if she didn't, who would?

CHAPTER NINE

Saturday, August 17, 2019
Didsbury, Manchester

Jayne sat down in front of the computer with a glass of wine. Mr Smith had already been let out through the patio doors to wreak his wicked ways among the female cats of Didsbury, and was last seen heading straight for an assignation at number nine. Either that or another house was feeding him, offering the dessert that Jayne refused to provide.

Throughout the rest of lunch, Rachel had provided the details of what she required Jayne to do. 'I want you to find out which of my ancestors came from Africa. To prove conclusively that my background is Ghanaian. When the *Sun* and the *Daily Mail* come hunting after the programme goes out, I want to provide them with all the details to celebrate my heritage in their pages. If I don't have the information, they will speculate and guess and intrigue as they always do – or go digging for it themselves.'

'When is the programme due to be broadcast?'

'Six days from today, at eight p.m. on Friday. I'll get the first phone calls from the red-tops the minute it finishes.'

'That's not a lot of time.'

'I know, but it's all there is.'

'I'll need the family history your brother compiled.'

'Does that mean you'll take the job?'

Jayne thought about it. She had already decided she could do with a break, and Iceland would be very attractive at this time of year. But a case searching for the answers to a DNA riddle and only six days to solve it? That was something she had never done before.

'Here's the money I promised you.'

Jayne looked down at a cheque drawn from Coutts with the figure '5,000 pounds' written on the front. She shook her head. 'I don't know if I can help you. I've never done DNA-based research before.'

'But you must. You're the only person I can turn to. My brother has already said he wants nothing to do with it.'

'You told him about the programme?'

She nodded. 'And Father. They both had to know.'

'What was their reaction?'

'They were livid with me, particularly my father. He said I had been a little fool, should never have agreed to the show and that the DNA must have been contaminated.'

'Well, they would say that, wouldn't they?'

'Please take the job.'

Jayne thought for a moment. 'I'll do it, but on one condition.'

'Anything.'

'You put your money away. If, and it's a big if, I can work out which ancestor of yours contributed the African part of your DNA, then you pay me. If not, then I will accept nothing.' Rachel tried to speak but Jayne held her hand up and continued. 'The reason is, I'm not certain I can do anything. It's not a normal investigation.'

Rachel smiled like a cat who had just discovered a whole gallon of cream. 'But that's exactly what Lord Radley said you were good at. Investigations that were out of the ordinary.'

Jayne knew she had been trapped. Rachel had an understanding of human nature far beyond her years. No wonder she was such a good actress. Jayne's motivation was always in the investigation, not in the outcome. In many ways, she was still a detective, only now she investigated family history not family violence.

'I'll start today. Can you send me the family tree your brother compiled?'

'It's a big file, as soon as I have access to a computer, I'll send it along.'

'Good. I'll call you in two days with an update.'

'There's one thing I have that might help you.' Rachel reached into her Birkin and pulled out a dark blue jewellery case. 'My mother gave me this before the cancer took her away.' She opened up the case to reveal a gold necklace with a variety of charms hanging from it. 'My mother said this had always been in the family, handed down from daughter to daughter. She told me she had added this charm to protect and guide me through life. I was to add something and give it to my daughter.' Rachel pointed to a gold lion dangling off the necklace. 'I'm a Leo, you see. Could it be of use?'

'If it's been handed down, it might be helpful.'

Rachel closed the box and handed it Jayne. 'But please don't lose it. It's one of the few things I have to remember my mother by.'

And that was it. They spent the rest of the lunch chatting about Rachel's job as an actress. She was a great story-teller with a theatrical love of gossip about the rich and pretentious. All told with a salacious glint in the eye that said, quite boldly, 'I don't take all this celebrity malarkey terribly seriously'.

It was only when they came to pay and Jayne offered to share the bill that the benefits of celebrity became apparent. The bill was put on Rachel's account. Not for her the ignominious presentation of a credit card machine.

Now Jayne was back at home in front of the computer, a strange sense of anticipation tingling through her body. What would she find out this time? Was there a hidden secret in the Marlowe history? Or was the DNA result false? Just another mistake by the testing lab?

That was the beauty of genealogical research; you never knew what you would find until you looked.

She logged into her Gmail account. There it was at the top, an email from Rachel with a large attachment. She clicked on it and waited and waited and waited.

Finally, the file opened. A quick glance showed that it contained 3774 names. 'He has done his research,' Jayne said out loud.

Starting at the bottom, she scrolled upwards. David and Rachel Marlowe. Sir Harold Marlowe and Lady Elspeth Marlowe, nee Brough. Two brothers and one sister for Sir Harold, one sister for Lady Elspeth. All annotated with dates of birth and death.

She continued to scroll upwards past grandfathers and great-grandfathers; cousins once, twice and three times removed. Name after name all linked together in the branches of a family tree. growing through the generations.

She scrolled further back through Victorian times, and Regency and Georgian, the Marlowe surname being passed from generation to generation. Past the Restoration and the Civil War, past the Wars of the Roses and the Black Death (the family had survived even that). Past Edward the First, the Hammer of the Scots, past the Warring Period of Stephen and Matilda, to just one name. Robert de St Malo, born 1042, died 1086.

And there it stopped.

Obviously, the name had changed through the ages, becoming more English as the family let their Norman heritage lapse. St Malo had translated into Marlowe, the name they still used today.

Jayne pulled back to see the whole family tree on one screen. A mass of name after name, branch after branch of a family who had resided in the same area of west Cheshire for over a thousand years.

Surely, the DNA result must be a mistake. This family could trace their line back through countless generations. And on checking the family tree, it looked like the line was unbroken through male heirs for the last millennium, at least.

This investigation was like looking for the proverbial needle in a haystack. Where should she start?

And then it struck Jayne like a Manchester bus. What if the African DNA had come from a marriage, not directly from a male Marlowe ancestor? Would that mean she needed to research every line that had married into the family too? An impossible task in just six days.

As she stared at the family tree with its long list of Marlowe descendants, only one thought dominated her mind.

Perhaps this job was too much, even for her.

CHAPTER TEN

Saturday, August 17, 2019
Didsbury, Manchester

After staring at the screen for fifteen more minutes, Jayne decided to sleep on it.

'Focus, Jayne, focus,' she said out loud to herself.

She couldn't possibly investigate all the marriage lines in less than one week, she had to concentrate her efforts. To her, the Marlowe family tree looked too perfect, too correct. And an unbroken male line for over one thousand years? It was possible – she was sure some aristocratic families might have such a lineage – but it was not that common.

She rubbed her eyes.

Tomorrow would be another day and she could attack the family tree then, comparing it with census results until at least 1841. After that, she would have to go into parish registers. With a family as prominent as the Marlowes, they would have strong links with the local church closest to Wickham Hall.

There was also the DNA test that Rachel had undertaken. What sort of test was it? And which company had performed it? She would have to ask Rachel for more details on that.

Jayne had first tested herself ten years ago, when DNA for genealogy was in its infancy, and had repeated the test with Ancestry.com three years ago.

Her test had revealed that she had Irish, Scottish and French forbears. She hadn't taken it any further, for the same reasons she hadn't investigated her own family tree up until then; she was always too scared to find out what she would discover. But after the recent events with her father and grandmother, perhaps it was time to look at her own DNA past again.

She had to know more, and that was when she thought of Tom Carpenter. She had met him after a talk she had given to the local family history society. He was a professor at Manchester University, specialising in DNA. She could give him a call tomorrow and pick his brains; she still had his card in her Rolodex.

Except tomorrow was Sunday. Would he mind being disturbed? She decided to send him an email. If he said no, she would have to find somebody else.

Hi Tom,

Remember me? It's Jayne Sinclair, we met at the Didsbury Family History Society when I gave a talk.

I remember you saying your specialism was DNA. I'm in the middle of a case at the moment and I wonder if I could ask you a few questions?

I know it's the weekend, but would it be okay to call you tomorrow morning at 10 a.m.? It's rather urgent, you see.

Don't worry if it's not convenient, I'll find the answers somewhere else.
Best regards,
Jayne

She sent the email and went to the fridge to pour herself another glass of sauvignon blanc. She knew it was sacrilege to keep her white wine in there, but she liked it cold, especially on a warm day like today.

As she was pouring the wine, her email pinged with a reply.

Hi Jayne,
Happy to hear from you and happier to help. Please call at 10 a.m. tomorrow morning, it won't be a problem.
All the best,
Tom

Wonderful! And at least she had made a start on the case. What would she discover?

She yawned, long and loudly, realising just how tired she was. But before she went to bed, she'd better find out more about the DNA test taken by Rachel before she rang Tom tomorrow.

She picked up her mobile and rang the actress. The call went through to voicemail.

'This is Rachel Marlowe. I'm either on set, sleeping or desperately avoiding people at the moment. If you leave a message I'll get back to you just as soon as I can.'

Jayne waited for the beep and then spoke. 'Hi Rachel, it's Jayne Sinclair. Do you have the details of your DNA test and can you send them to me? If you do, it could help shorten the research immensely. Thanks and goodbye.'

Jayne put down her phone. As she did, it occurred to her that in the last six hours she hadn't thought once of Paul or the divorce.

That was the beauty of genealogical research; you threw yourself into it and everything else vanished. All problems, all arguments, all issues. But eventually she would have to deal with it. Should she call Paul? Or simply hire a solicitor and handle everything through them?

She asked herself what was the right thing to do. And after just a few seconds, decided to call him tomorrow. Perhaps they could solve this amicably. Paul wasn't a bad man, nor was he a vindictive one, they just didn't love each other any more.

She drained the last of her wine and switched off the computer. She checked the patio doors and windows were locked before climbing the stairs to her bedroom. Mr Smith would come home in his own sweet time.

Just as she placed her foot on the bottom step, the phone rang. Was that Rachel returning her call? But it was her home phone ringing – how would Rachel have found that number?

Jayne was tempted to ignore it. But the ringing became more insistent. Perhaps it was somebody from her father's nursing home? She rushed back into the kitchen and lunged for the phone. If it was somebody calling her about double glazing, she would reach down the telephone line and wring the twerp's neck.

'Is this Jayne Sinclair?'

The voice was slow, with a drawl added to her last name as if the speaker was too lazy to finish the sentence.

'Speaking.'

'Jayne Sinclair, the woman who styles herself as a genealogical investigator?'

She didn't much care for the words 'styles herself as'.

'Yes, how can I help you?'

'My name is David Marlowe, I believe you met my sister Rachel this afternoon?'

'I did.'

'Good. Please don't be offended by what I have to say, Mrs Sinclair, but I'm afraid my sister has involved you in a waste of time. I researched our family history some years ago, and I can assure you there is no hint of African blood anywhere. We have lived in the area for over a thousand years, since my ancestor came over with William the Conqueror and defeated Harold at the Battle of Hastings.'

There was pride in the voice. Jayne decided to bring him down to earth.

'The science would suggest otherwise, Mr Marlowe.'

'Please, call me David. Are you talking about the DNA results?'

'The DNA would suggest you have a African ancestor somewhere in your past.'

'Rubbish,' he said loudly, before his voice softened and the charm returned. 'I am sorry to be so blunt, Mrs Sinclair—'

'It's Ms Sinclair, I am no longer married.' The words sounded so formal, so bitter to her own ears even as she said them.

'*Ms* Sinclair,' he repeated, as if spitting out a sour lemon. 'I am sorry to be blunt, but I had my own DNA tested two years ago and there was no hint of African ancestry. Mainly Anglo-Saxon, some Welsh and Irish, and a smidgeon of Viking. No other ancestry at all. The results from the programme must be mistaken. I would be quite happy to show you my DNA results if you so desire.'

Jayne thought for a moment. 'That won't be necessary, Mr Marlowe.'

'Good. So you will cease your investigation immediately and return my sister's money to her.' Again, the voice expected to be obeyed.

'I'm afraid that won't be possible, Mr Marlowe. Your sister is my client and only she can tell me to cease my work.' He began to speak but Jayne carried on. 'And for your information, I have accepted no money yet from your sister. Is that clear?'

There was silence at the end of the phone. The response, when it came, surprised Jayne.

'Why don't you come down to Wickham Hall? I can show you my own DNA results and take you through the family tree I compiled. You can even meet some of the ancestors.'

'Meet your ancestors?'

'The family portraits. It was a tradition to have them done in our family. We still have some of them. One is by Gainsborough.'

'I don't know, Mr Marlowe.'

'If I can't persuade you to cease the investigation, Ms Sinclair, at least do me the courtesy of allowing me to present my side of the story. It's only fair, isn't it?'

Jayne felt herself being manipulated by this family again. 'Well, I...'

'Good, that's decided. Shall we say three p.m. tomorrow at Wickham Hall? We can take afternoon tea together.'

Jayne heard herself saying yes and then asking where the Hall was.

'You'll find it in most of the guidebooks. We open the gardens for people to wander around in the summer.'

'You must find it tiresome to have hordes of tourists trotting through your home?'

'I quite enjoy it actually.' And then the voice changed, becoming harder. 'I'm very proud of my family and its history, Ms Sinclair. I wouldn't want it to be sullied in any way.' And then back to Mr Charming. 'I do look forward to meeting you tomorrow. Genealogy is one of my favourite subjects, it will be interesting to discuss the various research methods. See you at three.'

The phone went dead. Jayne stood there a moment, wondering why she had said yes to driving all the way to the countryside of Cheshire to meet this man. Was she becoming soft in her old age?

CHAPTER ELEVEN

Sunday, August 18, 2019
Didsbury, Manchester

Jayne was awake bright and early on Sunday morning, as was Mr Smith. As soon as she entered the kitchen, he miaowed loudly and went to stand next to his bowl.

This cat had a bottomless pit for a stomach, but apparently didn't put on weight. Jayne fed him and then made an espresso for herself from the machine.

She sat down in front of her computer and switched it on, listening to the machine as it booted up and inhaling the aroma from the coffee.

What was it about coffee and mornings? Somehow the two had fused themselves together and now she was unable to begin the day without her strong espresso.

The computer gurgled into life and she entered her password. Checking her mailbox, there was another email from Rachel with the DNA results enclosed in the Ancestry.com format.

She replied, thanking her client, and then waded through the rest of her emails – advertising from fitness clubs; an invitation to make a speech to a local genealogical society; three messages from friends whom she had not seen in a long while, complaining about her lack of contact; and twenty other sorts of advertising junk mail which she immediately deleted. She then checked her Facebook, Instagram and Twitter pages, avoiding most of the rubbish that people posted on social media. She had a particular aversion to pictures of food. Why people persisted in photographing every meal they ate was beyond her. But she knew she also had her own preferences. She was a sucker for a cute cat or dog video.

She glanced at the clock: 9.50 a.m. Could she call Tom now? It wouldn't hurt to try. He answered after three rings.

'Tom Carpenter.'

'Hi, Tom, it's Jayne Sinclair.'

'Hi, Jayne, how can I help you?'

She quickly explained the case and asked him to explain what DNA testing was in words of less than one syllable.

'I'll try, Jayne. Basically, DNA – or deoxyribonucleic acid – is a self-replicating material which is present in nearly all living organisms as the main constituent of chromosomes. It is the carrier of genetic information and is the building block of every human being, genetic material being handed down from each ancestor and stored in the DNA molecule. With me so far?'

'I think so. So everybody has it and they get it from both parents.'

'Correct. There are a few exceptions, but that's generally true. I'll email you some reading material after this call.'

'Great, so when it comes to genealogy, why do we test DNA?'

'With DNA, we're really looking for the DNA inputs that constitute every human being. For people interested in genealogy, there are three main tests available. Y-DNA testing, Mitochondrial testing and Autosomal testing.'

'Whoa, big words, all with more than one syllable.'

'Don't worry, the tests themselves are fairly straightforward. Y-DNA testing looks at the DNA in the Y-chromosome, a sex chromosome that is responsible for maleness. All biological males have one Y-chromosome in each cell and copies are passed down virtually unchanged from father to son in each generation. As a woman, this wouldn't be available to your client as she doesn't have a Y chromosome. But she could test her brother and her father.'

'It definitely wasn't that sort of test for my client.'

'The second kind of test available is the Mitochondrial test. This looks at female ancestry handed down through the mitochondria in the biological mother's egg. Mitochondria, or mtDNA, is passed down by the mother, unchanged, to all her children, both male and female. A mitochondrial DNA test can therefore be taken by both men and women. Are you with me?'

'Yes, got it.'

'The third DNA test is an Autosomal test and, from your description, it sounds like this is the one your client took. Most of the big companies like Ancestry.com use it. The 22 pairs of chromosomes that we inherit from both parents are called autosomes. Each pair is inherited from the father and from the mother. The chromosomes they pass on to their children are a mixture of the ones they inherited from their own parents. So you can use it to trace either side of your family. Autosomal DNA testing is much more information-rich than either Y-DNA or Mitochondrial tests, since it can reveal more about your ethnicity and who you are related to.'

'So that's how they could come up with the percentages for my client? 56% Anglo-Saxon, 22% Irish, 10% Viking and 6% African.'

'I would be less confident in the numbers on the actual percentages.'

'Why?'

'To take a complicated procedure and condense it into one sentence: testing companies look at a large amount of genetic data in a bunch of different ways and come up with the best possible ethnicity numbers. They then compare this data to a reference population of DNA samples from modern individuals living in various regions. Essentially, they are using modern-day populations to help make predictions about where our ancient ancestors lived.'

'Okay, I get it.'

'The best way to use ethnicity estimates is to combine them with traditional genealogical research methods. As more people get tested and contribute both their DNA test results and their family trees to online databases, scientists like myself will be able to identify additional patterns and draw more accurate conclusions. The accuracy has improved immensely over the last five years and will continue to improve exponentially.'

'How far back is the Autosomal testing accurate?'

'Each person gets roughly fifty per cent of their DNA from Mum and fifty per cent from Dad. But that means fifty per cent of each parent's DNA gets left behind. Also, what gets passed down and what gets left behind is completely random. That's why even siblings can have different ethnicity estimates. With each generation, your odds of inheriting DNA from any one individual in your family tree decrease. So your family tree is actually full of people who might not show up in your DNA test results, but they're still family. This is especially true the further back you go in the tree. Because of the way it is inherited, autosomal DNA can only help you go back about six or seven generations.'

'Great, so if Rachel was tested using autosomal testing, her African ancestor must have been alive within the last six or seven generations.'

'Correct.'

'Thank you, Tom, you've been really helpful.'

'No worries, Jayne, glad to be of use.' There was a pause at the other end of the phone. 'If you're free for dinner one night, I'd love to tell you more.'

Was that the offer of a date?

'I'd love to, Tom, but I'm a little busy at the moment. Maybe in a few weeks?'

'Great, I'll call you. Good luck with the research.'

The phone clicked off. Jayne held the receiver in her hand. She liked Tom, he was a good man, but she didn't know if she liked him in that way. She put the phone down.

Don't overthink it, Jayne Sinclair, it's just dinner. Remember, you still have a divorce to sort out.

The thought of Paul sent a shiver down her back. Time for another coffee and then she'd call him. She couldn't put it off any longer.

CHAPTER TWELVE

July 08, 1842
Wickham Hall, Cheshire

Emily could breathe more easily now that Henry and his wife had finally left for London that morning, after much hustle and bustle.

Probably a business deal, more financing of the new railways or the building of larger factories. How her brother had changed from his youth! These days, his one obsession was money; its acquisition and protection.

No doubt he would also visit the apothecaries there and find some new potions, tinctures or tablets for her to swallow. Every time he went away, he seemed to come back with a new draught, stronger than the last.

No matter, she would use this time to write. She had so much to say and so little time left in which to say it.

1819 – Barbados

It was over three years later, in the spring of 1819, that I said goodbye to Mother. The war in Europe had ended and the despot Napoleon was safely exiled to the island of St Helena, and Father thought it was about time for myself and my brother to receive the benefits of an English education.

'You have spent far too long on the estate, Emily, growing wild as a result and lacking in the refinement expected of a young lady of your station...'

'But Father...' I tried to interrupt him, but once he had fixed his mind on a topic, little could dissuade him.

'Your brother will study the business so that one day he might make a fruitful contribution to the development of our mercantile endeavours. You, on the other hand, will learn the refinement necessary for a lady. How to embroider, make small talk, manage a household and, most importantly, be a willing and submissive wife who is able to support her chosen husband in his career.'

'But Father...' I interjected again, to no avail.

'But me no buts, Emily, my mind is made up. You will return with me when I take ship on Saturday to Liverpool.'

'It is for the best, Emily.'

It was the first time my mother had spoken. I saw she had tears in her eyes as she said the words, but without her support, there was nothing I could do but obey as women have always obeyed; reluctantly and unwillingly.

The ship stood in Bridgetown harbour, having discarded its cargo of goods from Europe; wine, fine silks, cotton goods, dresses and china. All those essentials from England and the continent that Mother found so necessary to support her life. The old import of slaves from the Gold Coast had stopped twelve years ago, so Father was forced to adapt his trade and change his ships. Gone were the irons and manacles for the slaves, now the cargo was far less perishable. The holds were quickly filled to the brim with rum, molasses, sugar and mahogany bound for England.

'This lot will fetch a pretty penny, you mark my words, Emily,' he said to me. Then he turned to bellow at the dock labourers, 'Hurry along there. We must not miss the tide. I have had reports from the harbour master of prices dropping in England. The sooner we are at home, the better.'

He turned back and whispered, 'Prices are rising, but we won't tell them that, hey. It's the early fisherman who catches the bait.'

Father went forward to chivvy the captain and the crew to even greater heights. I stood with Mother on the dock. Henry had long since vanished into the bowels of the ship to discover what treasure lay beneath the wooden decks.

'Have you your woollen coat, Emily? It will be cold in England.'

'It will be June when we arrive, Mother. Even England cannot be that cold in June.'

'It is better to be safe rather than sorry. The wind in England sits on the chest, creating bad humours that invade the lungs.'

'You make it sound like the English weather is our enemy.'

'It has taken off many young women in its time, Emily. Do not fight against it, you cannot hope to win. Instead, protect yourself constantly.'

There was silence between us for a moment before I asked, 'Why don't you come too?'

'Me?' she snorted. 'Your father does not want me to come. He wants me to look after our interests here.'

'But I will miss you.'

'Emily, you are now a young , beautiful woman of thirteen. Soon you will find a husband and go to live with his family. You have no need of a mother to nurse you every day now. It is time for you to grow up and face the future with joy.'

'I don't want to grow up.'

'Ah, there speaks the young girl.' She stopped for a moment and took my hands. 'Don't you see? The only proof that I have raised you properly is if you become a young lady in society.'

'Hurry up, Emily, we are to cast off now,' Father shouted from the quarterdeck.

Mother took my hands in hers. 'Make me proud of you, Emily. Make me proud.'

'I will, Mama, I will.'

'Emily, we are waiting.'

The foremast sails had been unfurled. Four dock workers were standing next to the gangplank leading to the ship. Others were holding on to the ropes wrapped around the bollards on the docks. A group of sailors stood at the bow of the ship. The captain, an old salt called Mr Ratchet, stood beside the rail.

All of them were looking at me.

I kissed my mother, lifted my skirts and ran up the gangplank. As soon as I had stepped aboard the ship, my last link to Barbados was removed and the deck resounded with the patter of sailors' feet as they furled sails, coiled ropes and performed the thousands of duties that enabled a ship to set off for sea.

I ran to the port side of the ship. Mother was still there on the dock, her hand raised and her primrose bonnet guarding her face from the sun.

I felt the ship glide away from the dock and the wind feather the ringlets of hair surrounding my face. I looked up to see the sails gently ruffle in the breeze as they caught the wind coming from the south east.

A mob of sailors ran up the rigging and across the guy line beneath the mainsail. As one, they undid the sail and it unfurled, flapping as it caught the breeze. The ship was moving quickly now, slicing through the blue waters of the harbour, seagulls squawking in its wake.

Bridgetown, my home, my love, was slipping slowly away behind us.

I looked back to the dock. Mother was still there, her arm still raised, becoming smaller and smaller as the ship moved out to sea. Around her the dock was empty, the ship and its needs long forgotten. Suddenly, she walked forward, still waving, and shouted something to me.

I stepped to the gang rail and called to her, 'What? What was that, Mother?'

She waved and shouted again.

I saw her lips move, but the words were seized by the breeze and taken off towards the far side of the busy town.

I shouted again, 'What, Mother? What did you say?'

But her lips never moved. She just stood still, waving her arm in the air.

I never saw my mother again. She was taken off in the outbreak of yellow fever that decimated Bridgetown in 1822.

Of course, we wrote to each other often when I was in Liverpool. Probably not as often as I would have liked – my mother was a poor letter writer – but I never felt the touch of her hands on my face again, nor the warmth of her body as she held me close.

I will always remember her, though, standing there on the dock, her arm raised high as if to touch the blue sky.

But now, as I think about it, I'm not sure whether she was waving goodbye or if she was waving for me to come back.

I suppose I will never know.

CHAPTER THIRTEEN

Sunday, August 18, 2019
Didsbury, Manchester

Jayne dialled the number for his mobile phone. It rang and rang and rang. She was just about to give up when a sleepy voice answered, 'Yeah.'

'Hi, Paul, it's Jayne.'

'Hi, Jayne.' The voice was instantly more awake and she could hear a touch of wariness.

'You sound tired.'

'A late night, too much to drink.'

She decided to press on. If she didn't sort this out now, it would just fester.

'I received the solicitor's letter asking for a divorce, Paul. I would have thought you'd have the courtesy to call me first.'

She instantly regretted saying the last sentence. She had wanted this conversation to be positive, not one full of recriminations.

'I wanted to make it official, Jayne. We've been separated for more than a year now. And I've met somebody else.'

So, there it was, out in the open. Not surprising really. When was the last time they had talked? A month ago, maybe?

'I see,' she replied. 'So you want to get married again?'

'We're thinking about it. She wants kids and neither of us are getting any younger.'

Jayne thought how to respond. The truth was that she never wanted to have children with Paul. She felt neither of them were grown-up enough to handle the responsibility of raising a child. They both gave too much to their jobs. She finally said, 'Well, I won't stand in your way, Paul. I think the only issue between us is the house.'

'I've instructed my solicitors to be fair, Jayne. We both paid for the mortgage, with me probably paying more, but I'm happy to divide the money fifty-fifty when we sell it. Property prices have risen considerably in Didsbury from when we bought twelve years ago.'

'But I don't want to sell, Paul.'

'Ah…' was his only response.

Jayne continued. 'I'm happy here, it's my home as well as my office. I like the area and it would be difficult to find a house as good as this again. You're okay living in Brussels, your company gives you a housing allowance.'

'Then I think we have a problem, Jayne. I want to buy a home here with my fiancée, and the proceeds of the sale of the place in Didsbury would help me.'

She knew it was silly, but his use of the word 'fiancée' hurt and angered her. Did their time living together in this house mean nothing to him?

'I don't want to sell, Paul,' she said again.

'Let the solicitors work something out, we don't have to discuss it now.'

She heard a voice in the background.

A woman's voice.

'You're right,' she snapped, 'it's obviously the wrong time to call, you're busy. I'll instruct my solicitor to contact yours. But understand me, I don't want to sell this house.'

Before he could respond, she switched off her mobile.

'Well, Jayne Sinclair, you didn't handle that very well,' she said out loud. She sipped her coffee and decided to use the time before she left for Wickham Hall to research divorce solicitors on the net. Or perhaps she should ring Wendy – didn't she get divorced last year from that beast of a husband? She would know who to use.

Reluctantly, Jayne picked up her mobile again. She had enough on her plate without fighting with Paul about the house too.

Why couldn't love, and life, be easier?

CHAPTER FOURTEEN

July 09, 1842
Wickham Hall, Cheshire

With Henry away, Emily wrote during the day, leaving strict instructions with the servants that she was not to be disturbed.

'But what about food, and your medicine, ma'am? Your brother left strict instructions that I was to make sure you ate and took the laudanum,' the housekeeper, Mrs Trevor, whined.

'They don't matter. I'm not hungry and I don't need the tinctures that Dr Lansdowne has prescribed.'

'But I'll lose my post if I don't follow his instructions. He was very clear to me.'

Emily's eyes flashed with anger. 'Fine, leave them outside my room. I will eat as and when I am hungry.'

'And take the doctor's medicine?'

'I will take the laudanum as well.'

'Thank you, ma'am.' Mrs Trevor turned and walked away, leaving a trail of cheap perfume behind her.

Emily closed her door and shuffled to the dresser to retrieve her notebook. She began writing, remembering the details of her life as the words leaked on to the page once more.

1819 – Liverpool

Mother had been right. Even though it was supposed to be summer, the weather in Liverpool was cold and blustery on the day we arrived, swirling through the drab warehouses and whipping my skin with its vicious lashes.

The voyage had been calm and quiet. The Atlantic was a smooth pussycat, not the tiger I had read about in my books. Even Captain Ratchet had been surprised by the ease of the journey.

'She be quiet this month, too quiet. Building up her strength for a storm, you mark my words.'

The captain had the natural pessimism of all sailors. The glass was always half empty in his eyes, the slaves weak and valueless, the cargo a waste of time and money, the weather ever ready to change for the worse.

I spent most of the time sitting in the small cabin I shared with my brother, reading the books Mother had thoughtfully bought for me in preparation for my journey. Emma *by Miss Austen was a wonderful read even if I did not care too much for the title character. I much enjoyed Mr Scott's* Waverley, *starting it again as soon as I had finished it. However, I do think Mother would have been more thoughtful with Miss Burney's latest book,* Tales of Fancy: The Shipwreck. *Not the sort of book that should be given to somebody just beginning a long voyage. Nonetheless, I enjoyed the story and resolved to read the author's half-sister Fanny Burney's diaries when I had the opportunity.*

I didn't see Henry that much, except at meals and in the evening when he slept. He spent most of his time with Father and the captain, going over statements of account and understanding the complexities of the new trading arrangements. After the abolition of the slave trade in 1807, Father was no longer allowed to take part in the triangular trade: gold and trinkets to the Gold Coast; slaves to the Caribbean; sugar, rum and tropical woods to England. He had successfully branched out, trading finished goods with Philadelphia, Baltimore and Charleston in exchange for the cotton and tobacco for which England had an insatiable demand, and going even further afield to Russia and India.

How do I know all this?

My brother often left his books open in the cabin for me to see. Father would have been appalled if he ever found out I had been reading about trade, but I found the subject fascinating and a welcome diversion from the continual pursuit of eligible husbands that seemed to dominate every page of Miss Austen's novels.

One day my brother returned early, catching me reading The Wealth of Nations by Mr Smith. He stared at me a moment before reaching forward and closing the book. 'What are you reading that for?' he said.

'It's interesting,' I answered weakly.

'Interesting? The only interest it has for me is to send me to sleep within five minutes of opening it.'

'Father expects you to read it.'

'He doesn't expect you to read it. I would prefer to spend time with Mr Scott or Captain Marryat, not with that old Scottish bore.' He threw the book on his cot.

I decided to change the subject. 'What will you do when we finally get to England?'

'Father has decided I am to join him in the company. It is to be renamed Roylance and Son.'

'Isn't that good?'

'It is if you like account books and ledgers and profit and loss and insurance and banking and—'

'What would you rather do?' I interrupted him before he could list an encyclopaedia.

He sat on his cot, sending it swinging back and forth. His face became animated as he spoke. 'I want to become a soldier. I haven't told you about what happened when we rode out from the estate the day of the rebellion.'

'I thought you didn't want to tell me.'

'It's not that, it's just I never understood it until recently. Listening to Father and the captain has helped me.'

'What happened?'

He leant forward. 'Well, we met up with the rest of the militia that had been called out from around the island. There was about two hundred and fifty of us all told, mostly overseers but a few estate owners like Father and myself. We were joined by Colonel Codd with his four hundred troops and the two hundred soldiers of Lieutenant Colonel Armstrong's West Indian brigade.'

'Black soldiers?'

'They fought very well, destroying the first charge of Bussa's men.'

'Go on...'

'Well, we arrived at Bailey's Estate and found them waiting for us. They charged with rakes and scythes and knives, straight into our guns. The men were rock solid, calmly pouring volley after volley into the mass of the rebels. The smoke and din and screams were terrifying. The rebels soon broke under our fire and retreated to a nearby farm. There we surrounded them and poured fire into their ranks until they surrendered. Some escaped, of course, but we caught most of them later when we scourged Saint Philip County.'

I thought at this point of telling him about my encounter with King Wiltshire, but I decided to remain silent.

He continued, laughing. 'We chased those rebels all over the island. Like a hunting party, it was, the dogs in front, howling and yapping, the men behind drinking and shouting.'

Remembering the bodies of King Wiltshire, Jacob and his family hanging from the gibbets in Bridgetown, I asked him what he did when he caught the rebels.

'Why, we killed them, didn't we?' he said, as if surprised by my question. 'We strung them up over the nearest tree and let them swing in the wind.'

'Did none get a trial?'

He shrugged his shoulders. 'A few did, but why waste the time of the courts? They were going to hang anyway.'

I opened my mouth to protest but he carried on speaking.

'That's why I want to become a soldier. Colonel Codd congratulated me on my alacrity and keenness on chasing and capturing the rebels.'

'Did you kill anybody?'

He shrugged his shoulders again. 'I'm not sure. I shot one rebel in the leg, but my horse reared and I lost track of him. Maybe somebody else caught him.'

I stayed silent.

'I hope Father lets me become a soldier.'

The bell sounded on deck.

He stood up. 'Time to eat. I do hope we don't have salt cod again.' He looked at me. 'Please don't tell Father about my desire to soldier, not until I have spoken to him myself.'

I promised I wouldn't.

We went up to Captain Ratchet's cabin. It was indeed salt cod again. It was the captain's favourite food.

My brother and I never spoke about his ambitions again.

I often wonder whether he ever summoned up enough courage to ask Father. I feel he didn't, because as soon as we arrived in Liverpool, he became obsessed with trade and growing the business and the family wealth almost to the detriment of everything else. Perhaps in his own way he became a soldier for the family, donning his merchant's uniform of worsted every morning and going off to wage war in the Liverpool Exchange.

Only later, when we moved to Cheshire and Father had died, did he become involved with the militia.

Adam Smith wrote of the invisible hand that guides the markets. I wonder if the same invisible hand guided my brother. It's one more thing I will never know.

Anyway, I am losing my thread. I often find my mind wanders these days. But I must keep its meanderings in check if I am to finish this account before my brother returns.

As I was saying, we arrived in Liverpool. I remember stepping off the ship into a bleak and grim city, with the wind running down the Mersey and whipping at my thin skirt. If this was the height of summer, how would I handle *the depths of winter? I buried myself even deeper into my woollen coat and wished that I were back in Barbados, bathing in the warmth and sunshine and smiles of the island.*

As I stepped into the carriage Father had ordered to meet us on the dock, I looked back over my shoulder at the grey, forbidding skies and the dark, leering faces of the men working on the docks.

What was to become of me in this dark and desolate land?

CHAPTER FIFTEEN

July 09, 1842
Wickham Hall, Cheshire

1819 – Liverpool

Those first days in Liverpool were not the happiest of my life.

We stayed in Father's house on Hope Street. The red-brick building was quite new, built in the modern style that was prevalent in Bath, only Father had used red brick as Bath stone was an unwanted extravagance in his eyes.

The portico led on to an entrance furnished elegantly to exhibit the restraint of his wealth. Of course, Father wanted to display more ostentation but the decorator he employed insisted that if Father was to entertain in the modern style then he must avoid displays of opulence, as all that had gone out of fashion.

For once in his life, Father acquiesced.

My rooms were on the second floor; a simple bedroom with attached dressing and morning room.

My new maid, Rosie, had introduced herself as soon as I arrived. 'I'm to be your ladies' maid, milady. Rosie's the name, from Dublin originally, if you are wantin' to be knowin'.'

'Where's Dublin?' I asked.

'It be in Ireland, milady, across the sea.'

'Oh,' I answered, never having been addressed as 'milady' before.

'You'll be wantin' to change after the long voyage.'

I looked down at the hem of my dress. It was covered in dark, dank mud even though I had only walked from the ship to the carriage and the carriage to the front door of our home. My shoes were in an even worse state, the silk covered in dirty black grime.

Rosie noticed where I was looking. 'We'll need to get you some overshoes, milady. Can't be buyin' new shoes every day of the week, can we? Even though your father could probably afford it,' she said as an aside.

After changing my clothes, Rosie showed me to the dining room. The walls were lined with a deep red wallpaper and dominating all was a picture of my father, rosy cheeked and dressed in his finest waistcoat, his hand resting on a large globe in front of him. The artist had produced a fine, if complimentary, likeness, capturing the intelligence in my father's blue eyes. His not inconsiderable stomach had been reduced, though, a concession of the artist, no doubt, to make sure he was paid his fee.

Father was already sitting at the head of the long dining table when I walked in, my brother was sitting next to him and two strangers on either side of them.

'Gentlemen, I would like to introduce my daughter, Emily, newly arrived from Barbados.'

I curtsied as I had been taught to do by Mother. The greeting was returned by a slight bow of the head from the two gentlemen.

My father continued. 'Emily, this is Mr Dinsdale, my solicitor and legal advisor.'

I curtsied once more. 'It is a pleasure, Mr Dinsdale.'

He bowed, more deeply this time. 'The pleasure is all mine, Miss Roylance.'

The other gentleman was eyeing me strangely, almost leering. Father introduced him next. 'And this is Superintendent of Trade for the city, a most important man, Sir Archibald Sutton.'

'It's a pleasure to meet you too, Sir Archibald.'

The man's florid face looked down on me. He turned to my father. 'You were quite correct, Jeremiah, she is going to be a beautiful young woman. I particularly admire the quality of her hair.'

It was as if I wasn't there.

'She takes after me, Sir Archibald. My hair was always being complimented when I was younger. Alas, these days the only compliments I receive are for my lack of hair. Such is life. Another glass, sir, I see yours is empty.'

A servant quickly ran round with the decanter of port.

'Emily, why don't you sit next to Sir Archibald? Henry, you move opposite and I will stay where I am.'

We all took our places around the table. The servants rushed in, and course after course followed one after the other. Fresh salmon, roast mutton, fricasseed rabbit, roast duck with peas, currant pie and syllabubs, and a dessert of strawberries, cherries and currants.

I had eaten my full after the rabbit, but the men continued wolfing down food as if the country no longer produced it, all washed down with copious glasses of port and claret. Only my brother did not join in. Like me, he stopped eating fairly early in the proceedings. Coming from an island where we ate rice and fish and the occasional chicken, accompanied by fresh fruit, such food was far too rich for my tastes.

After the currant pie had been served, Sir Archibald turned to me and said, 'You are not eating, Miss Roylance?'

'No, sir. I have eaten my limit already.'

'You young ladies have such dainty appetites, I wonder that you manage to live through the day.'

I felt something touching my shoe under the table. I looked across at my brother sitting opposite, thinking it was him, but he was talking to Father and the solicitor. The pressure on my foot increased and I moved it away.

'A man's appetites are always more insatiable, don't you agree?' Sir Archibald said.

I was about to answer that I was unacquainted with the depths of a man's appetites when the pressure on my foot increased once more, pressing on my toes. I moved my foot away again, answering, 'I'm not sure' as his eyes gazed steadily on mine.

He put his knife and fork down. 'Oh, come now, Miss Roylance, I'm sure you have a stronger position than that.' His right hand vanished beneath the table and seconds later I felt it squeeze my thigh as one would squeeze the haunch of a pig. 'We all have appetites, don't we?'

He licked his lips and I brought the tines of my fork down on the back of his hand. He let out a small squeal of pain and the hand was instantly retracted.

'Is something wrong, Sir Archibald?' asked my father on hearing the noise, 'you made a noise as if you had been hurt.'

'No, sir, it is nothing. Do not trouble yourself. A little yelp of pleasure at the wit of your daughter's conversation.'

Father frowned at me. 'She will start at Miss Fanshawe's Academy for Young Ladies in the near future, as soon as she has acclimatised to the weather of Liverpool. Perhaps there she will learn to curb her wit and acquire the refinement required of a young woman.'

'I do hope not, sir. I always like women to have a certain fight in them. If they are too submissive, it makes for a dull marriage.'

'You are too modern, Sir Archibald, but I understand your words. Carpets and women should both be beaten at least once a month. A glass to you, sir.' Father raised his wine. 'To trade – may she make our city prosperous and free.'

'To trade,' the three other men, including my brother, echoed.

I stood up. 'I'm feeling tired, Father. May I retire?'

Father smiled. 'It seems the pleasure of your company has exhausted my daughter, Sir Archibald.'

'I'm sure it has, Jeremiah, but I have no doubt we will be seeing each other again.'

All the men rose from their chairs and I left the room.

As the door was closing, I heard Sir Archibald intone in his high voice, 'What a charming daughter. Thirteen, isn't she? Time for you to find her a husband, Jeremiah.'

I only had one thought in my head as I marched upstairs to my bedroom:

Lord save me.

CHAPTER SIXTEEN

Sunday, August 18, 2019
Wickham Hall, Cheshire

The drive up to Wickham Hall was long and winding, bordered on either side with a long avenue of lime trees. The Hall revealed itself as Jayne turned the last corner. Somehow, the afternoon light caught the limestone pillars of the Palladian building, giving it an ethereal, almost fairy-tale-like appearance. It was as if this were some prince's home from a Hans Christian Andersen story.

She slowed down for a minute, turning off Bowie in mid-howl, and just drank in the beauty of the place. What a wonderful home to have grown up in. Rachel must have had an extremely privileged upbringing.

A man with a broken shotgun in the crook of his arm and a scowl on his face stepped in front of her car. 'You can't park here, visitors is round the back in the car park.'

'I'm here to see David Marlowe.'

He scowled again. 'Like I said, visitors is round the back.'

'It's okay, Goddard, Mrs Sinclair is visiting me. Park over here if you please.' A patrician voice, used to giving orders and being obeyed. He wore a white straw panama, a light green jacket and khaki trousers, like a model out of the pages of some country gentlemen's catalogue.

As she drove forward, he pointed to a place in front of the house.

'You must be Jayne Sinclair?' he said as she stepped out of the car. He took off his hat and held out his hand. 'I'm David, welcome to Wickham Hall. Sorry about Goddard. Our gamekeeper is very protective of the family, particularly against visitors.'

She took his hand, enjoying the firm handshake. 'You have a beautiful home.'

He stepped back and looked up at the house. 'It is rather wonderful, isn't it? An absolute bugger to maintain, though. You should see my bills for the roof.'

Jayne looked around her. 'I don't see many visitors.'

'The house is closed on Sunday, just the gardens are open to visitors today. Although I love my customers and their entrance fees actually pay for all this, we do need some downtime to maintain the property and the gardens. I like to call this "Downtime Abbey".' He leant towards her and in a stage whisper said, 'And I do enjoy the peace and quiet when they're not here.'

He took her elbow and gently guided her to the front entrance. 'Shall we go in? Mrs Davies has thoughtfully provided us with some tea and scones. You must be famished after your drive from the big city.'

'It didn't take me long, less than an hour.'

'It always amazes me that Wickham Hall exists less than sixty minutes from Liverpool and Manchester, two of the biggest cities in

England. I like to think of this place as a little oasis of grace, civility and good manners.'

'That's a little old-fashioned, Mr Marlowe.'

'Please, call me David. Is it? Perhaps, but I don't mind if it is. I sometimes think we have forgotten some of those English values we hold so dear in our rush to acquire stuff, and more stuff, and even more stuff.'

Jayne bit her tongue. It was easy to espouse such a view when you already had lots of 'stuff', a bit more difficult if you had nothing.

They crossed the threshold into a spacious double-height vestibule, tiled in black and white with a simple round Georgian table in the centre bedecked with flowers. Behind the table, a curving red-carpeted staircase wound its way up to the second floor past paintings of austere men and one or two women.

David saw where Jayne was looking. 'The ancestors spend their time looking down on us. It's both a blessing and a curse. A blessing in that we can see who they were and what they looked like, and a curse in that they know exactly what I'm doing with my life.'

'It's like your whole family was sitting there, watching and judging you?'

'Exactly. Take Henry.' He pointed to a painting of an austere Victorian gentleman with lush mutton-chop whiskers. 'He was an entrepreneur and investor, a visionary in his own way, built most of the railways in the north west and encouraged the industrialisation of both Liverpool and Manchester. He achieved so much with his life.'

Jayne stared up at the hard-eyed man with sallow skin. An image from her O levels and Charles Dickens suddenly appeared in her head: Mr Gradgrind. '*Now, what I want is Facts. Teach these boys and girls nothing but Facts. Facts alone are wanted in life.*' A shiver went down her spine. She hated school, wanted to leave as soon as she was able, even though the teachers and her mother urged her to stay and go on to university. Only her stepdad, Robert, had supported her. 'You do what you feel is right, love. You can always go back later if you want.' She had joined the police the very next day.

Her memories were interrupted by David Marlowe.

'I think Mrs Davies has laid our tea out in the library. It's this way.'

Once again, he touched her elbow, gently guiding her off to the left. 'Did you and Rachel grow up here?' she asked.

He nodded. 'When we weren't away at school. It was always a wonderful place to come back to during the hols. So many places to discover and enjoy in the summer. Do you ride?'

'Motorbikes, yes. Horses, no.'

'What a pity. We have a meet here on Sunday, of the local hunt.'

'I thought fox hunting was banned.'

'It is, unfortunately, but we still meet to ride out with the hounds. Another example of the nanny state legislating to take over our lives.'

Again, Jayne bit her tongue as he opened the door to the library. Her jaw dropped as she entered a perfect room: at least sixty feet long with mahogany bookcases stretching from door to ceiling along three sides. In each bookcase, rows of neat volumes were bound in leather and titled in gold. Against each wall, a ladder was attached to the ceiling so that an avid reader could reach the books on the top shelf. On the left, a utilitarian table and a chair and a desktop computer were the only indications that this room belonged to modern times.

In the centre of the room, two comfortable armchairs were arrayed around a small table laden with cakes, teapots and cups.

David raced across the room with all the grace of a child in a sweet shop. 'Mrs Davies has done us proud. You must try the strawberry jam. She makes it from the fruit we grow in the walled garden. The cream comes from one of the tenant farmers' herd of Jerseys. Best cream in the world, I think.'

Jayne was still standing at the entrance, staring at row upon row of books. 'It's a beautiful room.'

David glanced around himself. 'I suppose it is. Grandfather was a bit of a collector. At the back you'll find the rarer books – we even have a first folio of Shakespeare, but that's kept at the bank. Personally, I think it should be in the library, but the insurance is so prohibitive.'

Jayne noticed one of the bookshelves in the middle was barred and locked. Through the bars she could see one title highlighted in gold: Newton's *Principia*. 'Have you actually read any of these?' she asked.

David laughed. 'I tried. One summer – I think I was thirteen or so and had just come down from Eton – I decided, in the arrogant way of all thirteen-year-olds, to read every book starting from A and ending at Z. I think I got to Aesop before I gave up and went fishing instead. Do please sit.' He gestured to one of the armchairs.

Jayne walked over and sat down, feeling herself being swallowed up by the comfort of the green silk cushions.

He sat down next to her, taking off his hat and placing it on the table. 'Darjeeling or Earl Grey?'

'Darjeeling, I think.'

'Good choice, my favourite too.'

He poured the light straw-coloured liquid into the china cups. 'This is a single estate Darjeeling White. It goes wonderfully with the strawberry jam and also with bacon butties. None of the latter today, though, more's the pity.'

She caught him looking at her over the top of his spectacles and smiling. She tasted the tea; it was light and refreshing with just a hint of astringency, and as she swallowed the taste changed, revealing a herby, almost grassy character. It had all the complexity of wine. 'It's delicious,' she said, instantly feeling that this was one of the most banal things she had ever said.

'Help yourself to the scones. I can't resist them.' He had already slathered half a scone with cream and was now placing a spoonful of jam on top. 'I always prefer the Devon way myself.'

'Devon?'

'Of eating scones. Cream first, jam later. Cornwall has it in reverse, of course. A shocking waste of good jam, I think.'

She helped herself to a scone, enjoying all the rich, crumbly creaminess of the cake, and relaxed back into the comfort of the armchair. She could spend hours in a room like this, surrounded by the scent of books and the aroma of knowledge. On her left, she caught David watching her over the top of his glasses.

He spoke first. 'I'd like to apologise to you, Mrs Sinclair.'

'That isn't necessary, Mr Marlowe.'

'David, please. I think it is. We got off on the wrong foot yesterday. My sister is always accusing me of being too abrupt with people. I'm afraid it's one of my less endearing character traits.' He flicked the hair off his face. 'Please accept my sincere apologies if I offended you in any way.'

This man had perfected the Hugh Grant approach to English charm down to a fine art. 'No apology is necessary, Mr— David.'

'Do have another scone…'

She was about to reach for another delicious morsel when she stopped herself. She wasn't born yesterday. All this charm and hospitality were being lavished on her by David Marlowe not because she was a lovely person, but because she had been appointed by his sister to investigate the family history.

She placed her china cup, its Darjeeling White tea still radiating good health, back on the saucer. There was a faint ring as the two pieces of china touched each other. 'Thank you for the excellent scones, but I didn't come all this way to drink tea nor to take up too much of your precious day. It's time to work. You were going to show me the family tree you compiled, I believe?'

David's face went through three emotions in the space of two seconds. Shock. Irritation. Annoyance.

'You can be very blunt, Mrs Sinclair.'

'Do call me Jayne. I suppose I can, but I've only been given a week to solve this puzzle by your sister and today is already the second day.'

The schoolboy charm appeared again. 'I don't suppose I could persuade you to change your mind?'

'About?'

'Working for my sister. Frankly, she's a wonderful actress but a bit of a diva. She was always indulged by our mother. She should have settled down long ago, in my opinion.'

Jayne couldn't stand this any longer. 'By settled down, you mean found a man, had children and ran the home like a dutiful wife?'

'There are worse things to do.'

'And there are better. But I think we shall have to disagree on women's role in society. You were going to show me your family research,' she said, standing up and smoothing down her dress, 'but if it's not convenient then I'll start the long drive back to Manchester.'

He stood up too, the mask of civility slipping. 'You are an impatient woman, Mrs Sinclair.'

'And a bloody difficult one. Or so my ex-husband says. But I'm rather proud of that. It's always funny how a woman becomes "difficult" the moment she is seen to be good at what she does.'

David rolled his eyes at her little speech. 'The chart is rolled out in the anteroom. Follow me.'

He strode off without touching her elbow this time. She knew she had been rude but it was quite deliberate. She could never play these people's games. She had to be herself; a blunt northern ex-copper who got the job done. And she only had five days left to do it.

David Marlowe opened a concealed door in one of the book-cases and stepped through into a long room with a central oak table that took up most of the space. On the table, a parchment scroll was unrolled and weighted down with glass paperweights in each corner.

'I commissioned this from Debrett's in London. Of course, my research was only on the most recent members of the family. The original research was completed by a famous herald from the 1850s, a Mr Fairbairn, during the lifetime of Henry Marlowe, my great-great-grandfather – the man in the portrait,' he added, by way of explanation.

'Why did he commission the research?'

David Marlowe shrugged his shoulders. 'I don't know. As far as I can work out, it was actually commissioned by Henry's wife, not himself. Henry was a busy man. One of the bloody railways he built still runs across my land.'

Jayne listened attentively. She would have to look into this Mr Fairbairn and check out his work.

David sniffed. 'Now, if you'll excuse me, I have an estate to run. You can call Mrs Davies if you require anything.'

'Thank you, I won't be long. You also said you had a set of your own DNA results?'

'They are in the drawer.' He pulled out a printed set of results from Ancestry.com, passing the pages across to Jayne. 'As you can see, no African ancestry.'

Jayne quickly scanned the printout. Irish, Welsh, English and a touch of Viking, but definitely no African. 'Thank you, Mr Marlowe.'

'But I already knew I had no Ghanaian ancestry.'

'How could you be so sure?'

He tapped the stiff parchment that was unrolled on the table. 'Because this family tree tells me I don't.'

He stared at her for a moment before turning to leave. As he reached the door, he stopped and turned back to her. 'My family and its reputation are very important to me, Mrs Sinclair. I will stop at nothing to ensure they are not sullied in any way.'

CHAPTER SEVENTEEN

July 09, 1842
Wickham Hall, Cheshire

1819 – Liverpool

I started at Miss Fanshawe's Academy for Young Ladies two weeks after my meeting with Sir Archibald and his wandering fingers.

It was not far from my house on Hope Street, just opposite the Cathedral. On the first morning, Rosie dressed me in a simple calico shift and soft canvas boots. She sat me down at my dressing table and proceeded to arrange my hair in ringlets.

'You must be so excited, milady, going to school and all that.'

'Why? All they will teach me is how to make small talk, embroider, manage a home, serve my husband and hang on his every word.'

'And so you should, milady. How else do you expect to find a good husband unless you can do those things?'

'You can't do those things...'

'And I don't have a husband.'

'But you have me.' I turned round and gave Rosie a hug. In the short time I had known her, Rosie had already formed an unbreakable bond with me and, even though she was only six years older, the maid had become a replacement for my mother; somebody to whom I could tell everything.

'Now, you come along, milady, school and Miss Fanshawe are waiting. We will walk there together.'

'Don't bother, I know the way.'

'Oh, milady, a young woman cannot walk the streets on her own. Whatever would the men think?'

'They can think what they want.'

'No, they can't. I will accompany you to school every day, milady.'

'Please call me Emily.'

'Oooh, I couldn't do that, milady. You father would have my ears for purses if I did that. Better I call you milady, pretend it's your name. So let's be off, we can't keep Miss Fanshawe waiting.'

The Academy, as it was known locally, was a townhouse that had been converted into a school by Miss Fanshawe's brother. There were nineteen other girls in attendance on the morning I stepped inside, all tutored in the Madras system of education. That is to say, the girls were broken up into four groups of five, each headed by a senior girl who was the class monitor, teacher, disciplinarian and general factotum. All four groups were supervised by Miss Fanshawe, a stout, overdressed woman with a large bosom and a tendency to overheat even in the coldest weather. This could be attributed to her desire to have roaring fires in each room, fed by a relay of servants.

'Girls,' she used to intone regularly, 'it is a well-known fact that the human brain needs warmth in order to function. At Miss Fanshawe's Academy, we ensure the brain is kept in a snug, warm and nurturing environment.'

Unfortunately, the teaching didn't stoke much warmth amongst the pupils, all of whom were the daughters of the merchants of Liverpool and the surrounding districts. These modern men, determined to educate their daughters in order that they procure satisfactory marriages, filled up the places at the school *as soon as they became available. This was despite the manifest evidence from bishops and members of parliament that educating women merely served to give them ideas above their station. It was with these warnings in mind that Miss Fanshawe had designed the curriculum.*

Mornings were given over to the arts of sewing, embroidery and polite conversation. The afternoons were for dancing, general deportment and managing a household. Monday and Wednesday mornings were spent on religious education, whilst Tuesdays and Fridays were allocated to reading and writing. Arithmetic was taught as and when it became necessary, for example, when a butcher's bill was presented to the household accounts. Or when a servant's wages were divided into quarters from a yearly sum.

It soon became apparent that I knew how to read far better than my teacher, the class monitor – a girl of seventeen, Clarice Gladstone. She was the granddaughter of one of Liverpool's most famous merchants, but unfortunately the brains of the rest of the family had been omitted for her generation. She was, however, a particularly fine embroiderer, and we soon became firm friends.

'Emily, you take the class for reading. It tires me so.'

The book in question, The Art of Cookery Made Plain and Easy *by Mrs Hannah Glasse, had been assigned by Miss Fanshawe. While it may have been a fine book for a cook, it wasn't the best reading for a group of young girls.*

I had in my bag a copy of Mrs Stanhope's Madalina. *I took it out and began reading.*

These words were much appreciated by the other girls, so much so that we were joined by two other classes as I read them aloud. We soon formed our afternoon reading group unknown to Miss Fanshawe, who spent the time from two to four in the afternoon in her bedroom on the second floor, supposedly preparing the next day's lessons but in actuality taking a post-luncheon nap. None of the class monitors minded this arrangement, as it meant they could do what they wanted rather than waste time looking after a gaggle of young girls.

Over the next year, books were brought in by everyone and we took it in turns to read. Mrs Edgeworth's tales were appreciated for their morality and Mr Scott's Rob Roy *was shocking in its physicality. Indeed, the reader, a young girl of fourteen, blushed and stammered so much during the telling of the tale I had to take over from her.*

In March 1820, I took Miss Austen's latest to our reading club; Northanger Abbey *and* Persuasion, *both published after her death. We were all particularly taken by the story of the heroine, Catherine Morland, a young and naïve girl who entertains the reader in her journey to a better understanding of the world and those around her. In the course of the novel, she discovers that she differs from those other women who crave wealth or social acceptance, as instead she wishes only to have happiness supported by genuine morality.*

This led to many a spirited discussion amongst the girls about love. I was one of those who advocated the importance of happiness in marriage rather than an adherence to duty. I was shocked by how many of the girls disagreed with me. Clara, one of my best friends at the time, was a particularly fervent supporter of the duty faction.

One day, we were discovered by Miss Fanshawe as we debated the morality of the slave trade after reading some of Mr Wilberforce's pamphlets from earlier in the century. Again, I found myself in a minority of one as most of the girls argued that the benefits of being a slave far outweighed the disadvantages of a lack of freedom.

The memory of King Wiltshire lying in the shed with blood oozing out of his leg wound fortified my will to argue against my fellows, and I must admit to raising my voice at their lack of humanity. Unfortunately, my shouts must have awakened Miss Fanshawe because she came down to the drawing room and discovered us in mid-discussion.

'What is going on here?' she asked from the door, adjusting her linen sleep cap.

We all stayed quiet.

'What is going on here?' she repeated.

Of course it was me who answered. 'We are reading, Miss Fanshawe.'

'Reading...' she bellowed. 'Reading is bad for young girls. It is a well-known fact that the brain is stunted by reading and, even worse, the eyes grow milky and unfocussed from staring at the words on the page.'

'But, Miss Fanshawe—'

'But me no buts, Miss Roylance. Reading is henceforth banned from this establishment. We will have no more truck with books.'

'But, Miss Fanshawe, how are we to learn anything?' Again, I was the only one who spoke. The other girls just sat there with their mouths open.

'Do you need books to embroider?' she asked everyone.

They shook their heads.

'Do you need books to sew?'

Again, they shook their heads.

'Do you need books to be a good wife?'

The other girls hesitated.

'Well, do you?' Miss Fanshawe shouted.

All the girls shook their heads in unison.

'There you have your answer, Miss Roylance. There will be no more books at this Academy.'

'What about the Bible?' I asked. 'That is a book.'

Miss Fanshawe frowned at me and then pronounced, 'The Bible is not a book, Miss Roylance, it is the word of God. Remember that and you will go far in life.' She then flounced out, slamming the door behind her.

For the next five years at Miss Fanshawe's Academy for Young Ladies, we never saw another book. Everything was demonstrated first by the class monitors and we merely copied it. That's not to say we didn't read – we were not going to give up one of the pleasures of life. However, it wasn't allowed at school, so we did it in the evenings at my house while Father and my brother were still at the office or entertaining in their Club.

I left Miss Fanshawe's at the tender age of nineteen with an ability to sew, dance, make small talk and balance a book on my head, but with little other knowledge.

No wonder then that, when I met a well-read man, I embraced him with both arms.

Emily put down her pen and rubbed her eyes. There had been a knock on the door an hour ago, which she had ignored. Perhaps it was the servants leaving food for her?

For the first time in many months she actually felt hungry. She checked outside the door. A plate of cheese, pickle and bread lay on a tray accompanied by a small carafe of wine.

She took the tray inside her bedroom and devoured the food, finishing the carafe too.

That night she had the best sleep she could ever remember.

CHAPTER EIGHTEEN

Sunday, August 18, 2019
Wickham Hall, Cheshire

On the drive back to Manchester, Jayne decided a little Elbow was needed.

She put *The Best Of* CD in the player and chose *Lippy Kids*, skipping over the first track, *Grounds for Divorce*, for obvious reasons. The velvety strings kicked in, followed by Guy Garvey's lush voice. After a few moments she found herself singing along to the chorus; 'build a rocket, boys'.

One day she would build her own rocket and soar. Until then, the DNA problem presented by Rachel was becoming more and more complicated.

After David Marlowe had issued his threat, Jayne had knuckled down to comparing the scroll with the family tree sent by Rachel.

Both matched exactly, with every family member tracking back to the time of William the Conqueror.

She had only been working for fifteen minutes before there was a tap on the door. An older man entered, looking like an older version of David, wearing a similar jacket and having the same blue eyes. He had advanced towards her with his hand held out. 'I do hope I'm not disturbing you. I'm Sir Harold Marlowe.'

'Pleased to meet you, I'm Jayne Sinclair.'

'You're the genealogist my daughter hired?'

Jayne nodded.

'How is the research going? Not my field at all, more my son's hobby, I'm afraid. Give me a company spreadsheet any time.'

Jayne pointed to the unfurled scroll. 'You have illustrious ancestors. Not many families can trace their lineage all the way back to a vassal of William the Conqueror.'

Sir Harold sniffed. 'I suppose so. Doesn't interest me, I'm afraid. I find all the family history stuff a little oppressive. Nothing can be gained from staring into the past. Look to the future, I always say. That's where we should be heading, not glancing over our shoulder at the past.'

'Not a common view. Without the past, would you have all this?' Jayne gestured to the house and its contents.

'I find it all a bit of a burden, actually. Since my wife died, I moved out to a dower house on the estate. I found living here so uncomfortable. My father loved it, of course, and so does my son. The love of the place seems to have jumped a generation with me. Oh well, I'll leave you to your papers. If you need anything, just ask Mrs Davies.'

He then left the room, vanishing as quietly as he had entered.

As she drove down the M56, Jayne replayed the conversation in her head. A man with a long family history who seemed to hate the past. Why was that? Was there more to the family than she knew?

She had quite liked the old man, though. He had a shyness, a diffidence that was missing in his son.

Automatically, she signalled right to overtake a lorry pulling out in front of her. The family tree on its parchment scroll seemed to state conclusively that there was an unbroken line back to 1066, but was that true? How had the family survived for so long? And what about David and Rachel – why were the two sets of DNA results so different? Had the Ancestry.com labs made a mistake? Or had they simply missed the African element when they had tested David Marlowe?

She yawned. It was always so boring driving on motorways. Next time, she would take the A56. It was a slower road but at least there was more to see. Until then, Guy Garvey's voice would comfort her like a velvet blanket, singing, 'It looks like a beautiful day'.

And she realised that it was indeed a beautiful day because, despite Paul and the divorce, despite the Marlowes and their threats, and despite the problems of Rachel's ancestry, Jayne loved every moment of this. Research energised her.

She was good at her job. Scratch that, she was great at her job.

She was going to solve the riddle of Rachel's past.

Who was the Ghanaian ancestor?

CHAPTER NINETEEN

Monday, August 19, 2019
Manchester Museum, Oxford Road, Manchester

Jayne stood outside the doors of Manchester Museum. In her left hand she felt the weight of Rachel's necklace in its box. She had rung the museum yesterday, asking to meet with a specialist in antique jewellery.

'You'd want to speak with Mr Livesey. What he doesn't know about jewellery isn't worth knowing,' they had told her.

So she had booked a meeting with him and now here she was, outside the old Victorian building. It was a long time since she had been inside. Her last time was over twenty-five years ago when Robert had taken her on a visit here when she was fourteen or fifteen years old.

She had spent most of that week arguing with her mother, the typical fights teenagers get into with their parents. Her skirts were either too short or too long. Her hair at that time was styled in the curls of Kylie Minogue, which her mother said made her look like a poodle on heat. The final bone of contention was her boyfriend at that time, Gerry. A lovely lad who looked just like Jason Donovan and was an apprentice plumber.

One Saturday morning it had all kicked off.

'I'm having no daughter of mine with a man who spends most of his time up to his elbows in shit.'

'Mum, he spends most of his time making tea and laying bathroom tiles.'

'He's too old for you.'

'He's only twenty-one.'

'You told me he was eighteen!'

Jayne had forgotten the little white lie she'd told when she had first spoken to her mother about Gerry.

'He's too old. I'm not having it, understand, little lady?'

'Oh, I can see you're not having it, that's why you're so irritable all the time.'

Her mother stared at her for a moment before the arm came round in a wide arc and struck Jayne on her face.

The blow didn't hurt but the shock did. How dare her mother strike her? She went to lift her hand and strike her back when Robert caught her arm, ushering her out of the house before she did any real damage.

They ended up at Manchester Museum.

'Look, lass, your mother means well. She cares for you.'

'Hitting your daughter across the face is a funny way of showing you care.'

'Sometimes, people can't say the words...'

'By people, you mean my mother?'

'She loves you, Jayne.'

'How do you put up with her, Robert?'

At this time, Jayne had been going through her phase of calling him by his name. She no longer felt comfortable calling him 'Dad' as he was her stepfather.

'I love your mother, Jayne. Always have done, always will do.'

'Despite her temper?'

'Because of her temper.'

'You're a strange man, Robert.'

'And I love you too, always remember that, lass.'

They had gone into the museum and spent hours looking at the mummies in their cases. She realised later it was Robert's understated way of telling her that all the arguments would pass. Nothing lasts for ever. These 3000-year-old mummies had once lived and laughed and loved, and now they were nothing but shrivelled corpses in a museum.

He was a subtle man, was her stepfather.

And now she was here again, twenty-five years later, with an appointment to see Donald Livesey, curator of the jewellery section.

She sat down in his office and, after the usual introductions, pulled out the necklace Rachel Marlowe had given her and handed it over to him.

'Hmm, we don't see many of these.'

He was a dapper man, almost a caricature of a university don; spotted bow tie, horn-rimmed glasses, a tweed suit, brown brogues, and hair swept across the top of his head in a comb-over. He spoke with an accent that definitely wasn't from Manchester.

He took off his glasses and placed a loop to his eye in order to examine the necklace more closely. 'Fascinating.' He seemed to be oblivious of Jayne's presence as he peered through his loop, examining every element of the jewellery.

Finally, he looked up. 'Where did you get this?'

'It's from a friend. Handed down through the family.'

He laughed. 'Sounds like an episode of *Antiques Roadshow*.'

'Do you know where it might have come from?'

'A better question is, where doesn't this come from?'

'I don't understand.'

'See here, this barrel-shaped piece near the centre?'

Jayne leaned forward to take a closer look.

'Well, that's Roman, without a doubt. Rolled gold, and I bet we'll find a little message or curse inside.'

'What?'

'Something like "Mighty Jupiter, help me get the job with the procurator" or "Mighty Jupiter, make sure Caius Dodos Impator's left hand drops off because he's a thief". Nice people, the Romans. Pretty common piece, though. And here—' he pointed to another section shaped like an animal, '—it's hallmarked with the lion's head for London and the letter mark of an "E", so it was made in 1740. Yet over here is a piece also hallmarked, but this time with the marks for Edinburgh 1781. Although it's hallmarked Scotland, it's definitely French, again from the eighteenth century.'

'I thought it was just a charm necklace.'

'It's exactly that. And a very charming piece of jewellery, first one I've ever seen like it.' He pointed to another charm hanging from the gold chain. 'This is another French piece – art deco, from the look of it, around 1927. This is probably Dutch judging from the style. And this centrepiece with the stylised lion—' he pointed to the design at the centre of the necklace, '—is African.'

'African?'

'Ashanti, probably, from the area we now know as Ghana. Quite old and very collectible. These primitive gold pieces do very well in the auction houses.'

'Anything else you can tell me?'

'That's about it. All in all, a mish-mash of jewellery pieces and styles assembled from many different objects and put together by somebody wanting to create their own piece.'

'Any thoughts on the age?'

'Not really. The English and French pieces are eighteenth century, the Roman is probably fourth century, but the most modern piece is art deco. So somebody was adding to it after 1927. The African piece is difficult to date, but is probably late eighteenth or early nineteenth century.'

'It's a bit strange, isn't it, to have charms from all those places and dates mixed together?'

'I haven't seen a piece like it, to be honest. Wouldn't want it for the museum, though, too eclectic. You might sell it through a dealer, if you want.'

'Oh, I'm not interested in selling it, I just want to know where it came from.'

'I think the simple answer is everywhere. Not much help, I'm afraid.'

They shook hands and she left, not before thanking Mr Livesey for his time and knowledge.

Standing outside the Victorian building, she shook her head. The African piece of the charm necklace might hint at Rachel's past but nothing else did. What had she said about it? 'She told me she had added this charm to protect and guide me through life. I was to add something and give it to my daughter.'

Strange. Had it been handed down from mother to daughter over the years?

Perhaps. But how was it going to help Jayne in her search?

'Well, this case just gets stranger and stranger.'

A student walking past her suddenly stopped and walked in the opposite direction.

She really would have to stop talking to herself.

CHAPTER TWENTY

July 10, 1842
Wickham Hall, Cheshire

1827 – Liverpool

I remember the first time I set eyes on him.

My brother and I had been invited to a literary soiree. It was almost two years after I had left the and I had done nothing except read, embroider and pass my time in the frivolous pursuits of a young, wealthy girl in Liverpool. Occasionally, boredom had led me to go for long walks on my own, much to the consternation of my father and brother. These walks were probably the reason my brother had arranged the invite in the first place; anything to keep me occupied.

The soiree was supposed to one of the highlights of the literary year, organised by Mr Roscoe, the pre-eminent historian and banker who had fought long and hard to bestow the merchants of Liverpool with the benefits of his learning.

The candles flickered in their sconces. The dresses glittered as they twirled. The audience were hushed by the dulcet tones of Signor Panizzi as he lectured on the Italian poets, particularly Dante, at the Royal Institution.

Unfortunately, as he spoke no English, he lectured in Italian and as a result I spent most of my time yawning, as did the rest of the audience.

Next to me, Henry was sitting upright, his eyes unwavering from the speaker.

Bored, I glanced to my left and right. The great and good of Liverpool were at the Institution that evening, all intent on imbibing a dose of culture and learning they felt was their right as residents of one of the leading cities of England.

On my right, Sir Archibald Sutton sat with his sister. Still as fat as ever, he now presided over the expansion of the docks and the construction of the many fine new buildings that dominated the shoreline.

He waved at me, his chubby fingers like fat sausages wriggling on a butcher's block.

I immediately looked away, only to find another man staring at me from the other side. I nudged my brother. 'Who is that?'

My brother glanced away from Signor Panizzi for a second. 'That's Mr Carruthers, here to support his branch of the Anti-Slavery League. Can you imagine it? In Liverpool of all places?'

I looked at the man out of the corner of my eye, only to find him staring openly back at me. He was tall, dark and had curly black hair, and was wearing a jacket cut in the modern style favoured by Lord Canning, the new prime minister.

I decided to concentrate once more on Signor Panizzi's lecture. That good man droned on in Italian for the next quarter of an hour without pausing for breath. I hazarded another glance at Mr Carruthers. He was still staring at me and this time he had the temerity to smile.

I turned my eyes back to Signor Panizzi, avoiding Mr Carruthers' gaze completely by concentrating on the speaker's florid waxed moustache as it wriggled like a caterpillar under his nose.

When the good Signor finally paused for breath and we were given a break of ten minutes, my brother and I rose to walk to the lobby. Henry, on pretence of talking to one of the other merchants of the city, left me alone for a few minutes.

Out of the corner of my eye, I could see Mr Carruthers was watching me but I pretended not to notice. He hesitated twice before finally plucking up enough courage to approach.

He bowed clumsily in front of me. 'M-M-M-Miss Roylance, I presume?' he stuttered nervously.

'Have we been introduced, sir?' I asked in a voice that I thought sounded imperious but probably came out as a high-pitched squeak.

'N-N-Not yet, Miss Roylance, but by approaching you tonight, I hope to have resolved that problem. My name is Charles Carruthers, and I have the honour to be your obedient servant—'

'You are neither my servant nor my slave, sir. Unless we have been formally introduced, I—'

Mr Carruthers began to redden. 'I would have thought formal introductions were such things of the past. For a modern lady, I would have—'

'And who says I am modern, sir?'

'From what I have heard, the whole of Liverpool is agog with your exploits, Miss Roylance…your wildness of nature.'

It was true. Since I had left Miss Fanshawe's Academy more than a year ago, I had developed a reputation for being a young woman of independent mind and spirit. My father had often criticised me for wandering around the docks unescorted and unchaperoned. But life at home was so boring. How many books could one read? How many samplers could one embroider? And how many sermons could one listen to?

'My exploits, as you call them, have nothing to do with anybody but myself, Mr Carruthers. I wonder you have time for such idle gossip if you are here to expand your branch of the Anti-Slavery League in a city built on the proceeds of the whole system.'

For the first time I saw him smile and his voice became more confident. 'I am gratified, Miss Roylance, that you have enquired about my business even though you pretend never to have heard of me.'

I felt my face reddening, 'I—'

But he continued before I could respond. 'If you would really like to hear about my work, I am giving a public lecture on the case for the abolition of slavery tomorrow evening if you would care to come.'

A bell was rung to remind the audience to return to the auditorium. 'At least my lecture will be in the King's English.'

He handed over a card, which I took with my gloved hand. 'I'm afraid I am busy tomorrow evening, but perhaps another time, Mr Carruthers.'

'As you wish, Miss Roylance.'

The bell was rung for a second time. I could see my brother wending his way back through the crowd to rejoin me.

Mr Carruthers bowed once more. 'I am sorry for taking up your time, Miss Roylance.' He withdrew as my brother approached.

'What did he want?' Henry asked.

'He invited me to a meeting of the Anti-Slavery League tomorrow evening.'

'You're not going to go?'

I remember staring at the expanse of Mr Carruthers' back and his broad shoulders as he danced his way through the crowd of merchants. 'No, I don't suppose I will,' I answered.

Little did I know how untrue that statement was.

CHAPTER TWENTY-ONE

July 10, 1842
Wickham Hall, Cheshire

1827 – Liverpool

I stepped into the hall and was surprised to see that it was packed.

After attending the Sunday service where the Reverend White had spent two hours prattling on about the innate goodness of God, I had gone home and embroidered yet another sampler.

As the afternoon ticked away and the clock on the drawing room mantlepiece ticked along with it, I made my decision.

I stood up and told my father I was going to visit my friend, Alice Chambers, to discuss Signor Panizzi's lecture and to borrow a copy of Dante's Inferno *in translation.*

I don't know why I did it. Boredom, probably. Or that wildness of nature Mr Carruthers had mentioned yesterday. He had not been the most charming of men when he spoke to me. Indeed, I found him full of himself and his ideas. Why then did I go?

A woman approached me near the entrance, dressed in a severe black dress fastened at the neck with a single pearl button. 'You're here for the lecture?' she asked.

I nodded.

'And would you like to become a member of the Society?'

'I would like to hear what Mr Carruthers has to say first.'

'The Reverend Carruthers will begin his lecture in five minutes. If you would care to take a seat?' She pointed to an empty chair next to three old ladies.

I was surprised Mr Carruthers hadn't mentioned that he was a man of the cloth yesterday. Had I misheard him?

As I took my seat next to the old ladies, the oil lamps at the side of the stage dimmed slightly and a man walked on to a lectern. Mr Carruthers.

To my eyes he looked different from last night. Altogether more self-assured and confident. Not like the diffident, almost apologetic man who had approached me in the lobby of the Institute.

The audience quietened as Mr Carruthers assembled his papers on the lectern, then stared out over the assembled crowd.

For a moment, just as he began to speak, his eyes caught mine and he nodded imperceptibly.

'Ladies and gentlemen,' he began, his voice strong and resonant, 'we are gathered here this evening to meet as the Liverpool branch of the Anti-Slavery League.' He paused for a moment and a smile crossed his face. A smile I felt was solely for my benefit.

'You may be wondering why we have opened a branch in this city. After all, it is a metropolis built on the proceeds of the whole system of slavery.' Once more a smile and a glance in my direction. 'It is precisely because Liverpool owes its very existence to the institution of slavery that we have decided to goad the lion in his den, to be a biblical Daniel, taking the fight against slavery to the very centre of its corrupt web.' At the end of this line, his voice rose and his *hand clenched the lectern in front of him. The audience immediately began to applaud, understanding every word, unlike last night.*

Mr Carruthers paused again, drawing himself up to his full height and said, 'As a son of Liverpool, born here not so long ago, as were most of you, we will oppose the whole system in this den of inequity because slavery is a moral and ethical outrage against the laws of God. And let me tell you, what we will see in this great city is the triumph of the great struggle for the deliverance of the enslaved African from the most oppressive bondage that ever tried the endurance of humanity; thereby achieving a moral victory, ensuring that justice, freedom, the clemency of power and the peaceful glories of civilisation shall have a place in the hearts of these poor enslaved men.'

The last words were spoken with fervour, encouraging the audience to erupt in applause.

Mr Carruthers continued in a quieter, calmer voice. 'But such a victory will not be won lightly nor easily, for against us are waged the Gods of Mammon, many of whom reside here amongst us.'

The three old woman beside me were staring at the stage in awe. I found myself listening closely too, hearing the mellifluous tones and cadences of Mr Carruthers' speech, losing myself in the magnificence of his arguments and the moral strength of his convictions. Gone was the nervous creature I had seen last night, and in its place, a lion had arisen.

'Liverpool must purge itself from the stain which slavery has brought upon it. Slavery hated the light, slavery hated the truth, slavery hated knowledge and religion. Who would deny that slavery loved darkness? That it loved ignorance, that it sought concealment? Light would expose its enormities and would make it blush, and reason would hold it up to the universal execration of mankind.'

Here he lowered his voice again and spoke almost in a whisper. 'But it was said that the planters loved religion. They showed it by pulling down chapels. They showed it by punishing missionaries. They showed it by desecrating the Sabbath. The planters laughed at religion, desecrating the altars of God, and they, therefore, were mad...'

Then, in the middle of the audience, three men dressed in the rough clothes of dock workers stood up. One of them shouted, 'What about us? What about the workers whose lives depend on trade? What are you going to do about us?'

Mr Carruthers stopped speaking for a second. 'I understand your worries, my friend. But no human life can be dependent on the enslavement of another of God's servants for its wellbeing. No human has the right to enslave another. We are all God's children.'

'I ain't,' said the man, suddenly throwing a bottle which smashed against the lectern. Others stood up in the hall and began to throw rotten fruit and more bottles towards the stage. Stewards rushed in from the side to prevent them, waving their arms ineffectually to prevent the violence.

On stage, I could see Mr Carruthers pleading for calm. 'Gentlemen, please, there is no need for this. This is a peaceful meeting.'

On my left, the man who had heckled Mr Carruthers picked up a chair and threw it at a steward. Two other men, one carrying a short baton, began to strike the people around him, lashing out at anybody who came close.

One of the three old ladies screamed and collapsed on the floor. I tried to reach over the melee of struggling bodies to help her, then my waist was encircled from behind and I was lifted up into the air.

I tried to turn around to strike my attacker before I heard a voice.

'Miss Roylance, it is me, Charles Carruthers. I suggest you leave this hall immediately.' He looked over towards the door, where another group of rough-looking men were pushing their way into the hall.

'But I—'

He lifted me up on to the stage and climbed up after me. I stared out over the hall. The stewards were attempting to push the men out while the old ladies were sitting and shaking on their chairs, waving umbrellas above their heads.

'Come this way, Miss Roylance, there is a room at the back where you can hide while I sort this out.'

'I'm not hiding anywhere, Mr Carruthers.' I planted my feet on the stage, indicating I would not be moved.

He moved towards me then hesitated, glancing back towards the melee on the floor of the hall.

Then he turned and walked to the front of the stage, arms held wide, shouting in a booming voice, 'Gentlemen, gentlemen! Please ask your questions and I will answer them.'

For a second the noise stopped as everybody looked up towards the commanding figure of Charles Carruthers.

One man shouted from the middle of the crowd, 'Our jobs, what will happen to our jobs if you ban slavery?'

Mr Carruthers smiled and his voice dropped a register. 'I understand your fears. You're worried you might not be able to feed your family, am I right?'

The man nodded.

'That's what you all fear, isn't it? That trade will collapse and you will have no jobs left.'

An Irish voice belonging to a large, well-built man boomed out, 'Without the docks, there will be nothin'.'

The pushing and fighting had stopped now and everybody was staring towards the stage.

'Oh, I agree, sir,' Mr Carruthers responded. 'Without the docks Liverpool would have nothing, but let me tell you this sir, stopping the slave trade won't decrease jobs. On the contrary, it will increase them. Won't sugar still be needed?'

The Irish man nodded. 'I suppose so.'

'Won't cotton be needed by the mills of Lancashire?'

There were a few mutters of agreement from inside the hall.

'Won't Ireland still be exporting cattle and wheat and potatoes to feed the people of the new mill towns?'

The sounds of agreement increased across the hall.

Charles Carruthers paused for a moment before smiling. 'And won't rum still be drunk in the ale houses of Liverpool?'

'It will… too much,' came a voice from the back.

'Too little if you ask me,' answered the Irish man.

Charles Carruthers raised his arms higher. 'The one thing that will increase the welfare of everybody is free trade carried out by free people living in free nations.' He now spoke to the Irish man directly. 'Now, sir, would you like to sit down and listen to what I have to say? If at the end you still disagree with me, we will shake hands on our disagreement and go our separate ways, firm in the knowledge that we have heard the arguments for and against this malicious trade in human beings. Why, weren't your own countrymen sent against their will to the self-same islands of the Caribbean by Cromwell as indentured servants?'

'Don't listen to him, Mick,' shouted the man who had started the fight.

The Irish man sat down. 'I want to hear what ye man has to say.' His supporters, the men who had pushed their way into the hall, sat down with him.

On the other side of the room, the thug who had started the fight, seeing he had no support, stormed out through a side door.

The rest of the meeting proceeded calmly, with questions asked and answers given. I looked on from the side of the stage as Mr Carruthers rebutted each and every argument put to him with strength and politeness, listening carefully and answering simply and directly.

At the end of the meeting, he stood in the centre of the stage and said, 'Dear friends, I know I have not convinced all of you this evening but I hope in some small way I have made you ponder the opportunities that the abolition of this iniquitous enslavement of our fellow human beings allows us. If we decide to go forward with this emancipation, mankind in future ages shall point to the abolition of colonial slavery as the commencement of an era that will be the most benign and brilliant the world has ever seen. I look forward to that day, ladies and gentlemen, with you and our God by my side.'

As he finished his speech, I felt my heart soar and I knew instantly I had fallen under the spell of Charles Carruthers' words.

Even better, I knew now I had a cause that would make my life, and that of those around me, meaningful.

I must convince my father of the rightness of Mr Carruthers and the Anti-Slavery League.

CHAPTER TWENTY-TWO

July 10, 1842
Wickham Hall, Cheshire

For a moment, Emily stopped writing as the memories flooded back. She remembered the fervour, the excitement with which she had gone home that night. Filled with passion for the cause, and the man, whom she now held dear.

With almost prescient clarity, she could remember the ensuing meeting with her father. She took up her pen and began writing again.

1827 – Liverpool

'You did what?'

'I went to a meeting of the Anti-Slavery League. Mr Carruthers was the speaker.'

My father rose from the chair and walked over to where I was standing, wagging his finger in my face. 'Those people are blackguards. They would ruin us, our company and Liverpool, and you have the gall to tell me you attended one of their meetings?'

I stood my ground, refusing to be intimidated. 'I listened to the arguments both for and against. It seems to me to be obvious and un-Christian. To enslave our fellow man is morally wrong.'

'Morally wrong,' he shouted. 'What do you think pays for this fine muslin at six shillings a yard?' He tugged at my dress. 'Or for this house? Or the food I put on your table?' He strode over to the fireplace and took a large gulp of wine.

I glanced over to my brother for support. He was sitting in a chair, casually examining his fingernails.

'Father,' he eventually said, 'it is important Emily understands the arguments on both sides of the slavery question. I will give her a pamphlet from General Tarleton to help her understand how slavery is beneficial to the economic and cultural wellbeing of the African.'

My father seemed to be satisfied with this until I could not keep quiet any longer and spoke again. 'How can selling a man, his wife and their children in a market be good for their economic and cultural wellbeing? How is it supposed to aid them?'

'Go to your room, young lady. I will not be insulted in my own home. Remain there until you are called for.'

I looked across at Henry, still playing with the end of his fingers. He indicated with his head that I should leave.

'Locking me in my room won't change my mind, Father. I have decided to support the Anti-Slavery League in its efforts in Liverpool.'

After this speech, I opened the door and left the room, running upstairs as fast as my skirts would allow me. Father was not going to browbeat me this time. My mind was made up. I would support Charles to rid Liverpool of the pernicious evil of slavery.

I stopped on the landing and listened, hearing both my father and brother's voices. Silently I tiptoed down the stairs again. I was desperate to hear what they were saying about me.

As I neared the bottom of the stairs, I saw Rosie walk across the hall with a fresh decanter of claret. In the absence of the housekeeper, who was visiting her sister, Rosie must have been dispatched to serve it. She saw me on the stairs and I placed my finger across my lips.

She went in to serve my father and brother and left immediately she had finished.

'What are you doing, milady?' she asked.

'I want to find out what they are saying. Keep a lookout for me,' I whispered.

She nodded and placed herself at the entrance to the servants' quarters.

I tiptoed to the door and placed my ear to the keyhole.

My brother was talking. '...do not be too worried by this outbreak of independence, Father. I see the malign influence of a man in this, influencing the emotions of a young girl.'

'Who?' asked my father.

'Mr Charles Carruthers. I saw them talking at Signor Panizzi's soiree the other evening.'

I heard Father stride over to his desk. Oh, how I longed to see what he was doing but the only evidence I could rely on was that of my ears. I heard rapid scratching and then my father said, 'It is time she was married off. I've made a list of suitable candidates. Sir Archibald, the superintendent of docks, seems to be the best. I've seen the way he looks at her.'

Dear reader, I was tempted to push open the door and shout, 'I will not marry that lecherous man, whatever you order.' Luckily, my brother was of the same mind but for different reasons.

'Too old, too fat and too stupid. One of the Gladstone sons would be a better match for both the company and for trade. Let me sound them out at the Club tomorrow night.'

'Very well. In the meantime, what are we to do with her?'

'I think a little trip into the country would do her good, away from the distractions of Liverpool. Didn't she make friends with the Marlowes at school? Perhaps I could arrange an invite to their house at Wickham Hall?'

'Remind them I helped the father with a large loan last year. They owe us a favour.'

'I will, Father. And if they ask for more money?'

'Give it to them. They are as poor as church mice but parade around with all the airs of the aristocracy. I've had my eyes on their house for a long time. Do they have an eligible son, by any chance?'

'I'm afraid not, only a daughter. A plain woman – Clara by name. She went to school with Emily.'

I remembered Clara well and my brother had described her exactly. I was surprised he was acquainted with her, though.

'Perhaps a month or so in the country would do her good. Fresh air and boredom. Always a good antidote for a young woman with an active imagination.'

Then Father rang the bell for more wine and Rosie had to go downstairs to fetch it before anybody else answered the call.

'There is one other matter we have to discuss…' my brother continued. He seemed to be the one leading the conversation rather than my father. How he had changed in the time he had been in Liverpool.

'The anti-slavery movement is gaining strength throughout the country. We will not be able to resist them for ever.'

'They are just a bunch of Quakers who love to hear their sound of their own voices.'

'Don't underestimate them, Father. Why, even here in Liverpool the movement is gaining force and strength.'

'Did you send the men to their meeting yesterday?'

'I did, but they failed to stop it. The pacifism of the Quakers is their strength, and when combined with a messianic belief in the rights of men, well…'.

What was that about men? Had my father paid those men to barrack the meeting? It couldn't be true.

'We'll see them off, don't you worry. The trade is worth far too much to the Exchequer, plus we control Parliament through our paid men.'

'There is a desire to reform Parliament, though — to bring in the vote for property owners…'

'Property owners?' he spat. 'We'll own them as well as their property.'

'I would not be so sure, Father. And besides, we must look at the future of our estates.'

Rosie appeared by my side with the fresh decanter. I stepped back into the shadows to avoid being seen when she opened the door.

From my hiding place I could see Father and my brother in the room, discussing my future without a care in the world for my thoughts or feelings.

As soon as Rosie closed the door, I rushed back and placed my ear at the keyhole.

My father was now pacing up and down. 'Come on, out with it. Don't beat about the bush, explain yourself, Henry.'

'Since the passage of the Slave Trading Act in 1807, we have been unable to re-invigorate our slave stock. Bussa's rebellion was catastrophic for our interests.'

'We stopped 'em and killed the ringleaders, didn't we?'

'We did, Father, but perhaps we were too effective.'

'What do you mean?'

'The slaves are no longer as productive as before.'

'Just tell Mr Howard to flog them harder, then.'

'Productive in the sense of producing replacements for themselves and their work.'

'The slave trade was abolished twenty years ago and we have still survived!'

'But for how much longer, Father? We should look to the future and invest our money here at home rather than developing our estates, which have no future nor any labour.'

For a second something caught in my throat and I had to suppress my natural reaction to cough.

My brother had stopped speaking; perhaps he had heard me.

'Go on…' I heard my father urge.

Thankfully, Henry continued. 'Railways, cotton, banking, insurance. That's where our future lies, not in the production of sugar, rum and molasses. There's talk of a new railway from Liverpool to Manchester – that's the future.'

'A horseless carriage on rails? A mere toy?'

'But a toy that can move men and materials at the speed of twenty-five miles an hour to and from the docks at Liverpool.'

'We've always made our money in sugar and trade. Let that be an end to it.' I heard a chink of a glass and the sound of pouring liquid.. 'There is nothing to worry about with these anti-slavers, you mark my words. And as for your railways, they are just a fad. Haven't they already killed one government minister in Huskisson?' He drank a long draught of wine. 'Aye, with a bit of luck they'll get rid of a few more. They won't be missed either, you mark my words. The slave trade will still be making Liverpool rich when I'm in my grave pushing up daisies.'

Then I heard the sofa creak. 'You asked for my thoughts, Father, and I have given them to you. Now, I must be off to the Club. I will be seeing Gladstone. Shall I tell him about my sister's availability for marriage?'

My father was silent for a minute. 'Not yet, we'll see how she is when she comes back from the country.'

'Fine, but I wouldn't wait too long. I do not trust Mr Carruthers in this matter. I will take my leave, Father.'

At those words I rushed upstairs, desperate to make the landing before my brother left the room. I made it and looked down at the drawing-room door through the rowels of the stairs as he walked out, put on his coat and hat aided by Rosie, took his walking stick and left by the front door.

I sat there for a long while, thinking of my predicament. What was I to do?

CHAPTER TWENTY-THREE

Monday, August 19, 2019
Didsbury, Manchester

Jayne Sinclair stood outside Manchester Museum and had a choice. She could go to the solicitors Wendy had recommended last night or she could go to visit Robert and Vera.

It was no choice really. She went back to her BMW and drove out to see her stepfather and his wife in Buxton. The solicitors could wait for another few days and so could her ex-husband.

For once the drive was pleasant; the sun was shining, a few clouds skidded across an azure sky and despite it being Monday, the traffic was light along the A6.

Forty minutes later she parked outside Robert and Vera's nursing home and walked in to be greeted by Violet, the new girl on reception.

'Hello, Jayne, didn't expect to see you here today.'

'Last-minute decision. Are they in their usual spot?'

'Where else? They've finished the *Guardian* crossword and moved on to the *Times*.'

'Robert will be grumpy, he hates doing that one.'

Violet made a face. 'Vera's choice, I think.'

Jayne pushed her way through the fire doors and into the television room. A few of the residents were dozing while *Homes Under the Hammer* droned away on the television.

Robert had decided to come to the home after living alone became difficult. He had been diagnosed with early-onset Alzheimer's. Most days he was fine, but a few times he lapsed into silence, unaware of where or even who he was.

Luckily, he met Vera at the home and together they made a fine couple. Jayne's mother had died many years ago and Jayne was so happy when Robert finally found happiness with another woman.

She found them sitting outside under the shade of an old beech tree, arguing about a clue.

'It can't be the answer.'

'Listen,' said Vera, '"Old boys reportedly get to grips with a problem". Old boys is usually OBS, and so the answer must be "obstacle", because the end sounds like tackle.'

'Happen you're right, lass. I'm so glad I married a clever woman.' He went to give his wife a kiss.

Jayne coughed and, like two naughty teenagers, the couple pulled away from each other.

'Hi, Jayne, great to see you,' said Vera.

'Sorry to interrupt, but I thought I'd pop in.'

Vera glanced across at Robert. 'You're not interrupting, dear, we're just doing the crossword.'

'Actually, Vera's doing the crossword, love, I'm just inking in the letters.'

'But you do it very well, husband.' And this time she did kiss him.

Jayne sat down with them.

'You look a bit tired, love, what's up?' asked her stepfather.

'Nothing really, just a new client and not enough time, as usual.'

'People these days are always in a rush to get answers. Never take their time, do they, Robert?'

'No, love. What's the case?'

'It's an actress, Rachel Marlowe.'

'Ooh, I saw her in *Charles II*, she was one of his mistresses. Was it Nell Gwynn or the Duchess of Portsmouth? One of the two, anyway.'

Jayne explained the research she was doing. Robert understood the problem immediately. He had researched his own family extensively and introduced Jayne to genealogy when she was young.

'You know me, lass, a bit old school. Can't really get my mind around this DNA stuff. Give me a good parish register any day.'

'I tested myself a couple of years ago,' said Vera. 'Apparently I'm Irish and Scots with a bit of Scandinavian thrown in for good luck.'

'That's probably the bit I like,' said Robert with a twinkle in his eye. Vera pinched the back of his hand and he turned to Jayne. 'If I were you, I'd do it the old-school way, check out the parish registers. You'll be amazed what you find.'

'Anyway, enough of work. Let's have a game of Crib, shall we? I've had enough of the crossword.'

They spent the rest of the day playing cards until four o'clock, when Jayne announced that she should leave to avoid the rush hour on the A6.

'When are you coming again, love?'

'Probably after Friday. I'm going to be snowed under with this job.'

'Aye, I reckon you will be. Not many families can trace their line back to William the Conqueror. But one piece of advice from this old 'un – don't believe the family trees until you've checked every detail yourself.'

'I'll remember, Robert.' She kissed him on the forehead and Vera on the cheek before leaving them and returning to her car.

It always felt good visiting them and watching the beautiful way they reacted to each other.

Love didn't have to be difficult at all. It just took work.

There was hope for her yet.

CHAPTER TWENTY-FOUR

Monday, August 19, 2019
Didsbury, Manchester

Jayne stood up and stretched, checking the time on the kitchen clock.

8.30 p.m. Where had all the time gone? She had been sitting in front of the computer since her return home, checking out the family tree as Robert had advised.

It was funny how time seemed to vanish when she was researching. Hours went by in the blink of an eye as she delved deep into a family's history. It was a time she loved. When all that mattered was making sure the details and relationships were correct.

The problems of the outside world had temporarily vanished; her divorce from Paul, the cost of the solicitors, what to do with the house – all gone for a few precious hours.

She walked over to the patio doors and stared out at the small garden. The few clouds had passed and it was now a lovely summer's evening. A blackbird was singing from its perch in the tree opposite. Two doors away, a few children were playing hide and seek. In the distance, the chimes of an ice-cream van with its jangling song, 'Oranges and lemons, say the bells of St Clements' ringing through the still air. Perhaps it was the same van she had heard earlier.

She stared at her garden. The grass looked dishevelled and overgrown, and the flower borders were choked with weeds. Time to get the mower out and get down on her knees to work on it.

She loved her garden, just hated the constant care and attention it needed.

And for a second, a thought crossed her mind.

It was a bit like relationships. They needed constant care and attention too, and if that work wasn't done, they would become disordered and chaotic. Perhaps that was what had happened between Paul and herself. They had been so busy with their own lives they had forgotten to cultivate their relationship.

Mr Smith miaowed at her feet and strolled out into the garden, leaping on to the top of the fence and walking along it with his tail held high in the air.

'See you later,' she said as he wandered off. For a moment she felt quite lonely, as if the world was conspiring to isolate her. Then she shook her head to rid it of such morbid thoughts and went to get her phone.

She rang her client. 'Rachel, it's Jayne Sinclair. How are you?'

'Could be better. I've just done a scene where I'm dying from consumption. Spent the last four hours coughing my guts out. They don't tell you about this in acting school.'

'Sounds awful.'

'Plus my co-star has the worst case of bad breath since my Labrador, and is about as attractive as a haddock. How he was voted Britain's sexiest star is beyond me.'

Jayne found herself laughing. 'My day was quiet in comparison.' She then told Rachel of her visit to the museum and her research into the family tree.

'So what are the next steps?'

'I've exhausted the census returns, and the registration of births, marriages and deaths only began in 1837. If I want to go back further, I need to research in the parish registers. With a family as prominent as your own, the records will have been entered into the local church. It's called St Peter's.'

'That's where I was baptised.'

'Great, I'll give the vicar a call and arrange a time tomorrow.'

'Can I go with you? I've a day off. Mr Dog Breath has to do his close-ups and has a few scenes where he breathes on his mistress.'

'Well, I—'

'The vicar knows me and I could help open a few doors that otherwise would be closed. And besides, I have to go back to Wickham Hall anyway, you could give me a lift.'

Jayne laughed at the chutzpah of this. She was now not just a genealogical investigator but a chauffeur too. Amazingly, she found herself saying yes.

'Great, that's confirmed. Pick me up from the Hilton at ten?'

'Could we start a little earlier?'

'I'm not at my best before then, I'm afraid. I need to drink gallons of coffee and put on my face. A girl has to maintain her standards.'

'Well, ten it is. See you tomorrow.'

'Great. You'll love the vicar, he's a bit of a character. Loves his archaeology, but Father won't let him dig the estate. See you at ten.'

Jayne put down the phone, shaking her head at what she had agreed. Rachel had a certain charm about her that made saying no quite difficult. Nevertheless, she would be able to smooth the way with the vicar, which could be very useful.

She stared at the fridge. Was it too early for a glass of sauvignon blanc?

'It's never too early,' she said out loud. Once she had poured a glass, she would ring the vicar and research divorce solicitors. She was desperate to remain living in the house, whatever happened.

Bloody Paul. Why did he have to be so difficult right now?

CHAPTER TWENTY-FIVE

Tuesday, August 20, 2019
Didsbury, Manchester

Jayne's eyes flicked open. Had she heard a noise?

She glanced across at the alarm clock beside her bed.

3.00 a.m.

Had she been having a nightmare? Was that why she woke up?

The bedroom was silent. Moonlight poured in through a small gap in the curtains, throwing the whole room into a charcoal drawing of light and shadow. Was there something there in the darkness beside the wardrobe?

A loud hiss, followed by a shriek outside her window and a long yowl.

She switched on the bedside lamp. Was that Mr Smith? He sounded like he was in pain.

Still in her t-shirt and knickers, she leapt out of bed and ran down the stairs into the kitchen. She switched on the light, and there was Mr Smith in front of the patio doors, his back arched and the hackles on his fur raised.

She hurried over to the door and unlocked it. Instantly, Mr Smith rushed in, running between her legs. Instead of heading to his bowl as he usually did, he ran into the hall and up the stairs.

She stared out into the garden. It seemed quiet. 'Is anybody there?' she shouted.

No answer.

She switched on the garden light. Instantly, a strong beam illuminated the long grass and weed-strewn borders. She listened for movement but the only sounds were those of the night: the soft rustling of the breeze in the trees. The hum of traffic in the distance. The clicking of a nightjar off to her left.

She stepped out on to the patio and said again, 'Is anybody there?'

No response.

Mr Smith must have met a fox scavenging for food in the bins. Poor fox, I wouldn't want to meet the cat as he returned from a night on the tiles. Must have scared the life out of the poor thing.

She turned to go back into the house when her eye caught a trampled rose bush in the border next to the patio.

'I'm sure that wasn't broken before.' She bent down to lift it up, noticing a large footprint in the soil at its base.

'That definitely wasn't there before.'

Then her training as a police officer kicked in. She gently moved away the trampled rose bush, revealing the full print of a large shoe, probably a trainer and at least a size ten, she thought. It couldn't have been the window cleaner as he hadn't been for a couple of weeks and, besides, he was always so careful with the plants.

Then she stood up and checked the lock on the patio door. Were those scratch marks? Or had they been there before?

She breathed on the glass next to the lock. In the moonlight she could see a large palm print for a second, before it vanished as the condensation from her breath disappeared.

The palm print was far bigger than hers. Somebody had definitely been outside her patio door.

A burglar? She hadn't heard of any break-ins in the area recently. She would give the local nick a call to check tomorrow morning.

Should she call them right now?

She imagined the voice of the call-centre operator.

'You think somebody was outside your house because your cat yowled?'

'Yes, plus there's a palm print on the glass and a footprint in the soil.'

'Has there been a break-in?'

'No.'

'Nothing has been stolen?'

'No.'

'There is no sign of an intruder in the area near your house?'

'No.'

'Are you in danger right now?'

'No.'

'Are you sure, madam?'

'Yes.'

'Okay, we'll send an officer down just as soon as one becomes available. It will probably be in the morning.'

With the recent cuts, her sort of call would not be a priority. Possible burglaries were classed as non-urgent cases.

She decided there was no point in reporting it. The police had enough to do and, besides, she was confident she could handle anybody who tried to break in. They'd soon regret going anywhere near her house.

She went back inside and checked the time. It was now 3.30. She didn't feel like going back to bed. Perhaps a good cup of coffee and a check of the news before she drove out to pick up Rachel?

As she made her coffee, one thought nagged away in the back of her mind.

Why now?

Why had somebody been trying to get into her house now?

CHAPTER TWENTY-SIX

Tuesday, August 20, 2019
Manchester

Jayne drove into the city centre along the A56, heading towards Deansgate where she could pick Rachel up from her hotel.

She had stayed awake since earlier that morning, fortified by coffee, the inanities of early morning radio and baking some bread. It was time to relax a little and let her subconscious mind think about Rachel's problem. There was a wonderful release in kneading the dough for the bread. She found it tactile and tiring, just what she needed. But inevitably, questions flooded her mind.

Where had Rachel's Ghanaian ancestry come from?

Which ancestor was it?

And who had been outside Jayne's door?

What did they want?

She had no answers at the moment, but she knew they would come eventually. At nine in the morning she had showered and then dressed in a very conservative outfit of jeans and a sensible jacket, adding just a dash of eyeliner and lipstick to give herself a natural look.

Jayne knew she was not a beauty in the conventional sense, but she made the best use of what she had; sparkling eyes and pronounced cheekbones. And she did it to make herself happy and feel good. Nothing else mattered.

Rachel was outside the hotel, smoking a cigarette and looking amazing; tall, elegant, beautifully made-up and as thin as a stick insect.

As soon as she saw Jayne, she stubbed her cigarette out in a plant pot and rushed over to get in the car.

'A ridiculous habit, I know, but one I picked up at my expensive boarding school. It was our one revolt against authority. Now I can't start my day without a coffin nail, it sort of jolts me awake.'

Jayne had never been a smoker and could not see the attraction. Paying some company a lot of money to fill your lungs with tar-soaked smoke? No thank you.

She put the car in gear and headed back the way she had come, looking for the signs to the M56 to take them into deepest, darkest Cheshire.

'I called the vicar last night and have arranged an appointment for eleven fifteen. We should arrive in plenty of time.'

'I'm looking forward to seeing old Arbuthnot again. Did I tell you he baptised me? Apparently, even then he was a bit unsteady on his feet and managed to dunk my head in the font. No wonder I'm scared of water, it's all his fault.'

'You're scared of water?'

'Aquaphobia. I turn to jelly when I see the sea or a lake. Can't help it. Probably why I love the mountains and skiing.'

They chatted for the next fifty minutes. Or rather, Jayne concentrated on driving while Rachel told her about work, gossiping mercilessly about the eccentricities and foibles of Britain's most famous people. This man wears a hair piece. Another wears make-up. A third can't ever remember his lines, so they hold up cards with the words written on them for him just off camera.

Jayne found herself laughing uncontrollably until Rachel asked, 'And what about you? Who's the real Jayne Sinclair?'

'You're looking at her. An ex-police detective, now a genealogical investigator.'

'Nooooo, I mean you *personally*. Who's the real Jayne Sinclair? What's in your family tree?'

Jayne told her about her father and the research into her grandmother and the SOE.

'That's so fascinating. I'd love to play a character like her – your grandmother, I mean. Imagine parachuting into occupied France with the only weapons being your wits and your beauty.'

'I think she had a revolver as well.'

'You know what I mean. It would make a wonderful film with little ol' me in the starring role.'

'Very funny.'

'I'm serious. It would be perfect for me.'

Luckily, they arrived in the village of Little Marden before the conversation could go any further.

She parked in a pub car park opposite the church and they walked together across the road and through the lychgate. The church itself sat on a slight rise in the ground and dominated the village, with its clock tower showing the time as four o'clock even though it was just after eleven.

The vicar was waiting for them at the entrance.

Jayne was surprised to see Rachel run up to the old man and gave him a big hug.

'It's been a long time, Rachel. I wondered when you were going to come back.'

'Too long, Reverend Arbuthnot.' She stepped back and gestured towards Jayne. 'This is Ms Sinclair, she's my genealogical researcher.'

They shook hands. Jayne noticed the vicar's touch was icy cold as if made from marble.

'I thought your brother had already finished your family tree. The Marlowes have been here for ages, benefactors of St Peter's long before I was the incumbent, and will be long after I'm gone. Your father has continued the tradition, donating very generously to the clock-tower fund.'

Rachel reached into her handbag and produced a cheque for five hundred pounds. 'Here's my contribution, Reverend.'

The vicar held up his hands. 'I couldn't possibly accept, Rachel.'

She folded it up and placed it in the pocket of his cassock. 'Think of it as continuing the family tradition.'

'If you insist. Now, Mrs Sinclair—'

'It's Ms Sinclair.'

'Of course, Ms Sinclair, would you like to see the church? It's Grade One listed, you know.'

'Don't let old Arbuthnot bore you, Jayne, he can speak for hours on the subject of his precious church. I've had so many lectures I can recite them by heart.'

'And I'm sure they helped you in your exams, did they not? Shall we go in?'

They walked through the entrance and immediately Jayne's eyes were led by the perspective of a row of arches to a small red-baize-covered altar at the end of the nave. The light had a soft, almost pinkish tinge that suffused the church with peace and tranquillity.

'It's mostly crafted in the Perpendicular tradition, but the north transept is in the Decorated style, giving the whole interior a slightly quirky but original effect.' Reverend Arbuthnot was now in full lecture mode. 'It's built from red sandstone and was mostly constructed in the fifteenth and sixteenth centuries, but one part – the Marlowe Chapel – was probably built as early as the fourteenth century.' He pointed to a small family chapel off to the left, with five old wooden pews and a picture of some long-lost ancestor of Rachel's.

'Look, there's the font you nearly drowned me in.'

'I didn't nearly drown you, Rachel, my hand slipped and you became wetter than usual. The whole point of a baptism is to get wet.'

For an instant, Jayne saw a tougher side to this old cleric, one that had scared many children in the past she was sure.

For the next thirty minutes, Reverend Arbuthnot guided them around the old church, his voice betraying pride at the beauty of his domain.

Eventually, Rachel spoke up. 'Thank you, Reverend, but we have another appointment with my father at one o'clock for lunch. Could we see the parish registers now?'

Again, Jayne saw a brief flare of anger in the eyes of the old vicar. 'Well, we mustn't keep Sir Harold waiting. Follow me. Some of the registers were stolen three years ago, but you can certainly look at the rest.'

The vicar led them to a small vestry behind a large oak door. He produced a large brass key and unlocked it.

'Was the door locked when the registers were stolen?' asked Jayne.

'That was what was so strange. I'm sure I locked it that day, but I must have forgotten. Old age creeping on me, no doubt.'

They walked into a large stone room with rows of books on shelves locked behind a long, barred bookcase.

'We added the security measures afterwards.' He pointed to the new bars and to a camera mounted in the ceiling. 'A bit like barring the gate after the horse has bolted, I thought, but the insurance people insisted on it.'

He walked over to the middle of the bookcase and produced a key from a bunch jangling at his belt. He unlocked the bars, opening them wide to reveal rows of thin old registers, each with a date in faded gold on its spine. 'Which year would you like to see? The earliest we have is 1723.'

'There are two registers I'd like to look at. The first is 1804,' said Jayne.

The reverend reached up and selected a thin, battered register. 'Here we are, 1804 to 1807. What's the record you want to see?'

'The birth of one of Rachel's ancestors, Henry Marlowe.'

'As one of the Marlowes, such a birth would have a unique page at the front.'

He leafed through the pages, but there was no special entry, and the births for that year covered just twelve pages of flowing copperplate writing.

'Can I look?' Jayne asked.

He handed over the book. 'You'll find the writing difficult to decipher.'

'It's not a problem, I'm used to this kind of script.'

She checked all twelve pages of entries. Nothing for any of the Marlowes.

'Are you sure you have the right year?'

'The census ages for Henry Marlowe were thirty-seven in 1841, and forty-seven in 1851. I suppose he should have been born in 1804. Can I check other years?'

The vicar handed her the book for 1807 to 1810, taking the 1801 to 1804 volume for himself.

They both pored over the registers, turning the pages slowly and carefully.

Finally the vicar shouted, 'Here's one.'

Jayne stood beside him, peering down at the wrinkled finger pointing at an entry written in an almost illegible script.

'Clare, is it?' he said. 'Or Dara? But it's definitely a female not a male, the big F is very clear.'

Jayne bent closer. 'Could it be Clara?'

'Possibly,' agreed the vicar, 'but I thought you were looking for a Henry.'

'We are. But I seem to remember Henry's wife was called Clara.'

'A coincidence. Common enough name in those times. Shall we keep looking for a son and heir?'

Jayne nodded and returned to her ledger, but there was no mention of any more Marlowe births, either male or female, for the period.

'Can somebody tell me what's going on?' asked Rachel.

'I just thought I'd check one of your ancestors, Henry. According to the census, and the family tree, he was born in 1804 but doesn't seem to have been registered. He had a sister, Emily Roylance, who was born in 1806 and appears in the census but not in the family tree. She also has a different surname, so perhaps she was a widow using her husband's name. Anyway, they were both described as living at Wickham Hall in the 1841 census. What happened to her?'

'I don't know. Never heard of her before.'

'It's a mystery we should solve.'

'Perhaps the births were registered in a different parish,' suggested Reverend Arbuthnot.

'But the Marlowe births and baptisms have always been celebrated at St Peter's. It's a family tradition,' said Rachel.

The vicar just shrugged his shoulders.

'Never mind,' said Jayne. 'The second area I'd like to research would be the period from 1830 to 1841, and we're looking for the birth of Royston Marlowe. According to the census, he was born in 1834. There was no registration of births until 1837, so the only way to trace the birth is through the parish registers.'

The vicar's shoulders slumped. 'I'm afraid we don't have any registers for the period from 1827 right through to 1842. They were stolen three years ago.'

'Stolen?'

'I'm afraid so. All the birth and marriage registers.'

'So there's no record of Henry Marlowe's marriage either?'

The vicar shook his head.

'Was anything else taken?'

'It was very strange, nothing else vanished except the registers. You see, we keep the gold crucifixes, plate and chalices locked away in a safe – even the chasubles are kept in a locked wardrobe, but I never thought anybody would steal some old books.'

Jayne noticed the vicar's eyes drift down to the ground for a second, and his feet shuffled nervously.

'That's a shame. Jayne, what are we going to do?' asked Rachel.

'Mr Arbuthnot, were the registers transcribed before they were stolen?'

'I can't remember. They may have been.'

'What does that mean, Jayne?'

'The Church of the Latter Day Saints, the Mormons to you and me, have been transcribing old registers for years. They may have the information we're looking for on microfilm.'

'Where can we see it?'

'Back in Manchester. There's a research centre in Wythenshawe.'

'All roads lead to Manchester. Can you visit them today?'

'I'll need to call first and check if they have a copy of the registers for the church.'

'And if they don't?'

'We'll need to order one, but that could take time – up to two weeks.'

'We don't have that long. The programme goes out on Saturday and it's Tuesday already.'

'Let's keep our fingers crossed.'

Rachel leant in and whispered so the old vicar couldn't hear. 'If you've finished here, we can call them from the pub. I'm dying for a glass of wine.'

Jayne nodded. 'There's nothing more here.'

Rachel strode over to the vicar and hugged him again. 'It's time to go, Reverend.'

The old man smiled. 'You must come again soon, when we get the clock fixed.'

'I will, I promise. You know I always love to see you.'

Rachel took Jayne by the arm and led her out of the vestry. Just then, an idea struck the genealogist. She stopped and turned back.

'Reverend Arbuthnot, did David Marlowe see the registers before they were stolen?'

The vicar hesitated for a second before answering. 'I… I think he did. He was going through the records at roughly the same time, I think.'

'Thank you, Reverend.'

Jayne and Rachel walked down the nave and out of the old church, hearing the vicar calling to them as they left: 'Please give my regards to Sir Harold, won't you?'

CHAPTER TWENTY-SEVEN

July 10, 1842
Wickham Hall, Cheshire

1827-30 – Liverpool

Over the next three years I disobeyed my father regularly, much to his unhappiness.

After that fateful first argument, I was sent down to Wickham Hall to spend time with Clara, my friend from school, and her father.

I must say she had changed in the intervening years, becoming bitter and old before her time. Her father was no better; a perverted man constantly railing at the imprecations of the modern world and the rudeness of his servants. He tried to importune me at every opportunity and I always had to be careful never to be alone with him, a task I accomplished by taking long walks or rides with Clara, and locking my door at night.

After a month or so, Father relented and I was allowed to return to Liverpool. I think he missed me even though I had sorely disappointed him.

I resolved on my return to play the dutiful daughter but, secretly and without his knowledge, began to work for the anti-slavery movement. I managed this for almost two years; attending meetings, talking with sympathisers, arranging Mr Carruthers' diary and being the unofficial secretary of the movement. I was helped in all this by Rosie, who covered up my doings, and by the use of a subterfuge which had worked for me before; the creation of an afternoon book club.

Myself and the sisters in the movement were able to meet and work out our plans without being disturbed. Indeed, the book club and its activities became so successful that we managed to recruit most of the eligible daughters of the merchants of Liverpool.

We were a trojan horse at the centre of polite society.

Mr Carruthers was able to attend meetings when he was in Liverpool. Unfortunately, his lecturing took him across the north as far as Manchester, Leeds, Hull and Lancaster. We kept up a lively correspondence in his absences, the letters sent in care of Rosie in case my father ever asked who was sending me mail.

In two years, the movement became stronger and stronger. We kept moving motions in Parliament, sending petitions and encouraging the people to make their views known.

Mr Carruthers was certain of our success, as was I. Together, we would win the day and help free our fellow man from enslavement.

All was going well, and I had managed to keep my subterfuge secret until one day my brother saw me in the company of Mr Carruthers after a meeting of the 'book club'. What he was doing in that area, God only knows. I hate to think he was tipped off by one of my fellow society members.

He accosted us at the entrance to the Philosophical Society, where we had been holding our afternoon meetings.

'Sir,' my brother asked Charles, 'what are your intentions towards my sister?'

Mr Carruthers glanced across at me. 'Sir,' he answered in return, 'I have no intentions towards your sister but, if she will consent, I would be the happiest man on earth if she agreed to be my wife.'

Well, reader, my heart soared when I heard these words. I had dreamt of such an outcome but never imagined it could actually occur. As a lady, I would have hoped the proposal had been made in more romantic circumstances but I had, at last, heard the words from his own fair lips.

'Emily,' my brother spoke to me, 'you are to return home with me immediately.'

'Henry,' I replied, 'I will not. You have no right to order me to do anything.'

I felt Mr Carruthers' hand on my bare arm. The touch produced a tingling sensation, the like of which I had never experienced before. 'Emily, you should return home with your brother. I will visit your house this evening and speak to your father.'

My first reaction was to say no and stand my ground beside the man I loved. But he spoke again. 'You must consider your reputation, it is better to return home.'

In the face of his words, my resolve disappeared like water off a hot stove. I nodded my head and walked back home with my brother.

Oh reader, I wish I had stayed by my true love's side.

CHAPTER TWENTY-EIGHT

July 10, 1842
Wickham Hall, Cheshire

Emily was feeling tired, her back stiff from the effort of bending over the desk to write. She had not realised that putting pen to paper was such hard work. Either that or living at Wickham Hall had softened both her muscles and her wits.

She stood up and stretched. Outside the weather was perfect, the light still shining as the swifts soared over the formal garden, their curved wings slicing through the air, each one calling shrilly to the other.

She checked outside the door. A tray of food had been placed there with some tea. She ate it ravenously even though the meat and the dumplings were cold, as was the tea.

She thought about ordering some fresh tea to be brewed but decided against it. The book would not write itself and she had such a lot to do before Henry returned.

She had to get her story finished before then.

1830 – Liverpool

The evening did not go well for me. As soon as I arrived home, I was sent to my room and told to wait.

I sat there alone for a long while, staring at the wall, hearing voices downstairs but unable to comprehend the words, until the housekeeper, Mrs Trevor, came into the room.

'Where is Rosie?' I asked.

'Rose has lost her position. She is no longer employed by this household.'

'What?'

'She was caught stealing and has been reported to the police.'

'Rosie? Stealing? Rosie would never steal from this family.'

'Your brother caught her with a pair of candlesticks in her bag.' The housekeeper smiled malevolently. 'That is the last we will be seeing of Rose McPartlan.'

'What's going to happen to her?'

'She'll be tried and sentenced as usual. Transported for life, I should imagine.'

'What is to happen to her family?'

'She should have thought about that before she stole.' Another smile crept across Mrs Trevor's face. 'You may be interested to hear that Mr Carruthers has just arrived. He's waiting in the ante-room for your father and brother.'

'I must go and see him,' I cried, rising from my seat in front of the dressing table. I rushed for the door only to find the route blocked by the housekeeper.

'You shouldn't go down. These things are best left to the men.'

'But I must see him.'

'Your brother has ordered me to keep you inside here, miss.' The housekeeper locked the door, placing the key in her pocket.

I lunged forward, trying to get at the key, but suddenly found myself in Mrs Trevor's ice-cold grip.

'You should do as you are told, miss, like a properly brought-up girl.'

I was pushed back roughly towards the bed.

'You will stay here, until the men have finished.'

As the housekeeper finished her sentence, I heard shouting from down below, followed by the slamming of a door and more shouts.

'It sounds like the men have finished their discussions. I will go down and see if the master requires a glass of wine.' She unlocked the door and went out.

I rushed after her, desperate to run downstairs and see Mr Carruthers, but I heard the key turning in the lock behind her.

I banged on the door and rattled the handle but to no avail. The housekeeper had locked me in: a prisoner in my own home.

What had happened downstairs?

The raised voices had not sounded good. Had Mr Carruthers already departed? Had Father sent him away, never to return? Would I never see him again? Never gaze upon that radiant face or his soft brown eyes? Would I never hear his voice again?

And poor Rosie, she would never steal from the family. Her one crime was loyalty to me.

For the first time in my short life, I felt totally alone.

What would become of me?

CHAPTER TWENTY-NINE

Tuesday, August 20, 2019
Little Marden, Cheshire

Jayne and Rachel sat in one of the small snug rooms of the village pub, the King's Arms.

'I had my first drink in here when I was fifteen,' said Rachel, sipping her glass of Chilean chardonnay. 'This place always brings back memories for me.'

'I think I had my first drink around that age too. A glass of snakebite, vicious stuff.'

'Half bitter, half cider?'

Jayne nodded.

'Been there, drunk that. Cheers.' Rachel clinked her glass against Jayne's lime soda. 'What are the next steps? I think we're running out of time.'

'Give me a second and let me call the family research centre.' Jayne picked up her mobile and scrolled through her contacts, hoping the number would be there. Luckily it was. Her call was answered on the third ring by a friendly voice.

After a short conversation, the man confirmed they didn't have the parish registers for St Peter's on microfilm and they hadn't yet been digitised.'

'When will the digital versions be available?'

'I'm sorry, I don't know, but all our records should be fully digital by the end of 2020.'

'I need the information earlier, I'm afraid. Thank you for your trouble and sorry for bothering you.'

Jayne looked across at Rachel, who was on her second glass of chardonnay, as she hung up. 'No luck, I'm afraid.'

'What's next?'

Jayne pulled out her laptop. 'We try online. There are a few sites which might have the records.'

'Do you want something to eat? I'm starving.'

'I thought you said you were meeting your father?'

'Oh, that was just a little fib for the reverend, otherwise he would have been lecturing on his flying buttresses and his architraves for the next year. So, what would you like?'

'A cheese sandwich would be great.'

'They do a wonderful ploughman's with a local artisan Cheshire from Chorlton's Cheese.'

'Sounds perfect, what are you having?'

'Another glass of chardonnay. But I'll watch you eat.'

While Rachel went to the bar to order, Jayne logged on to the pub's wi-fi. She then began to slowly trawl through the websites with Rachel looking over her shoulder.

After forty minutes, two more glasses of lime soda, and having finished her delicious ploughman's, she stopped.

'Nothing for St Peter's on the Findmypast, Ancestry or Familysearch websites. The Genealogist has some records, but not for the years we want. There are lots of Cheshire records but not many for St Peter's.'

'I think the Reverend is quite protective of the church's records.'

'Not protective enough if he allowed them to be stolen.' Jayne took a sip of lime soda. 'There's just one area left to look.'

'Where?'

'Perhaps we should have started there first,' she said as she typed in the web address. 'The Cheshire Archival and Local Studies office, which is a rather fancy title for a records office.'

The website appeared on her screen. She checked the pages. 'Well, it seems they have microfilm of the parish registers for St Peter's, but I'm not certain if they have the years we need.'

'What are you going to do?'

'Let's give them a call.'

Jayne spoke to the duty archivist. 'Well, it looks like they may have something but they'll be closed by the time we get there, so I've booked an appointment for first thing tomorrow morning. Do you want to come?'

'Try stopping me.'

Jayne stood up. 'Great. I'll take you back to Wickham Hall now, I'd like to get an early night tonight.'

Rachel drained her glass. 'Let's just have one more for the road.'

'One more lime juice and my lips will turn blue.'

'Have a glass of wine then.'

'Not when I'm driving. Seen too many accidents caused by stupid drunken drivers ever to drink and drive myself.' She sat down again. 'But you go ahead, there's one more piece of research we can do while I've still got some battery power on the laptop.'

'What's that?'

'This woman, Emily Roylance – there's something about her that intrigues me. Let's see if we can find anything.'

'Lead on, Macduff.'

'I thought it was "Lay on, Macduff".'

Rachel made a moue with her mouth. 'Respect. How did you know that phrase is from *Macbeth*?'

'O levels, 1990. I got a B in English even though I hated school. It never leaves you.'

CHAPTER THIRTY

July 11, 1842
Wickham Hall, Cheshire

Emily woke up late.

Her body, her eyes and her head hurt. She had finally stopped writing at two in the morning when the candle had burnt down to its quick and she hadn't wanted to wake the housekeeper to ask for a new one.

She checked out of the window. It was a perfect summer's day; the birds were singing and the leaves were gently rustling in the breeze.

A gentle knock on the door.

'Come in,' Emily said. As the door opened, she realised she had left her book open on the desk.

The housekeeper was bustling into the room carrying a tray.

'We've got a pot of tea, some soft-boiled eggs, some of Cook's bread and a pat of freshly churned butter from the dairy.'

The housekeeper carried the tray over to the bed and laid it on top of the sheets.

'Did you sleep well? By the look of you, you did not. The circles under your eyes are growing darker. The sooner Dr Lansdowne comes to look at you, the better.'

Emily glanced across at the book. It was still on her dressing table, open for all to see, but apparently Mrs Davies hadn't noticed it.

The housekeeper leant over her, tucking in the sheets and adjusting Emily's nightdress. 'Now, you eat it all up and I'll send Prudence up to fetch your tray. We have heard the master will be home tomorrow with Mistress Clara. It will be good to have them both back, don't you agree? Anyway, I must be away to prepare the house for their return.' She walked over to the door, stopping with her hand on the handle. 'Do eat, Miss Emily, we are concerned about how thin you have become in the last few months.'

And then she was gone.

Emily heaved a sigh of relief, pushed the tray to one side and leapt out of bed. What had the awful woman said? Henry was returning tomorrow…

She had to finish her book before then.

She sat down at the dressing table and took up her pen, dipping it in the ink, and began to write.

1830 – Liverpool

The next two months were the worst of my life; I wasn't allowed to leave the house, my father and brother refused to have any contact with me, my movements were watched day and night by Mrs Trevor and, even worse, I heard nothing from Mr Carruthers. My days were filled with inertia and sadness, my nights with the dreams induced by the liberal doses of laudanum administered carefully by Mrs Trevor.

At times like these, my thoughts ran amok.

Had Father scared Mr Carruthers off? Had he abandoned me? Why had he not tried to get in touch?

I knew nothing other than that which Mrs Trevor deigned to tell me.

'You will be pleased to hear Mr Carruthers has left Liverpool,' she announced one day. 'Apparently, you weren't the only young lady he was courting.'

'That's a lie, Charles would never behave in such a manner.'

'Your brother has the evidence. Apparently, he proposed marriage to the Danvers girl and some trollop of an actress.' She sniffed. 'Your father and brother have been unable to hold their heads up in polite society.'

I was left alone with my sorrow for the next week. Had Mr Carruthers really behaved so badly? Had he made love to other women besides me? I didn't know the answer. In fact, I knew nothing any more, except that I was a woman alone in the world. But I resolved to find out the truth, for nothing else but my own peace of mind.

A week later my father called me into his study.

'You have behaved stupidly, Emily. It doesn't surprise me, Carruthers took advantage of the frailty of mind of your sex. I shouldn't be disappointed but I am. The sooner you are married off to a good man, the better.'

'Father,' I said in my sweetest voice, 'I realise I have disappointed you and I promise to commit myself to regaining your trust. I hope you will forgive me.'

He finished his glass of wine. 'It is to be expected from your sex. I blame your mother, she gave you far too much freedom as a child.'

At the mention of my dead mother, my eyes naturally filled with tears.

Father saw this and poured another glass from the decanter, hastily mumbling, 'You have been chastised enough now, you may eat with the family this evening.'

'Thank you, Father. I have looked forward to this day for so long.'

'Now leave me, I have work to do.'

I bowed obediently, and tiptoed gracefully to the door, stopping just as I was about to leave. 'Father, would it be convenient to go to the bookshop? I feel I need to improve my education on the correct way to behave. There is a new edition of the Mirror of Graces *by A Lady of Distinction available. I feel it would help me immensely.'*

My father pondered this idea for a moment. 'I suppose it would be a good idea, as long as Mrs Trevor accompanies you as a chaperone.'

'Thank you, Father.' I ran back and kissed him on the top of the head. He reddened, swatting me away playfully and exclaiming, 'I have work to do, woman.'

But at least I now had his agreement to leave the house. This I did the following day, accompanied by my shadow, Mrs Trevor.

But what neither she nor my father knew was that Mr Collins, the bookseller, was an active supporter of the Anti-Slavery League. If I could get a second alone with him, I was certain he would be able to tell me the truth about what had happened.

As we entered the bookshop on Old Hall Street, a bell above the door rang loudly. Mr Collins ran out from behind the counter. 'Welcome, ladies, what can I do for you?'

He was a small, thin man with a pair of pince-nez perched on the end of his large nose like a cow straddling a stile.

'We would like to see some books on the moral education of young women, preferably written by somebody reliable,' said Mrs Trevor officiously.

As the bookseller came closer, he peered at me over the top of his glasses. I saw he was about to greet me by name and I raised my finger to my lips, before saying, 'Something uplifting and Christian, if you have it, Mr...?'

He nodded at me once. 'My name is Collins and I am at your service, miss. You are in luck, this morning we have received a new consignment of the latest Christian texts from the estimable writer, Mrs Ponsonby.' He led us towards a table piled high with books.

While Mrs Trevor buried herself in the prose, looking for something suitable, the bookseller announced, 'There are some more suitable books over here, miss. Perhaps, you would care to peruse them.'

I strode over to join him at a bookcase close to the window. 'Have you heard from Mr Carruthers?' I asked under my breath.

He glanced back at Mrs Trevor. 'He is still in Liverpool. The society is going strong but we have missed you over the last few months.' Then he corrected himself: 'Carruthers has missed you.'

'I heard he departed the city, leaving behind a trail of broken hearts.'

'The only broken heart is his own and he has remained here despite the need to work and lecture and organise across the north.'

My hopes soared at the news. 'He is still here?'

The man nodded. 'Come here this time next week and I'll make sure he will be in the stock room.' His eyes then glanced across to Mrs Trevor, who was advancing towards us, a book in her hand.

'Good lady, Mrs Fazackerley's Morals for Female Angels, what a fine choice. That is a special reader's copy provided by the publisher. This week it is only threepence halfpenny.'

'So inexpensive, sir.'

He leant in towards her. 'A price reserved for ladies of your own elegance and comportment.'

Mrs Trevor blushed at the compliment, but it meant that every Tuesday we returned to the bookshop to find the latest 'reader's editions'.

Each week, whilst Mr Collins showed these new books to Mrs Trevor, I was left alone in a stock room with Mr Carruthers. We only had ten minutes together but, dear reader, it was time I looked forward to with anticipation every week. We talked of love, life, the movement and our feelings towards each other whilst outside, Mrs Trevor selected her favourite books.

Even guided by Mr Collins, she had appalling taste in reading matter, but I didn't care so long as it afforded me time to spend with the man I loved.

One day, six months after our little subterfuge had been in operation and Mrs Trevor was buried deep in the Christian words of Mrs Tyrack, Mr Carruthers surprised me.

He knelt down on one knee and said, 'Dear, dear Emily, will you do me the honour of becoming my wife?'

You can imagine the shock and delight the idea gave me, but I could only think of the obstacles. 'What about Father? What about my brother?'

'Do not worry. Let us elope to Gretna Green and there we will marry. Once we are legally bound to each other for life, they will then accept us for what we are. Man and wife.'

So the next week, on a Tuesday, while Mrs Trevor was snoring soundly and my father and brother were both at their clubs, I stole out of the house and took a stage to Lancaster and then to Gretna Green.

Dear reader, we were married two days later on Thursday, September 23, 1830, over the anvil in the famous blacksmith's cottage by the Reverend Albert Smith.

I became Mrs Charles Carruthers.

I wish I could say we lived happily ever after, but I'm afraid I could not lie to the person reading this, because we did not. My father and brother saw to that.

CHAPTER THIRTY-ONE

July 11, 1842
Wickham Hall, Cheshire

1830 – Liverpool

The first days after Gretna were filled with both happiness and sadness for my beloved and I.

Happiness in that we were together, delighting in each other's company and staying at his rooms in Argyle Street. There were no servants and I busied myself with making breakfast; burnt toast, lukewarm tea and eggs that were still liquid inside. But it somehow didn't matter. We gorged on our love for each other, food was not important.

Sadness, though, soon followed. After one week and no communication from my family, I decided to pay them a visit. I knocked on the door and was met by a woman who smiled sourly as I stepped inside. Mrs Trevor had vanished – was that a result of my disappearance?

I told this new woman that Mrs Carruthers wished to see her father and brother. She kept me in the hall, the hall of my own home, while she went to communicate with my family.

The answer was not long in coming.

'Mr Jeremiah regrets that he is not aware of any acquaintance by the name of Mrs Carruthers.'

My face flamed with anger. 'Will you please tell my father that his daughter is waiting to see him.'

She smiled again and was joined by a burly footman. 'Mr Jeremiah anticipated your request. He has told me to tell you he has no daughter.'

I stood still in the hallway, my father's portrait staring down at me from the wall. All I could manage was a very weak, 'Pardon, what was that?'

The woman opposite me sighed. 'Mr Jeremiah has no daughter,' she stated bluntly. 'He is not receiving visitors today.'

'What about my brother?' I blurted out. 'I want to see my brother.'

'Mr Henry also informs me he has no sister.'

With that, the footman advanced and began to gently push me out of the door.

'Don't you dare touch me,' I shouted.

He stepped back.

The new housekeeper simply said, 'James has his orders to remove you from the house.'

'Who gave such orders?' I demanded.

'Mr Jeremiah and Mr Henry agreed. Now, are you going to leave peacefully or do I have to ask James to throw you out?'

I pulled down the hem of my morning jacket and strode back to the door. Before I left, I turned and said, 'Please inform my father that I will never grace this house again.'

'You mean to say Miss, you will never disgrace *this house, or this family, again.'*

I felt my face reddening. 'I have no family,' was the only response I could think of before I left, slamming the door behind me.

A similar misfortune had befallen Charles, but at least his family had agreed to meet with him. Apparently, they had decided that they could not be allied with a slave-trading family such as my own. Charles had argued fiercely that the sins of any family should not be visited on their daughter. However, they remained steadfast. They felt their reputation as Christians was at stake. They would not support or accept me into their household.

When Charles returned and gave me the news, I cried for a long time, my heart broken by the cruelties that families can inflict on each other.

Charles comforted me. 'It's fine, my love, we will be our own family from now on.'

'But what are we to do? What is to become of us?'

'I fear we can no longer stay in Liverpool, my dear. The city is set against us, both traders and abolitionists. We would be shunned whenever we came into contact with polite society.'

'Damn polite society,' I shouted, 'we will be our own society.'

He sat down beside me and took my hand. 'And what will we live on, dear? You have no money and my meagre allowance would not keep us in books, let alone food, rent and all the other necessities of life.'

I hadn't thought of money. It had simply never occurred to me.

'Listen,' he said, 'I have been offered a post in Manchester as secretary of the Anti-Slavery League there. The salary would not be large, but at least it would keep us alive and I would be doing the work I love.'

'But it would mean leaving Liverpool and home.'

'You have no home now, Emily,' he said gently, 'your home is with me.'

I thought about what he had said. It was all true, I had no family and no home any more. 'You are right, Charles, my home is with you, my family is you.'

'We have work to do, Emily. The Reform Act will change the nature of Parliament, it will no longer be controlled by the sugar men and their bought MPs. We have a chance now to free all the slaves in the colonies. Mr Clarkson and Mr Wilberforce are adamant, one more push will finally do it.'

'When do we leave?' I said as brightly as I could, but inside my heart was shrinking at the thought of living in that dark, dank, dirty town. I would miss my home in Liverpool, with the tang of the sea and the breeze off the shore cleansing the city. Instead, I would get used to the stench of cotton waste and people, always people.

CHAPTER THIRTY-TWO

Tuesday, August 20, 2019
Little Marden, Cheshire

'Give me a second.' Jayne took out her laptop and logged on to the Ancestry.com website. She quickly found the 1841 census and brought up the page she had saved for Wickham Hall.

NAME	AGE	PROFESSION	PLACE BORN
Henry Marlowe	37	Independent	F
Clara Marlowe	35	Independent	Cheshire
Royston Marlowe	7	Scholar	Lancashire
Emily Roylance	35	Independent	F

'See, there's Emily Roylance. Who is she and what relation was she to Henry Marlowe? We couldn't find her birth records in the church.'

'Nor could we find Henry's. They were probably baptised somewhere else like the reverend said.'

'You could be right. See the last column in this census? It says "Where born, locally or in Scotland, Ireland or Foreign Parts"?'

'Yes, there's a large F there.'

'It means they were born overseas. This enumerator didn't record the birthplace, just wrote an F for "foreign" in the column. Did any of your ancestors serve overseas?'

'Not that I know of. I always thought we were proud Cheshire folk.'

'Interesting.' Jayne typed in a general search for Emily Roylance. She clicked the exact button for the names and then typed in 1806 for the birth date. 'That's the one given on the census but we won't specify it more exactly than that. We'll also start with the UK and Ireland; we can always broaden it later.' She pressed search and waited for the result. It came back in two seconds.

'Sixty-five hits,' said Rachel, 'is that good?'

'It's great. Sometimes you can get thousands of hits. Sometimes even more with a name like John Smith.'

Jayne scrolled down the page.

'What are you looking for?'

'The 1841 census. Here it is.' She clicked on it, but instead of going straight to the image she checked the suggested links. A new page came up with more names, most of which connected to Henry Roylance.

Jayne scanned the page. 'Hmmm, this is interesting.'

'What is it?'

'It's a link to a Gretna Green marriage site for the years 1794 to 1895.'

'Gretna Green? The place in Scotland where people used to run away to get married?'

'The one and only.'

Jayne clicked on the link and a single result popped up on the screen; a picture of a book with copperplate writing.

Jayne zoomed in and scanned the result.

Charles Carruthers of the parish of St Nicholas in Liverpool, Lancashire, and Emily Roylance from the parish of St James in Liverpool, Lancashire, were married before these witnesses George McReady and Helen Shipton, this twenty-second day of October, Eight hundred and thirty.

'What does it mean, Jayne?'

'It's pretty obvious. Our Emily Roylance, if we have the right person, was married to Charles Carruthers.'

'But why run away to Gretna Green to do it?'

'In those days, it was usually because the bride was underage, but if Emily was born in 1804 that would not be true in this case. Perhaps she was pregnant or the family disapproved of her new husband. I suppose we'll never know.' She stared into mid-air for a moment. 'Hang on, I've an idea. It's a long shot but you never know.'

Jayne opened a new tab and typed 'Roylance + Liverpool' into Google.

A link to a Wikipedia entry was the first result.

Jeremiah Roylance of Liverpool, merchant.

Mr Roylance was a merchant involved in the Russian, American and, after the disestablishment of the British East India company in 1814, the Indian trade, through his company, Roylance and Son of Liverpool. He helped establish and develop the harbours and wharves of Liverpool, owned plantations in Barbados and Trinidad, and was Chairman of the

West Indian Association, representing their interests as MP for Liverpool from 1824 to 1832.

Little is known of Mr Roylance's origins, but he seems to have been the son of a humble carter born in 1762 in Sefton, Liverpool. In 1780, aged 18, he was appointed the overseer of the Success Estate in the Bahamas. From this post he developed the trading of sugar, molasses and rum, eventually buying out the owner of the estate and changing the name to Perseverance in 1793.

In 1796, he embarked on a year of travelling, developing his contacts in Boston, St Petersburg and along the West African coast. He was one of the major importers of slaves into the Caribbean, building a fleet of ships, in partnership with other traders, to transport slaves across the Atlantic. After the banning of the slave trade in 1807, these ships were used to trade along the Eastern seaboard of America and later to carry cotton and other goods to Liverpool.

In 1816, Mr Roylance was one of the major actors in the quashing of the slave rebellion in Barbados. The largely non-violent rebellion was brutally crushed by the estate owners under the militia of Colonel Codd, of which Mr Roylance was a founding member. They killed many slaves: estimates of the toll from the fighting range from 100 to 250. After the insurrection was put down, the government sentenced 45 men to death, and 27 were executed. The executed slaves' bodies were displayed in public for months afterwards as a deterrent to others.

After the rebellion, Mr Roylance returned to Liverpool in 1819, living there for the rest of his life but retaining his interests in the plantations on Barbados and Trinidad.

He devoted himself until his death in 1835 to trade across the world, and to ensuring that Liverpool became one of the most successful ports and cities of the period. He had two children; Henry and Emily. Their mother was Dolores Sharpe, who is reported to have died in Barbados during a cholera epidemic in 1822.

Jeremiah Roylance died after a short illness in his beloved city and is buried in St Luke's Cemetery. After his death, his papers were donated by his son, Henry, to the city. They are presently kept in the International Slavery Museum on the waterfront. After the Slavery Abolition Act in 1833, the company was closed, ceasing to exist by 1838. Little is known about his family after his death. They seem to have left Liverpool and never returned.

'The man was a slave merchant?'

'Sounds like it. Remember, Liverpool at this time was England's biggest port involved in the slave trade.'

'But I thought we abolished slavery?'

'We abolished the trade on slaves in 1807 but slavery itself continued in the colonies until 1834.'

'But what has this woman got to do with my family?'

'I don't know, Rachel, but we need to find out. I think we have to go somewhere else besides Chester tomorrow.'

'Where?'

'Liverpool. And to be more precise, the International Slavery Museum.'

CHAPTER THIRTY-THREE

Tuesday, August 20, 2019
Wickham Hall, Cheshire

As they drove back up the long drive to Wickham Hall, Jayne was struck once again by how beautiful the house was. The Georgian entrance was beautifully flanked on either side by two elegant wings, the proportions so precise and created to please the eye. The grounds on either side of the drive created the perspective, leading the eye to the elegant front door.

Jayne stopped the car in front of the house. David Marlowe came out to greet them. 'Rachel, such a surprise to see you. Father will be pleased.'

'Father is here?'

'He's in the library. And hello again, Mrs Sinclair, still chasing your wild goose? I thought you would have given up by now?'

'Don't be a boor, David, and actually, we think we have found some interesting leads today at the church.'

Despite all Jayne's warnings, Rachel had blurted out exactly what they had been doing. Jayne stared at her; she who was now biting her lip as if she had realised her mistake.

'Have you? I went through those registers three years ago. I didn't notice anything out of the ordinary. What is it?'

Jayne got out of the car before Rachel could answer. 'We're not certain and it may be nothing, a misreading of the source. We need to check it out further.'

'I wouldn't waste my time if I were you. Would you like to stay for tea, Mrs Sinclair?'

'No thank you, I must be heading back to Manchester.' She turned to Rachel. 'I'll pick you up at nine tomorrow.'

'Okay, looking forward to it, Jayne, even though it will be a bit of a struggle that early in the morning.'

'You're continuing with the search tomorrow?' asked David.

'Off to Chester and Liverpool this time.'

David's eyes narrowed. 'Why are you going there?'

Rachel glanced across at Jayne. 'We're just following up on some new information.'

'I guess it's your time and your money. Personally, I wouldn't be wasting either.'

'See you tomorrow.' Jayne got back into the car and started the engine. As it turned over, Jayne leant forward to place a Mott the Hoople disc in the player, noticing a shadow at the upstairs window of the house as she did. It ducked down as soon as Jayne looked up.

Was somebody watching them?

CHAPTER THIRTY-FOUR

Tuesday, August 20, 2019
The M56 to Manchester

Jayne accelerated into the middle lane of the M56, past a slow-moving lorry on the inside lane.

She was feeling pleased. 'All The Young Dudes' was blasting out of the car's speakers, the road was pretty quiet and the sun was shining. They had definitely made progress today. The visit to Liverpool tomorrow should clear everything up.

Tonight, when she got back home, she would go online and see if she could find out more about the Roylances. If they were a prominent family, as it seemed they were, then there should be some information. At least she could check the 1841 and 1851 censuses.

The only cloud at the moment was the impending divorce action with Paul. She had been so busy over the last few days she had done nothing since their phone call. And, as the whole day would be spent in Liverpool tomorrow, she would have to find time to call the solicitors Wendy had recommended to her. She added this to her mental to-do list.

The one saving grace of the Marlowe case was it had made her so busy she didn't have much time to think about Paul and the divorce. She thought at one time that they would grow old together, become one of those wrinkled couples who hold hands as they walk down the street. They were happy once, but that seemed such a long time ago now, as if it had happened to another person entirely.

No point in blaming anybody. They had simply grown apart rather than grown together. Luckily, there were no children, so the pain of the divorce was solely on them. As long as they both acted like adults, there should be no problem.

The only issue was the house. She really didn't want to move. It was her home, her office her refuge from the world, and she didn't want to lose it now. Hopefully, Paul would be nice about it and they could come to some sort of an agreement.

A light in her rearview mirror caught her eye. Some idiot was flashing his headlights at her. 'Just overtake me in the outside lane,' she said out loud.

The Range Rover accelerated towards her, still flashing its headlights.

'Okay, okay, I get the message.' She checked in her mirror and signalled left to go back into the inside lane.

The Range Rover pulled alongside her and matched her speed.

What was he doing?

She tried to look across at the driver but the windows were blacked out.

Up ahead, a slow-moving container truck was in front of her. She began to slow down. The Range Rover slowed too.

'What are you doing?' she shouted across at the car towering over the BMW.

As if he had heard her, the driver began to move closer to Jayne, his car gradually moving into her lane.

Jayne banged her horn twice.

The Range Rover kept moving over.

Up ahead, the container truck was getting closer and closer; she could see the large 'D' on the back of the truck and its foreign numberplate.

Still the Range Rover crept closer and closer, its dark grey wing almost touching her BMW.

'So that's how you want to bloody play it?' she snarled.

Jayne checked in her rearview mirror, then slammed on the brakes, swinging the BMW into the middle lane so it was now directly behind the Range Rover.

She memorised the registration number. ST14 VUW.

The Range Rover picked up speed, accelerating past the container truck. Jayne followed it, feeling the power in her BMW as she stepped on the accelerator.

Suddenly, the Range Rover's rear lights flashed on. Jayne jammed on her brakes, hearing them squeal against the hard tarmac of the road.

The red lights were getting closer and closer. She pulled the steering wheel to the left only to hear a loud blast from the horn of the container truck.

She pulled the wheel back to the right, staying in the middle lane. She glanced quickly in her right hand mirror but a car was speeding down the outside lane, accelerating towards her.

She was boxed in. The Range Rover was still stationary in the middle lane, its red brake lights bright in the late evening light.

She was going to hit it. She braced for the impact.

The container truck raced up on the inside, the driver in his cab staring down on the two cars in the middle lane.

Time slowed for Jayne.

The Range Rover was still stationary, the red lights bright. Her tyres were squealing against the road, screaming out for more grip.

She was getting closer, closer. She was sure to hit the car in front.

Then her tyres finally gripped the road. She stopped inches behind the Range Rover.

Its lights flashed off and it accelerated away.

She put the BMW in gear and chased after it. Nobody was going to play these games with her.

She stamped her foot on the accelerator and the car responded. The Range Rover was going fast, but she was going faster. She was gaining on him.

She moved into the outside lane. Getting closer now, she wanted to see who the driver was and why he had driven so stupidly.

Suddenly, without warning, the Range Rover swung right across the front of the container truck, across yellow lines and up on to an exit road.

Jayne was still in the outside lane and moving fast.

The driver looked across and waved. She'd never seen him before. Who was he?

She checked up ahead; the next exit was eight miles away. Even if she left the motorway then, the driver would be long gone before she should drive back and find him.

Jayne slowed down. Still, she had his numberplate. She would ask one of her old friends in the police to put on a trace at the Driver Licensing Authority in Swansea.

She would pay this man a visit and give him a piece of her mind. Just because you owned a big Chelsea tractor didn't mean you also owned the road. Driving like that could kill people.

Jayne stared down at her hands. They were gripping the steering wheel tightly, her knuckles white with tension.

Calm down. Take three breaths.

Jayne obeyed her instructions to herself, breathing deeply and concentrating on her stomach.

And then it occurred to her. Why had this happened today?

CHAPTER THIRTY-FIVE

Tuesday, August 20, 2019
Didsbury, Manchester

By the time Jayne arrived home, her breathing was back to normal and her face was no longer reddened with anger. She had calmed down, helped by some soothing classical music from Elgar. After the incident with the Range Rover, Mott the Hoople had somehow felt all wrong.

On the drive back, more questions had flooded her mind. Why had the Range Rover targeted her? She had done nothing wrong that day and her driving had been exemplary. The was no excuse for road rage. Had he chosen her deliberately, trying to attack her on a part of the M56 he knew would be quiet?

Or was it linked to the Marlowe case? David Marlowe had heard they had made some new discoveries and were going to the archives tomorrow. Had he tried to frighten her off?

If he knew Jayne's character, he would have realised that was exactly the wrong thing to do; it only made her more determined to get to the bottom of this mystery. Who exactly were the Roylances? And how were they linked to the Marlowe family and Rachel's heritage?

As soon as Jayne walked through the door, Mr Smith greeted her as usual, rubbing his body against hers. She picked him up and nuzzled her face into his fur. He miaowed and managed to wriggle out of her arms, racing to his bowl.

It could only mean one thing; he was hungry. She fed him quickly and opened a bottle of good rioja. She definitely needed a glass of wine after what had happened.

After a few sips of wine, and with the cat eating his food happily, she sat down in front of her computer.

She reopened the Wikipedia entry on Jeremiah Roylance and read it through once more. It was interesting that he had a son called Henry too. Was it a coincidence? It was a very common name back then, particularly among the middle classes.

She checked both the 1841 and 1851 censuses for the Roylances of Liverpool.

Nothing.

No entries that even vaguely mentioned a Jeremiah, a Henry or an Emily Roylance. It was exactly as the Wikipedia article said.

Little is known about his family after his death. They seem to have left Liverpool and never returned.

Were the Roylance and Marlowe families linked?

But there was nothing in the Marlowe family to suggest any relationship or marriage with somebody called Roylance. However, they had been involved in the slave trade. Was this the connection to

Rachel's past? Had one of her ancestors owned estates in Barbados and Trinidad?

It was all very strange.

Jayne began to think that the incident with the Range Rover that afternoon was no coincidence. Hadn't it happened just after Rachel had revealed they were on to new leads? Was David Marlowe trying to scare her off to protect the family's name and heritage?

Jayne searched online and found the number for the International Slavery Museum in Liverpool. She would reserve a seat to look into the archives of the Roylance family for tomorrow afternoon.

It was shaping up to be a busy day. Chester in the morning and Liverpool in the afternoon. Luckily, both places were not that far apart.

Perhaps the answer lay, at it usually did, somewhere in the archives.

CHAPTER THIRTY-SIX

Wednesday, August 21, 2019
Wickham Hall, Cheshire

The following day, Jayne was up early to feed Mr Smith and drive to Wickham Hall. Of course, when she arrived just before nine she found that Rachel was not yet ready.

David Marlowe greeted her at the entrance. 'My sister is not generally a morning person, Mrs Sinclair. Would you care for some breakfast while you wait for her?'

'No thank you, but a coffee would be wonderful.'

'Oh, we have plenty of that.'

He walked her to a small dining room which was laid out for breakfast. Harold Marlowe was already sitting down reading the *Financial Times*. As she entered, he stood up. 'Good morning, Mrs Sinclair, it is good to see you again.'

David walked over to a row of chafing dishes on the side table. He lifted the lids. 'Eggs Benedict, scrambled eggs, kedgeree, sausages, toast. Mrs Davies must have known you were coming. Are you sure you wouldn't like to join us?'

Jayne shook her head.

As she said no, an old woman appeared in the doorway carrying a pot of coffee and another pot containing hot milk. 'Miss Rachel will be down in five minutes,' she said, placing the pots on the table, 'but personally, I think it is going to be closer to fifteen minutes.'

'Thank you, Mrs Davies.' David poured a cup of coffee for Jayne and then began to serve himself from the chafing dishes.

His father put down his newspaper and eyed Jayne over the top of his bifocals. 'I hear you're off to Liverpool to follow a lead, according to my daughter.'

Rachel had obviously been talking to her father. Jayne simply answered, 'That's correct.'

'I wish you every success in your endeavours.'

David placed his breakfast on the table. 'Liverpool? The family have never lived there. What do you hope to find?'

Jayne smiled. 'Just following a lead.'

'I think you will be wasting your time, Mrs Sinclair. As far as I know, the family has no links to Liverpool, except for helping to fund various railways that went to the place. Henry Marlowe and his son, Royston, believed in free trade as a way of increasing the wealth of the country.'

'And of increasing their own wealth too, I expect.'

David smiled. 'Of course. Before those two, the family had tended to be simple country folk; hunting, fishing and farming. But after them, we became very involved in the mercantile growth of the country. It was to be expected in the Industrial Revolution, of course.'

Rachel appeared in the doorway, dressed and made-up perfectly. 'Sorry I'm late, Jayne. Shall we go?'

'You don't want to eat, Rachel?' asked her father.

'No thanks, Papa, Mrs Davies has made me a flask of coffee instead.'

Jayne drained her cup and stood up. 'Thank you for the coffee.'

'Good luck with your wild-goose chase, Mrs Sinclair,' said David Marlowe, without looking up from his kedgeree.

Outside, they got in the car and took the road to Chester. Jayne waited five minutes before speaking to Rachel.

'Last night, somebody tried to run me off the road. I checked the numberplate and the car was owned by Purview Estates.'

'But that's the name of the farming estates next to Wickham Hall.'

'Exactly. The car was a grey Range Rover.'

Rachel thought for a moment. 'There are two Range Rovers on the estate. Anybody can use them. I've driven them to the village myself.'

'Did you tell anybody what happened with our research yesterday?'

Rachel shook her head.

'I was attacked an hour after I left Wickham Hall.'

'I never spoke to anybody until much later, I promise, Jayne.'

Jayne checked in her rearview mirror. Was somebody following them, and was that how David Marlowe knew of their movements?

She would be careful today. If she caught the man who was watching them, he would be lucky to escape with his life.

CHAPTER THIRTY-SEVEN

Wednesday, August 21, 2019
Chester, Cheshire

It was close to ten o'clock before they parked in Chester. It had been seven months since Jayne had visited this area and she was tempted to go in to see the archivist of the museum, Reg Atkinson, who had helped her with the Roberts case last Christmas. But time was of the essence and she decided to do that another day.

With Rachel in tow, they walked to Duke Street, a long row of Georgian and early Victorian houses in the middle of the city. The archive itself was housed in what looked like an old brick warehouse or mill.

They walked in and marched up to an archivist on the front desk.

'Hello, my name is Jayne Sinclair. I rang earlier about looking at the parish registers.'

'It was for St Peter's, wasn't it?'

'That's right.'

'I've found the microfilms for you. Unfortunately, some of the years are missing…'

'Let me guess. 1832 to 1841?'

The archivist's eyebrows rose. 'How did you know?'

'A wild guess.'

'The registers for earlier in the century are still available. I've pulled out the ones from 1800 to 1810 for you.'

'Didn't we see those with Reverend Arbuthnot yesterday?' Rachel asked.

Jayne nodded. 'Do you have anything else for the period?'

The archivist thought for a moment and began to shake her head, before an almost visible light bulb went off in her eyes. 'You could try the Bishop's Transcripts.'

'Bishop's Transcripts?' asked Rachel.

'Copies of the parish registers were sent each year to the Bishop of Chester. Researchers often use these records when the original is difficult to read or is missing.'

'So the 1832 to 1841 records will be in the Bishop's Transcripts?'

'I don't know, honestly, but they could be. It all depends whether the vicar at that time was diligent in his duties. I'll pull out the microfilms for you anyway.'

She vanished into a room behind her desk and returned minutes later with an armful of microfilms.

Jayne thanked the archivist and took them to a reader, inserting the first of the Bishop's Transcripts reels into the machine.

'You're not looking at the register?' Rachel asked.

'We've already seen it at the church and time is running short. This place closes for lunch at one and we have to get to Liverpool for two. It's only in the Bishop's Transcripts that we will find new information.'

She scanned the records quickly, looking for any sign of St Peter's. There was nothing in the first reel or the second. Finally, she inserted the third and final reel into the reader, crossing her fingers as she did so.

'I didn't know you were so superstitious, Jayne.'

'The gods of genealogy are a fickle bunch. It's best to keep them onside.'

She scanned this last reel more slowly. After twenty minutes, just as her spirits had begun to ebb, a title card appeared on the screen.

St Peter's Church, Little Marden

'Bingo, we've got it,' said Rachel.

Jayne moved slowly through the birth records, which started in 1822 and stopped in 1842. They read all the entries, even though the handwriting was a terrible scrawl which only improved with the obvious arrival of a new vicar in 1836.

Nothing.

There were a lot of familiar Cheshire names, but no Marlowe births were recorded. No mention of a Royston Marlowe.

'It looks like he was baptised somewhere else.'

'Or maybe the year was wrong?' Jayne went through the rest of the baptismal records until 1842 again.

Still nothing.

'What do we do now?'

Jayne thought for a moment. 'These Bishop's Transcripts also have marriage records. Let's check them.'

They scrolled to the end of the microfilm, finding the marriage records. Rachel was the first to spot it.

'Look! Clara Marlowe married Henry Roylance on February 14th, 1836.' She paused for a moment before adding, 'Is this the son of Jeremiah Roylance?'

CHAPTER THIRTY-EIGHT

Wednesday, August 21, 2019
Chester, Cheshire

Jayne advanced the microfilm. On the next page was the full entry for the marriage.

Marriage of Henry Roylance and Clara Marlowe

Groom's age: 30
Groom's residence: Hope St, Liverpool
Profession: Merchant
Groom's father: Jeremiah Roylance
Groom's mother:

Bride's age: 28
Bride's residence: Wickham Hall, Little Marden

Profession:
Bride's father: Sir Philip Marlowe
Bride's mother: Lady Anne Marlowe

Jayne Sinclair whistled under her breath. 'No wonder we couldn't find Henry Marlowe's birth records…'

'I don't understand, Jayne. Henry's name is Roylance, not Marlowe? But the family tree says he was born in 1804 as Henry Marlowe?'

'This proves he wasn't. His real name was Henry Roylance and he lived in Liverpool.'

'But… but how did he get the name Marlowe? Did he take his wife's name?'

'I'll show you.' Jayne jumped up and strode towards the archivist. 'Do you have a copy of Phillimore and Fry?'

'The Index of Name Changes? I think so, let me find a copy of it for you.'

A couple of minutes later the archivist returned with a red, leather-bound volume.

As Jayne opened it, she explained to Rachel Marlowe what she was doing. 'This book was printed in 1905 and it's an index to all name changes that were announced or occurred through Royal Licence after 1760.'

'Will Henry be in there?'

'We're going to find out.'

She opened the yellowing pages of the book and went through the index for M.

'Markeloff, Marker, Markham, Markland, Marks, Markwick, Marlow… Here it is.' Her finger jabbed the page. '"Marlowe: Roylance, Henry, on his marriage to Clara Marlowe". February 14th, 1836, and September 12th, 1837. I think the second date is when the name change took effect.'

'And what's "LG 898 and LG 1053"?' asked Rachel, peering at the page.

Jayne didn't answer the question but instead asked the archivist, 'Do you have a computer I could use?'

The archivist pointed to an empty desktop on the right. 'But you'll have to be quick, we close for lunch in fifteen minutes.'

Jayne rushed over to the desktop with Rachel following closely behind. She sat down and typed the web address for the *London Gazette*, the LG in the reference. 'This is the newspaper where all official notices were printed by the government. It's still used today. We'll just search their archives for 1837, pages 898 and 1053.'

Jayne typed quickly and one entry appeared on the screen. 'Bingo.'

Whitehall, 12 September, 1837

The Queen has been pleased to grant unto Henry Roylance, of Liverpool in the county of Lancashire, Gentleman, his Royal Licence and Authority that he and his issue may henceforth use the name and arms of Marlowe in lieu and instead of that of Roylance, being the ward and presumptive heir of Sir Philip Marlowe of Wickham Hall, Little Marden, in the county of Cheshire.

And to Command that the said Royal Licence and Authority be recorded in his Majesty's College of Arms, otherwise to be void and of none effect.

Signed
Sir Ralph Norris

'There's another page, LG 1053, let's check that too.'

Jayne typed in the next page reference. Again, just one entry popped up.

VICTORIA R.

Victoria, by the Grace of God of the United Kingdom of Great Britain and Ireland, Queen, Defender of the Faith, To Our Right Trusty and Right Entirely Beloved Cousin Henry Duke of Norfolk, Earl. Whereas Henry Roylance, of Liverpool in the county of Lancashire, Gentleman, hath by his petition humbly represented to Us that through wardship and marriage he wishes to adopt the surname Marlowe. The Petitioner therefore most humbly prays Our Royal Licence and Authority that he and his issue may take and henceforth use the surname of Marlowe in lieu and instead of that of Roylance. Know ye that We of Our Princely Grace and Special favour have given and Granted and do by these presents give and grant unto him the said Henry Roylance Our Royal Licence and Authority that he and his issue may take and henceforth use the surname of Marlowe in lieu and instead of that of Roylance, provided that this Our Concession and Declaration be recorded in Our College of Arms, otherwise this Our Licence and Permission to be void and of none effect.

Our Will and Pleasure therefore is that you, Henry Duke of Norfolk, to whom the cognisance of matters of this nature doth properly belong, do require and command that this Our Concession and Declaration be recorded in Our College of Arms to the end that Our Officers of Arms and all others upon occasion may take full notice and have full knowledge thereof. And for so doing this shall be your Warrant.

Given at our Court of Saint James the Twelfth day of September, 1837 in the first year of Our Reign.

By Her Majesty's Command
(Signed) H. A. BRUCE

Recorded in the College of Arms, London, pursuant to a Warrant from the Earl Marshal of England.

(Signed) **GEORGE HARRISON**, Windsor Herald

Henry Roylance, Licence that he and his issue may take and use the surname of Marlowe in lieu and instead of that of Roylance.

'Sounds like Victorian mumbo-jumbo to me.'

'It's really simple. Your ancestor Henry changed his name by Royal Licence from Roylance to Marlowe.'

'He adopted his wife's surname? Why would he do that?'

'I think the word "wardship" in the explanation gives us a reason. He must have been adopted by your ancestor, Sir Philip Marlowe.'

'But why?'

Before Jayne could answer, she felt a gentle tap on her shoulder. It was the archivist.

'I'm sorry, I have to close up now, it's close to one o' clock.'

'Thank you, sorry for being so long,' Jayne replied. Turning back to Rachel, she said, 'Let's find a café somewhere and have a quick lunch before going to Liverpool. There may be one more document that should explain everything. With a bit of luck, it will be online.'

CHAPTER THIRTY-NINE

Wednesday, August 21, 2019
Chester, Cheshire

After leaving the Cheshire Archives, Jayne and Rachel quickly found a café.

Jayne pulled out her laptop and logged on to the internet.

'This is so exciting, Jayne. We now know Henry Roylance adopted the surname Marlowe when he married into the family. What are you looking for?'

Jayne's fingers tapped at the keyboard. 'It's a bit of a long shot, but according to the family tree, Sir Philip Marlowe – Clara's father – died in 1837. I'm hoping that as a rich landowner, he left a last will and testament. Luckily many of the historical Cheshire wills are kept online.'

Rachel looked over Jayne's shoulder as the landing page for Findmypast appeared. Jayne pulled up the Cheshire Wills page and typed in the name 'Philip Marlowe' and the date '1837'. There was a pause as the search engine looked for the answer.

Then just one response appeared on the screen. Jayne clicked on the name and a copy of the last will and testament slowly formed.

Rachel read out the words, occasionally stumbling as the copperplate writing became too florid for her:

"'I, Sir Philip Marlowe, of the parish of Little Marden in Cheshire by this will and testament give and bequeath to my dearest adopted son, Henry Marlowe, everything of which I may possess including the house and estate of Wickham Hall, my house at 23 Cadogan Square, London, all my chattels, appurtenances and moneys, with the following exceptions and after the payment of all my funeral expenses.'"

"'To my dearest and only daughter, Clara, I leave 1000 pounds plus an income of 150 pounds for life to be spent as she sees fit. To the church of St Peter in the parish of Little Marden, I leave 500 pounds to be spent on the upkeep of the church and its surrounding graves including my own. This money must not be used for the upkeep of the minister. He has had enough money off me during his tenure of the benefice and has done little work to justify the cost. To the poor of the parish of Little Marden, I also leave 500 pounds for the construction of homes for the old and sick. These homes to be constructed on estate land by my manager Alfred Smith.'"

Here, Rachel paused for a second. 'I know those houses. They still exist on Chester Road, just as you leave the village.'

She went back to reading the will.

"'To the afore-mentioned Alfred Smith, I leave the sum of 100 pounds as well as an income of 10 pounds per year to be paid annually, for his loyalty and advice when the estate was suffering penury and blight. Finally, to Mrs Amelia Gaynor, who provided such support and comfort for me after the death of my wife, I also leave the sum of 100 pounds and an income of ten pounds per year to be paid annually."

"'I appoint the said adopted son, Henry Marlowe, as executrix of this, my last will and testament." It's signed by Sir Philip Marlowe and dated April twenty-seventh, 1837.'

'The will makes it clear. Henry was not Marlowe's legitimate son, but was adopted when he married Clara.'

'Meaning?'

'That long family tree with male heir after male heir is tosh. The line was broken in 1837 because Sir Philip had no male heirs.'

'My brother won't be pleased when I tell him.'

'Don't let him know for the moment. We should make sure of our facts first and provide a true family tree for him.'

'How are you going to do that?'

'The key lies with this man.' Jayne pointed to the screen. 'Henry Marlowe, also known as Henry Roylance.'

'Didn't his name come up when we searched in the pub? How are you going to find out more about him?'

Jayne thought about telling Rachel of her search for the Roylances on Wikipedia, but decided against it. She could give Rachel the article to read in the car on their way to Liverpool, she had realised that nothing remained secret for long once Rachel knew about it.

Instead, she said, 'It's the reason we are going to Liverpool now.'

'Oh, Jayne, this sounds so exciting. A proper detective story, and instead of acting in it, I am actually living it.'

But Jayne wasn't listening. One other thing was troubling her about the Marlowe family tree. If Royston was born in 1834, but his parents weren't married until 1836, was he illegitimate? That may explain why there was no birth record in the local parish church. But it didn't feel right to Jayne. If Royston were illegitimate, surely

Henry Marlowe would have legitimised the birth to avoid anybody contesting the will?

Rachel had stopped talking. 'Did you hear what I said, Jayne?'

Jayne shook her head.

'I'm going to wangle a day off filming tomorrow too, just in case anything comes up.'

'Are you?'

Rachel's face suddenly became white and tired, her back arched and she began to wheeze and cough. 'I'm so sorry, I seem to have caught the flu. Can you reschedule around me? If you can't then I will, of course, come in... *Cough, cough.* Could be one of my better acting performances.'

Then she brightened up, transforming back into the usual Rachel. 'That should do it, what do you think?'

CHAPTER FORTY

July 11, 1842
Wickham Hall, Cheshire

Emily had continued writing as if her life depended on it. Now even the ink was running low. Could she ask the housekeeper to fill it up, or would that reveal her secret?

She didn't care.

Her book had to be finished today. Once her brother had returned it would be difficult for her to complete it.

She thought of her son, now aged nearly eight. He looked like a miniature version of Henry now; top hat, waistcoat and trews, all in the modern style. But he hardly smiled any more. It was as if all the fun had been sucked out of his body and replaced with a vat of seriousness.

Had she made the right or the wrong decision in returning to this hellish house?

She wondered if she had, but they would have starved in Manchester had they stayed. Would Liberty have had to live on the streets? Or even worse, slave from dusk till dawn in one of those factories that were springing up like mushrooms after a rainstorm.

She had made the right decision, hadn't she?

She picked up her pen.

Don't think of that now, Emily. Finish your book. Tell them what happened next.

1833 – Manchester

Manchester was not as bad as I expected. True, there was an obsession with making money and the manufacture of 'things', and I greatly missed the culture of Liverpool, but overall I was happy with my life in the city.

Since our arrival three years previously, we had lived in a house not far from St Peter's Square where the massacre of the citizens by the militia had taken place just thirteen years before. Even now, the event was spoken of in hushed tones, as if it were some dirty family secret that shouldn't be discussed in public.

My own family still disowned me, of course: I heard nothing from either my brother or my father. It saddened me to think of their estrangement from my life, but nothing could be done. I had made my decision to marry Charles and I didn't regret it for one second.

Charles was in his study preparing for the meeting that evening. The bill for the abolition of slavery was presently going through Parliament. Everybody was cautiously optimistic that it would be passed this time.

Having had my hopes dashed before, I was much less sanguine these days; my husband, however, was excited beyond measure. Even the prospect of facing Colonel Leith Hay this evening did not worry him. On the contrary, it gave him energy – as if it were the last battle he must face before victory.

Colonel Leith Hay had been travelling around the country, challenging the proponents of abolition to an open debate. His expenses had been paid for by the sugar lobby and his efforts were nothing but a transparent attempt to woo public opinion; a public who overwhelmingly, at least for those who were able to read, supported abolition.

Tonight was Manchester's turn and Charles, because of his prowess as a speaker, had been chosen to defend the cause.

'I'm ready, Emily. How do I look?'

Charles was wearing the latest fashion in clothes; a black frock coat with broad shoulders and a tightly cinched waist over a white shirt, accessorised with a dark cravat and anti-slavery tie pin.

'You look very fine, my dear. Do you have your notes?'

He patted his top pocket. 'I don't think I'll need them, though.'

'Better to have them anyway. Shall I call a Hackney?'

'We could just walk?' The meeting was to be held at the Friends Meeting House a short walk from their home.

'I think it better to make a show on arrival, Charles, we mustn't let the society down.'

'As you wish, dear.'

We arrived to a large crowd waiting at the entrance. As Charles entered the hall, he was patted on the back by a crowd of supporters like a champion boxer entering the ring.

Colonel Leith Hay was already waiting for him in the wings. His back was straight and his chest puffed out, all his years of military service in evidence through his bearing.

To me, he looked nothing less than a bantam cock at a country fair, displaying himself for hungry buyers.

On seeing Charles, he merely nodded once to acknowledge his opponent for the evening.

The hall was packed to the rafters. The sconces were lit. A four-piece orchestra played chamber music, its attempts at Mozart drowned out by the buzz of the spectators.

The chair of the meeting, Alderman White, banged a gavel on his desk. The music stopped and the crowd gradually became silent.

'As you know, ladies and gentlemen,' the Alderman said in his broad Manchester accent, 'we are here this evenin' to debate the pros and cons of the question of the abolition of slavery. The motion is "The Abolition of Slavery is good for the soul of England". Speaking for the motion will be Mr Charles Carruthers...' A cheer went up from the audience. 'And against the motion will speak Colonel Leith Hay.' Another cheer, but this time less wholehearted.

'I give you, Mr Charles Carruthers.'

'Wish me luck, dear,' Charles whispered to me before he stepped forward.

'You don't need it. Right is on your side.'

He kissed me on the forehead and then strode out on to the stage to thunderous applause.

'And the opposing speaker, Colonel Leith Hay.'

The colonel pulled down his jacket, adjusted the medals on his chest before twirling his moustache and striding out manfully on to the stage. He was met by loud cheers this time.

To my ears, the audience seemed to be divided evenly between the two sides.

'Mr Carruthers will begin for the motion, followed by the good colonel. Each will then be able to rebut the other's speech and finally there will be a conclusion of five minutes from each speaker followed by questions. Mr Carruthers, if you would care to begin...'

Charles stepped forward and, gripping the lapel of his jacket with his left hand and extending his right arm forward, began to speak. 'Ladies and gentlemen, people of the great city of Manchester...'

'And Salford,' added a voice from the audience.

'And, of course, Salford. Who could forget Salford?'

'You just did,' shouted the same voice, to laughter.

But Charles refused to be deflected from his speech. His voice was powerful and composed, daring anyone to interrupt him again. 'I come here today to talk about one of the most iniquitous punishments ever exhibited by one human on another; the enslavement of black Africans by their fellow humans. Now, I am not going to argue that this is an easy question to resolve. On the contrary, it forces us to ask ourselves a very basic question. How do we judge our own souls? Is the abolition of slavery good for the soul of England?'

He paused here for a moment and smiled, holding his arms open wide. 'It is a question of a difficult nature, where those with strong opinions, partly of a religious description, and partly founded on a philosophic view of the dignity of the human species, came into contact with deep convictions of the ruin and degradation which their enactment would cause to both property and persons. I will show in the course of my speech that the fears of my opponent are unfounded. There is a philosophic argument for the abolition of slavery and also an economic argument for its abolition.

'However, I would call upon my opponent to debate in a manner which requires forbearance, conciliatory spirit, and patient attention. A manner which Colonel Leith Hay has so far eschewed by his use of intemperate language…'

In the wings, I listened to Charles' voice with pride, my heart soaring. I no longer listened to the words; I knew the speech off by heart anyway, having written most of it for Charles myself.

Instead, I heard the music of his voice; the inflexions, the cadence, the subtle pauses that conveyed so much meaning. And behind it all, like a melody running through a concerto, was his passion. A love for his fellow man I had come to share and wholeheartedly endorse.

At the end of the speech there was a spontaneous burst of applause and cheering. It was almost two minutes before the cacophony quietened down and Colonel Leith Hay was able to begin his speech.

'I thank my learned opponent for his eloquent speech. I wish I had his turn of rhetorical phrase, but I am afraid I am but a humble soldier. My speech will only deal with my own personal experience and the facts of the case. I will not bother to use such calls to humanity and freedom and dignity. Instead, I will just use facts.'

Here he tugged at his moustache and began to prowl the stage from side to side, jabbing his fingers skyward as he rolled off his points.

'Fact one. The negro population of the British slave colonies are not yet prepared for the gift of freedom. They are at present an indolent and idle race, and it could not be expected that they would work unless there existed some means of making them.

'Fact two. Only one third of the slave population actually did any work. The children, the aged and the infirm, amounting to two-thirds of the whole, remain a burden upon the estates, cared for by the goodwill and nature of their masters. And, indeed, at a not inconsiderable cost.

'Fact three. The estate owners relied on the labour of their slaves to make the estates economic. Without this labour, they would close and then where would the slaves be? I'll tell you, destitute and starving.

'Fact four. Witnesses have recounted to me that immediate emancipation was altogether impracticable. Admiral Sir Charles Rowley has gone so far as to declare that "if born to a state of absolute labour, he would rather be a black man in Jamaica than a white labourer in England". There was a great deal of evidence to show that the habits of the negro had not improved after emancipation where the experiment had been tried. Saint Domingo, for example.

'Fact five. I am more acquainted with Barbados than the other slave colonies of this country. In that colony, there were 5,000 proprietors, owning in all 80,000 slaves. Of these 5,000 proprietors, not more than 1,500 possessed landed property, leaving 3,500 who possessed none and yet still owned 33,000 slaves. If abolition went ahead, their property would be taken from them.'

A voice called out, 'Are human beings property?'

'They most assuredly are, sir, as confirmed by the highest courts of law of this land. Slaves are property. And you, sir, would you have your property taken from you without a by-your-leave? Of course not, and neither would the people of Barbados. These are some of the kindest slave owners. It was notorious that the insurrection of the year 1816 in Barbados began upon the estate of a planter who was known throughout the island as the best master, the kindest and most affectionate in his treatment of his slaves in the colony.

'Fact six. Fully twenty-seven million pounds accrues to the Exchequer in taxes each year on the import of sugar, rum and other products from the slave colonies. If the islands are to be made destitute, how will the Exchequer replace the income? By taxes on you and me, my friends.

'Finally, fact seven. What will be the effect on England of such abolition? The incomes derived from the colonies are, for the most part, spent in this country. What would be the effect on trade and agriculture? How would the tiny hamlets fare that had sprung up into towns in consequence of the colonial employment and expenditure of colonial capital? Would the gentleman inform us whether Liverpool, Bristol, Manchester, or even London itself, have risen to importance in consequence of the advantages they have derived from the colonial trade? Why would he sneer at the observation that these cities would decline after abolition?

'Friends, I am not opposed to the negroes, but I am opposed to any action that deprives men of their property without any compensation, creating a precedent which might be applied to other types of property with equal injustice.'

He stopped prowling the stage and said, 'Now let me put some flesh on these facts.'

I stopped listening. I had heard these words far too often from my brother and father as an excuse for continuing slavery in other colonies.

I only started listening again when Charles took the podium once more, quietly yet forcefully demolishing each and every one of the so-called 'facts' one by one.

As I listened to his voice, I realised I loved this man with all my heart.

CHAPTER FORTY-ONE

April 08, 1833
Hope Street, Liverpool

'Damn the man, he's nothing but a blackguard.'

Two days later and Jeremiah Roylance was sitting in the front room of his house, reading the *Liverpool Mercury*. His son, Henry, was stretched out on a divan in front of the fire.

'Listen to this. "Liverpool man leads charge against slavery. Charles Carruthers of St Nicholas Parish was the main speaker at an event organised in Manchester yesterday evening. His opponent was the celebrated soldier, Colonel Leith Hay. Together they debated the motion that the abolition of slavery is good for the soul of England." Soul, did you hear that? England now has a soul. Never heard such poppycock in my life. Idiots, the lot of them, never worked a day in their lives. All the abolitionists should be strung up, traitors all.'

'Father, they are debating the final reading of the bill next week.'

'And we'll just mobilise our vote as we have always done to block it. Even with the new reforms, the sugar lobby still has the votes to defeat any bill.'

Henry sat up straight. 'I don't think it will happen this time, Father. There are many voices in favour of abolition, many of them from among the estate owners themselves.'

'Estate owners? You're telling me men from the Caribbean are going to vote for abolition? Why, it would be like geese voting for Christmas.'

Henry sighed. 'I have explained this many times. We cannot and should not block this bill.'

'Why? Tell me that.'

Henry turned to face his father and began to count the reasons off on his hand. 'Firstly, the system of slaves working our plantations is unsustainable, Father. After the slave trade was banned in 1807, we can no longer find enough new slaves or replace them as we once did.'

'Make them breed, then we will have more slaves and the value of our plantations will increase.'

'But that's just it, Father. They are not breeding in sufficient numbers, and we can't sustain our workforce through slavery any more.'

'So what would you have me do? Free them and then hire them back by paying wages?'

Henry paused. 'If you can, do that – but I have a better idea. Bring in indentured workers from India. Labour is cheap and plentiful and there will be no problems with the climate.'

'But that will take time to organise and implement.'

'Exactly, and that is why we have arranged for the former slaves to serve a five-year apprenticeship before they are completely freed from their current status.'

'Apprenticeship? What are we going to teach them, how to cut cane? They know that already.'

'True. But the word "apprenticeship" salves the consciences of our friends the abolitionists and it buys us time. They will be paid a pittance and still have to work in the same jobs. Our costs should go down.'

The old man put down his newspaper to listen to his son.

'Secondly, the trade is dying. Most of the plantations are mortgaged up to the hilt. Prices are falling and we are unable to compete with America, where slavery is still in force. Unless we change, we will die slowly.'

'We have already changed. Didn't I develop new trade with India and the East?'

'You did, Father, but it is not enough. The sugar trade is dying slowly.'

'And I suppose you have an idea where we should go?'

The son nodded. 'I do. It is here in England. The new railway between Manchester and Liverpool has opened and it is the future. Bringing goods into Liverpool, manufactured in Manchester and Birmingham, for export to the Americas and India and Africa and the East. We need to fund these railways, insure them, build transport services and provide finance to set up the factories to make the goods.'

'And where is this money to come from? Will it grow on trees?'

'It will come from the government in return for freeing our slaves.'

'The government will give us money? I don't believe it,' he snorted.

'They have already agreed. The Act, if it is passed, has set aside a sum of twenty million pounds to be paid to the owners of slaves in return for relinquishing their property.'

'But to do that they would have to accept that slaves are property in the first place.'

'That's the beauty of the Act. They have acknowledged our right to own these people and so they have to pay us if they wish us to free our property.'

'Twenty million, you say?'

'By my rough calculations, it means we should receive the sum of 23,234 pounds, six shillings and threepence.'

'And we don't have to share it with anybody?'

'The former slaves will receive nothing except their freedom.'

'And we will still own the land and our plantations?'

'Every last acre and iron nail and stalk of cane.'

The old man stroked his beard. 'It's a pretty sum. A man could do a lot with such a sum.'

'Indeed, Father, we will. After the money is paid, we will quickly put it to use to further grow our business. We will gradually wind down our involvement in the Caribbean, still trading but no longer having the costs of producing sugar or rum. Let others take that risk.'

'And the slaves?'

'They have their freedom, it is enough. A fair bargain.'

The merchant in Jeremiah saw the trade-off. 'So that is why you are supporting this bill.'

'Not supporting, no, we could hardly do that given our history. But not opposing either. It will be passed, Father.'

The old man shook his head. 'I never thought I'd see the day when we no longer had estates.'

'We will have land, Father, but not in the Caribbean. Here in England instead.'

The old man raised his eyebrows. 'How so?'

'I have a plan, Father, which should give our family the future it deserves, positioning it as far as possible from trade and sugar and ships. It concerns a friend of Emily…'

CHAPTER FORTY-TWO

Wednesday, August 21, 2019
International Slavery Museum, Liverpool

On arrival in Liverpool, Jayne parked the BMW and walked with Rachel to the Maritime Museum, an old warehouse next to Albert Dock on the waterfront.

The archive was on the second floor with the International Slavery Museum on the next floor above it.

'You've read the Wikipedia article. It seems the Roylances were one of the Liverpool families involved in the slave trade,' Jayne said as they waited for the lift.

'My ancestors were involved in the slave trade?'

'That's what we are going to find out.'

They took the lift to the second floor and approached the archivist.

'My name is Jayne Sinclair, I booked a table yesterday.'

'I remember the call, Mrs Sinclair. You were interested in the Roylance papers, I believe? There are seventeen boxes in total, but we only allow three boxes for each researcher at any one time.'

'Is there a catalogue of the items in each box?' asked Jayne.

The archivist pointed to a computer inside the research room. 'Please deposit your coat and bags in the lockers and sign in on the book. I'll call up the catalogue for you. Only pencils and pads are allowed in, I'm afraid.'

'Can I bring my laptop?'

The archivist thought for a moment. 'Yes, but without its bag.'

Jayne and Rachel placed all their things in a locker and accompanied the archivist to the computer.

'When you've decided what you would like to look at, I'll find the correct boxes for you. One more thing – what is the nature of your research?'

'Family history. I'm a genealogist.'

The archivist frowned. 'Funny, you're the second person this week to look at the Roylance papers.'

'Who was the other person?'

The archivist smiled. 'I'm sorry, I'm not at liberty to say.'

When she was out of earshot, Rachel leant in close to Jayne and whispered, 'A bit officious, isn't she?'

'Just doing her job. Let's check the catalogue and see if there is anything interesting, shall we?'

The first three boxes seemed to be account books and details of purchases on behalf of the various estates the Roylances owned in Barbados and Trinidad. The next five boxes were details of the numerous voyages undertaken by the ships of the company from 1787 onwards.

'Most of these seem to concern slave ships, with numbers of slaves bought and sold and the prices obtained,' said Jayne. 'Interesting, but not likely to advance our research.'

'A profit and loss of human misery,' said Rachel. 'I can't believe my ancestors were involved in such evil.'

The next two boxes concerned the company's expansion after the abolition of the slave trade, including new voyages to India, America, Brazil and China.

'It all seems very businesslike,' said Rachel as they finished going through the list of letters and books.

'This looks better. One volume on the activities of Mr Henry Roylance in Liverpool. There seems to have been a lot of correspondence with the Merseyside Harbour and Docks Board.'

'Wasn't he the one who married Clara Marlowe?'

'The one and only.'

'Let's order that box then. There's only one other left. "Miscellaneous letters and documents." Should we add that too?' asked Rachel.

'It could just be a lot of old accounts and invoices, but let's do it. I'll fill in the form.'

Jayne wrote down the numbers on the sheet of paper and handed it to the archivist. 'Are there any other boxes relating to the Roylance family?'

'Only what's in the catalogue,' the other woman announced, without looking up.

'So nothing after 1836?'

'If it's not in the catalogue, we don't have it. The company didn't last long after the death of the founder in 1835. I believe it was wound up in 1838.'

'How did you get the documents?'

For the first time the archivist looked up. 'They were found in a large donation of documents on slavery from the Carruthers family, which were given to us in 1903. I'm afraid we only got round to cataloguing the collection in the 1990s. I wish we had more people to help us but our resources are limited.

'How did the documents end up with the Carruthers family?'

The archivist shrugged her shoulders. 'We'd like to know too. The Carruthers family were active in the abolition of slavery movement in the 1820s and 1830s. Strange, though, that they would have papers from one of the leading estate owners and slave merchants of the period. The other researcher was interested in the Carruthers family too. I think he looked at box twelve.' She checked her computer. 'I was right, he checked out box twelve. Would you like it too?'

Jayne nodded.

'You'll have to fill out another form and I'll bring the boxes to you in about five minutes.'

Jayne did as she was told and then went back to sit with Rachel.

'This is all a bit of a long shot, isn't it? A Hail Mary pass I think they call it in America,' Rachel said.

Jayne shook her head. 'It's research. Going through the remains of the past to discover the truth. Sometimes it throws up nuggets of gold, at other times, handfuls of mud. But no research is wasted, because it helps us eliminate possibilities.'

'I don't think we'll ever find the truth. It's buried too deep in the past. I'll have to practise my "I haven't got a clue" face for when the tabloid reporters come knocking on my door on Sunday morning.'

'What will your brother do?'

Rachel thought for a moment. 'Deny everything, probably. He's very good at denial, goes with being a politician.'

Jayne thought it was time to lighten the mood. 'I always thought denial was a river in Africa.'

Rachel smiled. 'That is really one of the worst jokes I've ever heard.'

At that moment, the archivist returned from the storage area with their boxes. She placed them on the table, explaining, 'Please don't mix them up as you're looking at the documents, and I would be grateful if you wore these.' She placed two pairs of cotton gloves on the table and walked away.

'She frightens me,' whispered Rachel.

Jayne glanced across at the large numbers of documents in each box. 'These frighten me more.'

CHAPTER FORTY-THREE

Wednesday, August 21, 2019
International Slavery Museum, Liverpool

'Let's split the work. You take the first Roylance box and I'll take the second.'

'What am I looking for?' asked Rachel.

'Anything that mentions the Marlowes and the Roylances. The families must be linked somehow.'

Rachel frowned but opened the box, taking out the first document.

Jayne did the same. Her first piece of paper was a cargo manifest dated 1812, detailing the storage of rum and sugar in the vessel *Diane* on its voyage from the Bahamas to Liverpool. Jayne scanned it. The captain was a Mr Flood and the first officer a Henry Massey. But there was nothing else of interest.

She looked inside the box. There were many similar-looking documents; checking them all for any mention of the Roylances would take hours.

Jayne glanced across at Rachel, who was reading her document carefully. 'What do you have?'

'It's from 1822. A letter to a Sir Archibald Sutton of the Harbour and Docks Board asking why the wharfage fees have increased threepence for one of their ships. At least, I think that's what it says, the writing is difficult to read.'

After one hour they had barely touched the contents of each box.

'This is going to take years, Jayne.'

'I suggest you simply scan the heading of each document rather than read it all. You'll know fairly quickly whether it covers family or business matters.'

'I'll try.'

The pace sped up with this new strategy and by 3.30 Jayne had finished her box while Rachel had just twenty documents left in hers.

Neither of them, however, had discovered any mention of any family or personal matters.

They both began to feel despondent.

'I don't know if this is going to work, Jayne. So far there's been nothing in any of the boxes. If we go through all seventeen, we'll be here until next year.'

'Let's take a five-minute break and get some fresh air.'

They walked downstairs to Albert Dock, an inlet from the Mersey surrounded by old brick-built warehouses that were now home to cafés, tourist shops and restaurants.

'To think, these buildings and this dock used to be heaving with activity; ships thronging the harbour, rigging whistling in the wind, dockers shouting to their mates, sailors preparing for shore leave.'

Jayne stared out into the quiet waters of the dock and its surrounding buildings. 'Look at it now. Just a restaurant and café area…'

'With some expensive flats in the converted godowns,' added Rachel.

'How the world has changed.'

For a moment the quiet of the scene vanished for Jayne and she was transported back to Albert Dock in its heyday. A man in a top hat smoked a long cheroot. A bare-footed sailor knuckled his forehead as he accepted his wages. The soft sound of water lapping against wooden hulls and the caress of the wind across canvas sails. A young man joined the old man smoking the cheroot and showed him a cargo manifest. A young woman holding a parasol to shield herself from the summer sun joined them. A row broke out; what were they saying? She strained to hear…

'Jayne, JAYNE!'

Rachel was shouting at her.

Jayne shook her head, trying to dispel the image she had seen of the past.

'You were miles away. Like you weren't here any more.'

Jayne couldn't explain it. Occasionally, she felt such an affinity with a place or a time, that it was like she was swallowed up by it.

'It was nothing, Rachel, I was just thinking. When we go back, let's quickly finish the box you are working on and then jump to the ones from the Carruthers family. I feel they may be more useful to us. We can always go back to the Roylances later.'

'Sounds like a plan. I'm bored with cargo manifests.'

On their return to the archive, they scanned the remaining Marlowe box, finding nothing of interest. Jayne returned the finished boxes to the archivist and requested three more of those that remained.

While they waited, they started on the Carruthers box, taking it in turns to look at the letters and documents.

It was Rachel who spoke first. 'These letters are far more interesting. Listen to this, from a Charles Carruthers to the Quaker Meeting House in Manchester:

"Dear Mr Roughly,

"Thank you for hosting our meeting of the 23rd at your elegant establishment.

"The response to my speech was all I could have hoped for and more. Manchester does seem to be welcoming, nay embracing the anti-slavery message with open arms.

"I was particularly gratified to see the wide range of attendees to my talk. Not only the ladies and gentlemen of your estimable church but a goodly attendance from the men and women of the lower orders who listened attentively and calmly. Would that I could get the same reaction here in Liverpool. Usually, the merchants send parties of rowdy Irish or sailors to break up our meetings. But not in your city. There it seems open to new ideas and new ways of doing things.

"I thank you also for your tour of your factory and its new machines. To see all their activity and to hear the noise they produced was awe inspiring. Even Blake, I'm sure, would have been impressed.

"**I was disappointed, though, to see so many young boys and girls attending to the machines, some as young as seven years old. Wouldn't their future needs and those of Manchester be better served with attendance at school?**

"**I am sure you, as an enlightened employer, have considered the advantages of some sort of scheme of learning as they work, perhaps in the evening or before work? If we are to eradicate slavery abroad, surely we should also eradicate it at home too? But perhaps that is a discussion for when I return next month.**

"I hope you will be able to organise another meeting with an even bigger crowd for that time.

"I remain your obedient and faithful servant,

"Charles Carruthers.'"

Jayne sat back and thought. 'It does seem the Carruthers family were heavily involved in the anti-slavery movement. I wonder how that went down with the Liverpool merchants and slave owners?'

'Like a cup of cold sick, I imagine,' answered Rachel.

Jayne picked up another document from the box. She scanned the first couple of lines and whispered 'Bingo' under her breath.

'What was that, Jayne?'

'I think we've found it, Rachel. Listen to this.' And she read the letter out loud.

Sir,

I acknowledge your letter of the 16th.

Please understand that I am no less unhappy with the behaviour of my son, Charles, than you. I fear he has been led astray by your daughter, but eloping to Gretna Green and marrying there without my express permission is both unseemly and ungodly.

If I had any knowledge of their actions, and I assure you I did not, I would have immediately made sure, with all the force at my disposal, that he would have been unable to commit such a heinous act.

As for his actions being a slur on the good name of your family, let me remind you, sir, that your family has no good name. You have made your fortune from the enslavement of your fellow man and, as a Christian of many years standing, I cannot abide my family being linked to yours in any way, even through the tenuous links of marriage.

I have, therefore, disinherited my son from this day forth just as you have disinherited your daughter. Neither he nor his supposed wife will ever cross the threshold of our home, so long as I draw breath.

I remain your servant, sir,

James Carruthers.

'But what's this got to do with me?' Rachel asked. 'Emily Roylance ran away to get married to Charles Carruthers in Gretna Green… So what?'

'Give me a second.' Jayne took out her laptop and clicked on the saved record from the Gretna Green archive.

Charles Carruthers of the parish of St Nicholas in Liverpool, Lancashire, and Emily Roylance from the parish of St James in Liverpool, Lancashire, were married before these witnesses George McReady and Helen Shipton, this twenty-second day of October, Eight hundred and thirty.

Jayne thought for a moment, working it all out in her mind.

'Well, we know Henry Marlowe's name was originally Roylance, and somebody called Emily Roylance was staying with them at Wickham Hall in the 1841 census. A sister perhaps, given her age? We also know that Henry Roylance was living at the same address as the Roylances in Liverpool when he married Clara Marlowe. So it is more than likely that they were the same person.'

'But what's the link to my African ancestor?'

A researcher on the next desk made a loud shushing noise as Rachel spoke a little too loudly.

Jayne apologised to him and leant in towards Rachel, whispering, 'I don't know… yet. But I feel it in my waters, Rachel, there is a link – we just haven't found it yet. Shall we finish the box? There might be something else inside.'

CHAPTER FORTY-FOUR

July 11, 1842
Wickham Hall, Cheshire

Emily was tired. Her pen was still in her hand but the words on the page were swimming in and out of focus. She must get this finished, she had so little time left.

1833 – Manchester

Charles rushed into the parlour clutching a letter. 'It is passed, Emily, the bill is passed.'

I remember looking up from my embroidery. I was feeling slightly nauseous and had been suffering all week. I had not bothered Charles with my illness until I could visit a doctor, and I had done so that morning and received his diagnosis.

'It's passed, Emily,' Charles repeated, a look of sheer joy and happiness beaming from his face.

'What bill, dear, what are you talking about?'

'A letter from Mr Buxton. Parliament passed the bill on its third reading.' He scanned the letter. 'He apologises for taking so long to write to me, but he had a lot of work to do after the passage of the bill. It finally received Royal assent on August twenty-eighth. There have been celebrations in London. The sugar lobby is defeated, and the slaves are to gain their freedom next year, on August first, 1834.'

He looked up from the letter with tears in his eyes. 'All we have worked for all these years has finally come true.'

'That is wonderful news, Charles. Finally…'

'Mr Buxton writes that some concessions had to be made. The five-year apprenticeship and the payment of twenty million pounds to the slave owners, but the substance of the bill is exactly as it was designed by Mr Wilberforce and Mr Clarkson. The shackles will be broken, the slaves will be free. We should give praise to the Lord.'

He dropped to his knees and began to pray. 'Thank you, O Lord, for this gift of your compassion and understanding of your fellow man. Thank you for opening the hearts and minds of those who profit from this pernicious trade to finally accept the error of their ways and free their slaves. It is only through your divine power we have achieved our long-cherished goal. We thank you once again, O Lord, and praise your infinite wisdom and patience for your insignificant subjects here on Earth. Amen.'

He stood up, fervour showing in his eyes. 'I need to go and tell the congregation. We should organise prayer meetings to give thanks for the news this evening.' It truly is a gracious blessing from God. He turned to run out of the room.

'Before you go, Charles, I have news of my own.'

He stopped for a second and turned back.

'I am pregnant. Your child will be born next May, if the Lord so wills it. Are you pleased?'

He knelt down in front of me, grasping my hands. 'Two such pieces of news on the same day! I don't know what I have done to encourage such good fortune. Truly, the Lord must be watching over us this day.'

I smiled and leant forward to kiss him on the forehead. It had occurred to me that if slavery was abolished, what further need would there be for an organiser of an anti-slavery society?

I had quickly dismissed this idea before it took root in my mind. Today, was not the day to trouble Charles with my worries.

CHAPTER FORTY-FIVE

Wednesday, August 21, 2019
International Slavery Museum, Liverpool

They finished the boxes just before the archive closed, scanning the contents rather than reading every cargo manifest and trade letter. There was nothing more related to either Charles Carruthers or Emily Roylance in any of the other boxes.

'What next, Jayne?' Rachel asked.

The genealogist thought for a moment. 'It's a long shot, but let me see.' She took out her laptop and typed in the web address for University College London.

'Why are you checking a university?'

'Because it's home to the database for the legacies of British slave ownership. In 1834, the British government freed the colonial slaves by paying their owners a bounty for each slave.'

'Really?'

Jayne nodded.

'And what did the slaves get?'

'Nothing but their freedom.'

'Why would the government give the slave owners money?'

'Because slaves were classed as property and in those days, it was thought impossible for a government to deprive an individual of his property, so they were compensated.'

'Ugh, that's disgusting.'

'Not at that time. It was thought of as logical and legally enforceable.'

The search box came up and Jayne typed in the name 'Roylance'. Instantly, the results appeared.

'I thought so. The Roylances owned slaves and received money for them when they were freed.'

They looked at the results together.

Jeremiah Roylance

Address: Holt St, Liverpool
Awardee: Barbados
         Perseverance Estate 3926 11s 11d (178 enslaved)

         Trinidad
         Bulkeleys   2458 6s 8d (126 enslaved)
         Carmichaels   5006 3s 10d (231 enslaved)

Henry Roylance

Address: Holt St, Liverpool
Awardee: Barbados   5004 8s 5d (120 enslaved)
         Trinidad   9675 3s 6d (448 enslaved)

'The Roylances were paid all that money to free their slaves?' Rachel asked, shocked.

'Over twenty-three thousand pounds by my reckoning, which would be roughly three million pounds in today's money.'

'That's terrible, Jayne.'

'We shouldn't judge these people by our standards.'

'Why not?' The actress then sighed. 'We still haven't found my African ancestor.'

'No, we haven't, but the ownership of slave estates in the Caribbean gives us a link we can follow up on.'

'Does it? I don't know. I'm tired of all this. Take me home, Jayne. I've had enough for today.'

Rachel was quiet as they drove back from Liverpool to Cheshire. Once again, her brother was waiting for them as Jayne parked at the front of the house. He must spend his life checking the CCTV, she thought, or whoever was following them had already rung the house to warn him.

Whatever it was, Jayne was ready in case anybody pulled the same stunt as last night. This time she wasn't going to let them get away with it.

As Rachel got out of the car, David greeted her with a cheery, 'How was your day? Did you enjoy the wild-goose chase?'

'Not really,' Rachel sulked. 'We discovered a lot about a family called Carruthers, and another called Roylance, but nothing to link them directly to any African ancestors. I'm beginning to think you are right, David, it's just a wild-goose chase. The DNA results must be wrong.' She turned back to Jayne. 'You've got just two days left to discover the truth, Mrs Sinclair, before the programme goes on air. I hope we're not wasting my time and my money.' With that she flounced into the hall, without saying goodbye.

David laughed. 'Looks like you have an unhappy client, Mrs Sinclair. And knowing Rachel, when she's unhappy, she's not a nice person to be around.'

Jayne didn't reply, simply restarting the engine and spinning the wheels on the car to create a cloud of dust that enveloped the man. She had had enough of the bloody Marlowes to last a lifetime. She wished she had never taken this rotten case.

On the drive back to Manchester, she quietly seethed with anger, but kept her eyes peeled for any signs of danger.

There were no grey Range Rovers trying to run her off the road tonight. But she arrived back at home with her shoulders aching and her body tired from gripping the steering wheel too tightly.

CHAPTER FORTY-SIX

July 12, 1842
Wickham Hall, Cheshire

Emily woke up with her head resting on her open book. Outside, the early morning light was streaming in through the windows on another bright summer's day. She must have dozed off whilst writing. The last line on the page was smudged and ink had transferred to the cotton sleeve of her dress.

No matter.

Her brother was due back today. She only had a little time left in which to write, and it was the most important part of her story.

She took up her pen, dipped it in the ink and began to compose her thoughts.

1833–4 – Manchester

Unfortunately for me, the pregnancy was not a happy one. The morning sickness that I endured left me tired and morose, and later, the gradual expansion of my body left me lethargic and bitter. The baby seemed to suck the very essence out of me as it grew in my womb. Some days I found it impossible to get out of bed.

Added to this were my worries concerning Charles. As I had expected, the passage of the bill, even though it was not yet law, meant that the society began to cut back on expenses, the major one of which was Charles's salary and benefice.

He was told just before Christmas that his services were no longer required.

'What are we going to do, Charles?'

He took my hand as I lay in bed, fatigued by the baby growing inside me.

'Something will turn up, don't you worry. And in the end, there's always my family. I can always ask them for help to tide us over.'

Finally, after two months of seeking and failing to find another position, Charles did turn to his family for aid.

They rebuffed him with strong words. His father even went so far as to call me 'a jezebel who has tempted Charles with the forbidden fruit'.

Despite mixing up two completely different bible stories, I felt about as close to a jezebel as Lady Caroline Lamb was to an honest woman.

Charles, however, was not despondent. He tramped the streets of Manchester, calling on all the traders and merchants who had supported his work in the past, but to no avail. There really was no need for a preacher whose sole claim to fame was an ability to organise an anti-slavery society.

Soon we were given leave to quit our rented house when we could no longer afford to pay the landlord. And in the harsh early months of winter and the crueller months of spring, it was often better for me to stay in bed rather than risk the damp cold of the parlour and the sitting room.

'I could approach my father, or at least my brother,' I offered. 'I'm sure he would listen.'

Charles reluctantly agreed. I sent a letter out the next day and received a reply by return of post from my brother. The tones were rather cold and unemotional but the message was clear.

Dear Sister,

Thank you for your letter of the 24th.
It was gratifying to hear the news of your pregnancy.
Father is as well as can be expected.
I'm afraid he refuses to countenance sending you any money whilst you remain married to that man. If you will leave him, he will, of course, accept yourself and your child into our family.
I am to be married to Miss Clara Marlowe, probably next year as she has just embarked on a grand tour of Europe.
I remain your obedient and loving brother,

Henry

I read the letter four or five times, each time seeing less and less warmth in it. It was almost as if my brother was writing to a stranger. Had he changed so much, or had he always been so cold?

I didn't know the answer.

When Charles returned after his afternoon searching for a position, I hid the letter so he wouldn't see it. Lately, he had become more and more despondent and I didn't want to burden him with the news from my family. Somehow, we would get through these trials and tribulations together. Hadn't our marriage vows talked of 'to have and to hold, from this day forward; for better, for worse; for richer, for poorer; in sickness and in health; to love and to cherish, till death us do part, according to God's holy law'?

I would keep my vows whatever happened.

CHAPTER FORTY-SEVEN

July 12, 1842
Wickham Hall, Cheshire

1834 – Manchester

On April 6th, 1834, at nine o'clock in the morning, Charles died.

As I sit here and write these words my tears drop onto the page and stain the ink. Dear reader, you don't know how difficult it was for me to write those words.

At the time, all I remember was an immense numbness that seemed to suffuse my body and overwhelm my spirit.

We had moved into a small house in Ancoats, far from the comfort and security of our old home, but it was all that we could afford.

Charles, after much traipsing through the streets of Manchester, had finally found a position as a clerk with a firm of solicitors, but the hours were long and the pay meagre.

Gradually, he grew thinner and thinner as I think he forswore his own food in favour of feeding myself and our baby, who was yet to be born.

Within weeks of starting his new position, he woke up one morning vomiting and unable to control his bowels. At that time, I feared it was the pestilence, an evil miasma that inhabited the whole area.

We could not afford a doctor but a local lady came in and administered a poultice to his stomach. Unfortunately, it was too late.

My poor Charles passed away in my arms, a black evil dribbling from his mouth.

He was never going to see the final abolition of slavery, a goal he had spent his whole life working for.

He would never see our dear child, the soul for whom he had sacrificed so much.

He would never feel my skin next to his, nor hear my heart as he lay his head on my breast.

And me? I had lost so much too.

I would never listen to his voice, nor feel his touch, nor taste the beauty of his lips.

I wrote a letter to his family explaining the circumstances of his death but received no answer, and nor did I expect any.

At least I was given assistance by the congregation of the Quakers. Charles received a proper funeral and would not rest for eternity in a pauper's grave.

But what was to become of me and our child?

Mrs Cummins, the midwife, told me I was to give birth to a boy in the middle of April.

She had just prepared the dose of laudanum she had procured from the chemists. Apparently, the shock of Charles' death could adversely affect the baby, so I was to be dosed for the following week until the birth.

I did not like it as I spent my time dreaming of Charles and his smile like the dawning sun.

I wished that Charles were there by my side.

But he was not, and I was alone.

CHAPTER FORTY-EIGHT

July 12, 1842
Wickham Hall, Cheshire

1834 – Manchester

On April 18th, 1834, my baby was born.

A happy, healthy baby boy, as Mrs Cummins had predicted, weighing in at six pounds and twelve ounces.

I named him Liberty, after the achievement of his father and in honour of the year the slaves finally achieved freedom.

At least Charles will be remembered even though it broke my heart every time I said his name.

I remember feeling my baby lying in the bed beside me, his face screwed up tight against the world and a shock of black hair, just like his father, crowning his head.

I do not know what I would have done without Mrs Cummins' kindness. She had looked after me since Charles died, feeding me and caring for me to the detriment of her own family.

But I could not avail myself of her kindness for too long. Soon, I would have to leave that house and find a way of sustaining myself and my child.

At that time, I thought I could become a governess or offer lessons in reading and writing. It could be difficult with Liberty by my side, but I was sure we could find a way.

I was more positive than I had been ever since my pregnancy began. Perhaps it was the laudanum speaking, or perhaps simply the physical act of giving birth had relieved me of the burden of having a child inside me.

I did not know. But it was time to sleep before Liberty woke again and demanded to be fed.

We had to make our own way in the world from then on.

CHAPTER FORTY-NINE

Wednesday, August 21, 2019
Didsbury, Manchester

When Jayne opened the door to her home in Didsbury, Mr Smith didn't come out to greet her. She called his name, expecting him to rush out with his tail erect and his furry body pressing against her legs.

Still nothing.

She listened and called his name again.

No response.

Instantly the hackles on her neck rose. Something was wrong. She rushed into the kitchen to find the whole place in disarray; papers scattered everywhere, her computer shattered on the floor, the glass of the patio door broken.

In the corner, Mr Smith lay beneath one of her coats that had been thrown on the floor. He peered out cautiously, saw her and then rushed over. She picked him up, nestling her face in his fur.

'You're okay, Mr Smith, you're okay,' she whispered.

Her feet crunched over broken glass as she walked around the kitchen. Still holding Mr Smith, she picked up the bar chair that had been thrown to the ground. Next to it, her computer lay smashed, its screen and innards spilling out over the tiles. Luckily, she backed up all her files into the cloud and on to hard copy. Most of her paper files were scattered all over the floor, however; her life, her cases, just the detritus of some thug who had broken into her house.

It was then she looked up and saw the far wall. In big, bold, blue letters, the intruder had sprayed: '**LEAVE IT ALONE OR ELSE**'.

Leave what alone? Did they mean the case? Maybe this wasn't a burglary. And then she remembered her jewellery. She didn't have much, but Paul had given her a few things over the years. He particularly enjoyed the fine workmanship of classic watches and had given her a Rolex and a Cartier on their fifth and tenth wedding anniversaries respectively. Celebrations that seemed to belong to a different time and place.

Putting Mr Smith down in the hall close to his favourite windowsill, she ran upstairs and opened her dressing-table drawer, taking out her jewellery box.

She opened it but everything was there. Her watches were nestling on their velvet cushions, her diamond wedding ring still in its box from Chaumier, assorted gold and silver necklaces untouched.

Strange. Why would a burglar go to all the trouble of breaking in and then steal nothing?

Her detective training kicked in. She checked the house. All those items that should have been stolen – televisions, electrical appliances and the rest – were all still there. Nothing was missing.

She walked back into the kitchen. The desktop computer, easily the quickest item to sell if a druggie needed money, was lying broken and forlorn on the island counter where she had left it.

Then she looked again at the words sprayed on the wall. This wasn't a burglary but another warning. With a start, she remembered Rachel's necklace.

She raced over to the cupboard where she kept her work files. Stupidly, she had placed the necklace and its box into a manila envelope and put it in Rachel Marlowe's case file, ready to return to her.

She looked in the case file.

Nothing there.

The necklace, all her notes on the case and the Marlowe family tree, which she had so painstakingly recreated, was gone.

She knew now who had taken it. There was no point calling the police; she knew exactly who had done this.

And they were going to pay.

CHAPTER FIFTY

July 12, 1842
Wickham Hall, Cheshire

1834-37 – Manchester

For nearly three years my baby and I existed through the kindness of strangers.

Mrs Cummins and the congregation of the Quakers provided me with food and hand-me-down clothes. I took in washing and cleaned their houses, receiving pennies in return for my labour, but at least with what I earned I could buy fresh milk for Liberty.

After the first year, I moved from the house in Ancoats to a room in Angel's Meadows. There were no angels there, and precious little grass, but the landlady was a kindly old soul who rented her rooms to those women of a genteel disposition who had fallen on hard times.

'I know what it's like to be poor,' she said one day as we sat in her kitchen, warming ourselves in front of the range, Liberty drinking his milk in my arms.

'Before I married Mr Harcourt,' she continued, 'bless his soul, I had nothing but the clothes I stood up in. He rescued me from the streets and promised me the house when he died. A kindly man, but old. I thought that when I married him I didn't have long to wait. But blow me, didn't the old sod last to be eighty-two? Here was I thinking when he pops his clogs, I'll find myself a young 'un and have a bit of fun. But by the time he'd finally gone, I'd lost all the will. Bless me, ain't life a card, eh?' She laughed loudly at herself through a mouth absent of teeth but full of gums.

There were three other women in the house as well as myself. All had fallen on hard times for one reason or another, but I was the only one with a child.

Generally, Liberty enjoyed having four new mothers to look after him, but occasionally problems arose, particularly when he was teething and crying loudly every night. Mrs Harcourt, the landlady, wanted to rub gin on his gums.

'My love, I bought a pennyworth at the grog shop just for him. See, he likes the taste, don't he? And it'll help stop his infernal noise of an evening.'

I moved out soon afterwards, taking my son and my meagre belongings to another room in Chorlton-upon-Medlock.

Here I had a basement which wasn't as clean as Mrs Harcourt's house, close as it was to Arkwright's mill, but the rent was cheaper and the other residents didn't bother me at all.

Eighteen people lived in the same house, all sharing one outside toilet whose waste was taken away each morning by the gunny man for sale to the market gardens in Stretford.

I managed by taking in washing and writing letters for the other residents to their relatives back in Ireland.

'Sure, none of them have the reading, but the priest can tell them what's going on. Now, won't they be excited to just be receiving the thing, rather than reading it.'

It wasn't the perfect life for Liberty, but at least we managed and he ate well, growing into a strong, healthy boy, if prone to prolonged fits of crying for no apparent reason.

Then, one day, I fell sick.

It was the same illness Charles had contracted; fever, followed by vomiting and the sweats. Pestilence, the locals called it, but I knew it probably came from the bad water we were forced to drink.

I lay in my bed wasting away, Liberty beside me, his head buried in my sweaty hair. I had no money, no food and no energy to work any more. I had not paid the rent and the new landlord had already told me to pay up or leave.

In one of those moments of lucidity that occasionally occur in the middle of an illness, I woke one morning and, borrowing a pen and paper at the local church, wrote a letter to my father.

Dear Father,

I am your daughter, Emily. As you may be unaware, my late husband, Charles, passed away these three years now. Since then, I have had a son, Liberty, who is the spitting image of his father. I write to you in his name, not for myself or in desire of anything from you, but to beseech you to take him under your care and patronage. It pains me to say it, but in my present circumstances, I cannot give him the sort of upbringing and life he both deserves and desires as the grandson of Jeremiah Roylance.

I beg you, Father, whatever you may feel about me and the wrongs I may have trespassed upon you in the past, for my son's sake, forgive him even if you are unable to forgive me.

I ask you to change your mind and accept my son into the household as your grandson.

Your faithful and loving daughter,

Emily

I gave the letter to the coachman plying the Manchester to Liverpool route, along with the last shilling I possessed in the world. Neither myself nor my son would eat that night, but if it meant he could escape this life of meanness and drudgery, it would all be worth it.

For myself, I cared not a jot, but my son was my world. More than that, he was the living embodiment of my husband, a symbol of both our love and our commitment to each other.

If, by giving him up, I could create a better life for him, a life of privilege and education, I would do so willingly and without a moment's hesitation.

The answer came far earlier than I thought possible. Two days later, a liveried servant brought me a letter. I tore it open in my eagerness to read the contents.

Dear Sister,

It was pleasant to receive your letter addressed to Father after all these years. I am sorry you have fallen on hard times. Perhaps our Lord the Redeemer took the opportunity to remind you of the error of your ways when you went against the wishes of our father and married Charles Carruthers.

Nonetheless, it was gratifying to receive your news and I congratulate you on the arrival of your son. However, Liberty is a strange name for a boy; it has a dissenting feel about it.

There is one piece of bad news I must impart. Father passed away two years ago. After you left, he wasn't in good health and, if truth be known, he adapted slowly to the change in circumstances of our estates and our fortune since the emancipation of the slaves. The former has decreased and the latter increased exponentially.

I am now residing at Wickham Hall. I married your former classmate, Clare Marlowe, and am in the process of disposing of both the house and the business in Liverpool. Indeed, I am soon to adopt the name and title of Henry Marlowe, therefore all your future correspondence should be addressed to me by this title.

As for your request regarding your son, I am happy to say I will accede to it on three conditions:

The boy adopts the name of Marlowe is the first.

The second is that I will have full control of the boy's upbringing and education.

Finally, that you accompany him and come to live with us here at Wickham Hall. I will not have a sister of mine disgrace the family name by living in such conditions as you now find yourself.

Accordingly, I will send a coach to fetch you both to Wickham Hall in three days' time, at ten in the morning. If either yourself or your son board the coach, I shall presume you have agreed to my terms.

Your brother,

Henry Marlowe

Father was dead? Why hadn't Henry told me before? Why had he left me in ignorance until that day?

I looked across at my sleeping son, his chest rising slowly and his body thin beneath the rags covering him. In the half-light from the small window into the basement, he looked almost wraith-like, his skin white as parchment. A harsh cough erupted from his thin lips, but still he slept on.

I knew then what I had to do. My needs, my feelings, didn't matter any more. I had to do what was right for him.

Nothing else mattered.

CHAPTER FIFTY-ONE

July 12, 1842
Wickham Hall, Cheshire

1837 – Cheshire

It took one whole day to travel from Manchester to Wickham Hall.

Early that morning, I dressed Liberty and myself in our best clothes, the ones I kept at the bottom of the case for use at Sunday church.

The coach arrived and all the neighbours gathered to stare as it rattled down the cobbled street and stopped outside our house.

'Lady Muck's done alright for hersel'!'

'Can I get a ride, mister?'

'Where you goin'?'

I hugged Mrs Cummins, the midwife, who had come to see me off, and stepped up into the velvet-lined coach, helped by the kindly driver. Staring straight ahead with Liberty sitting upright beside me, they started off at ten o'clock precisely, stopping just once to change horses.

The coach was well constructed and comfortable, with the new elliptical springs that made the journey far less tiring than I remembered. Still, by the time we arrived at Wickham Hall we were both exhausted.

Clara took one look at Liberty and sniffed. 'He needs a bath?' The housekeeper stepped forward. 'Make sure he washes well, and burn those clothes. We don't know where they've been.'

'Hello, Clara,' I said. 'It's been a long time since school.'

'It has,' answered Clara curtly, 'and look at the state you have allowed yourself to fall into. All through marrying a most unsuitable man.'

Liberty was led upstairs, holding the hand of Mrs Trevor and glancing backwards towards me. I smiled to reassure him.

'Sister, we have something to discuss with you now,' said Henry.

'I am tired, brother, it has been a long journey.'

'I'm afraid this cannot wait. Come into the library with me.'

I followed him into the room which I remembered from my visit to Wickham Hall all those years ago, when I was young and naïve and foolish.

As soon as I approached the table in the centre, my brother placed a document in my hand.

'As I communicated in my letter, there are some agreements we must have from you before both Clara and I can allow you and your son to remain at Wickham Hall. You must sign them now.'

I slumped heavily in the library chair; around me all the books seemed to form a prison whose walls were made of words. 'What does it say, Henry?' I asked wearily.

My brother glanced at his wife before continuing. 'The details have been drawn up by my solicitors, but essentially the document states that we – that is, Clara and myself – will become the boy's legal guardians and have full control over his education and upbringing. As we are unlikely to have children of our own, I intend to make the boy my heir. He will inherit Wickham Hall and the estate.'

I was too tired to speak, so I just nodded my head. It was Clara who spoke next.

'Obviously a name like Liberty cannot be attached to the Marlowe surname, and so we will rename the boy. From now on, he will be known as Royston Marlowe. It was my grandfather's name and it reflects the proud traditions of my family. Do you agree?'

I thought of Charles. What would he want? In the split second I was given to think, I decided he would want the best life possible for Liberty, a life I was unable to give him myself.

I stared down at the table and nodded.

Clara smiled, adding, 'From today onwards, you will only call him Royston. Do you agree?'

I nodded again.

'Finally, you will, from today onwards, refer to yourself as his aunt, not his mother,' Henry added. 'Clara and I will retain the titles of mother and father for ourselves. You will live here with us at Wickham Hall, of course, as a member of my family.'

'But that is impossible. He will always know me as his mother, I gave birth to him.'

'In time he will forget, like all boys,' said Clara. 'Do you agree, or shall we instruct the coachmen to take you back to Manchester?'

I looked down at the hands lying in my lap. Once they had touched fine silk and embroidered intricate samplers. Now, they were red and chapped and wrinkled. Hands made tired and old in the constant struggle to feed and clothe Liberty.

Dear reader, an immense tiredness washed over me. I knew I could not do it any more. If I did not accede to their demands, both Liberty and I would end up in the workhouse and what would happen then? More than likely, my son would be taken away from me. At least now I could see him every day. Watch him grow and become a strong, healthy and happy man.

'Do you agree?' my brother insisted.

I nodded once more and whispered, 'I agree.'

'Then sign the document and let us have done with it. The boy, Royston, can start a new life.'

I picked up the pen in my trembling hands. I found myself hesitating before I signed, the sharpened point of the quill hovering over the page.

'Sign it,' Clara said.

I wrote my name.

My brother reached forwarded, snatching the document from me. 'It is done,' he said. 'Clara, will you show my sister to her rooms?'

In a trance, I stood up and followed Clara out of the library, up the stairs and into the room where I was to spend most of the next five years.

My own private prison.

CHAPTER FIFTY-TWO

Wednesday, August 21, 2019
Didsbury, Manchester

Jayne spent most of that evening cleaning the kitchen and throwing out all the broken glassware and crockery. She called the window repair service, who said they could only come in two days' time. Another hassle. She knocked out the rest of the glass and found a sheet of cardboard to paste over the empty space. It wouldn't stop a determined burglar, but the chances of another break-in were remote.

The words sprayed on the wall were impossible to remove. She was going to redecorate anyway, but this was just another expense she didn't need at the moment.

She thought again about calling one of her old friends in the police, but decided against it. The law could be slow and ponderous;

she was going to sort this out herself in her own way. It was time for it all to stop.

Jayne had won a reputation in the police as being particularly tough on men who attacked women. The other coppers had often made jokes about it in the canteen and the locker room.

'Here she comes again, Manchester's answer to the Yorkshire Ripper, except she takes men apart.' Or, 'It's the ball-breaker, hang on to your tackle, lads.'

She didn't care then and she cared even less now. Nobody, absolutely nobody, should attempt to scare or hit women. If they did, she would take them down.

After feeding Mr Smith she tried to let him out as usual to court the amorous cat at number seven, but he refused to go, sticking close to her.

'Okay, stay here then, but I'm going to take a long bath.'

She opened a classic New Zealand sauvignon blanc and poured a large glass, taking it upstairs.

Relaxing in the warm bath and drinking the wine made her think about Paul again. She really did have to contact the divorce solicitors. Now more than ever, the house was the most important thing to her. Strangely, it being violated made her even more determined to protect it in the future.

From Paul or anybody else.

As she lay in the hot water, she allowed her mind to wander over the day's events. She knew there was a connection between Emily Roylance and Rachel Marlowe, but how could she prove it? And even if she did, where was the link to African ancestry?

The puzzle still remained unsolved, and now there were just two days left before the programme was aired.

As Jayne's head began to sink beneath the water, an idea came to her.

Could that be the link? Could it be as simple as that?

CHAPTER FIFTY-THREE

Thursday, August 22, 2019
Didsbury, Manchester

The following morning Jayne was up bright and early.

After her bath, she had spent the rest of the evening thinking about the case and planning her course of action. She was pretty certain now who Rachel's African ancestor was; it was the only scenario that managed to fit all the facts.

It was also clear to her that only one person could have been responsible for the road-rage attack and for the break-in. It was time to move on to the offensive by making a couple of calls.

The first was to Rachel, waking her up.

'Er, hello?' her client answered sleepily.

'Hi, Rachel, it's Jayne Sinclair. I've finally solved your puzzle for you. Can I come to Wickham Hall to show you this morning?'

Rachel's voice was instantly more awake. 'Really? That's great news. Who is it?'

Jayne ignored the question. 'I'll be there at ten thirty. As it concerns your brother and your father too, could you make sure they attend, please?'

'I'll ask them, I'm sure they'll want to know. How did you do it?'

'I'll tell you when I see you.'

She then called the second number, that belonging to her ex-boss in the police. 'Hi Charlie, it's Jayne.'

'Hi Jayne, it's a long time since I heard from you. Still enjoying your retirement, are we?'

'Not really retired, I'm working harder now than I ever did.' She paused for a moment. 'Charlie, I have a favour I need to ask you.'

She explained the problem and worked out a course of action with her ex-boss, who was now a Chief Superintendent. Finally, after all had been agreed, she put down the phone and stood still for a moment, staring at the cardboard covering up the hole in her patio door. Mr Smith was at her feet, still staying close to her, not like his usual behaviour at all.

She reached down and picked him up, nuzzling his soft fur with her face. For once he didn't try to wriggle out of her grasp, but just lay there enjoying the attention.

'Nobody, absolutely nobody, gets away with trying to scare me,' she said out loud. 'Except you, of course, you old tom cat.'

CHAPTER FIFTY-FOUR

Thursday, August 22, 2019
Didsbury, Manchester

At the main entrance to Wickham Hall, she was met by Rachel this time, looking as lovely as ever.

'Hi, Jayne. Father and David are waiting in the library for you. They can't wait to discover what you've found out.'

'I bet they can't.'

'Have you eaten? There's still some breakfast left.'

'I have, thanks, but a coffee wouldn't go amiss.'

'I'll get Mrs Davies to bring some to the library. Shall we get started straight away? I have to leave before three and Father has an appointment in Chester at noon.'

Jayne smiled to herself. 'Of course.'

Both men were in the library. David was lounging on the sofa staring up into the air. His father was sitting more upright in the armchair, reading the *Financial Times* again, a pot of tea at his elbow.

When they entered, David immediately sat upright whilst Sir Harold Marlowe folded his paper neatly, placing it on the table next to the tea.

David stood up to shake her hand. 'Good morning, Mrs Sinclair, I believe you have some news for us. Finally solved the problem, have we?'

'I think I have, David.'

Sir Harold stood up too. 'Good morning, Mrs Sinclair. I do hope we haven't inconvenienced you too much, dragging you all the way into the wilds of deepest, darkest Cheshire.'

'Not at all, Sir Harold, I think you'll find what I have to say very interesting.'

They both waited for Jayne to sit before returning to their places. Rachel remained standing, hovering next to both of them.

Jayne placed her phone down on the table, opened her folder and began to read. 'It has been an interesting case – actually two cases…'

'I don't understand, Jayne. There's just my case, isn't there? I briefed you to find my African ancestor?' said Rachel.

'If there was one at all,' added her brother.

Jayne spoke firmly. 'No, there are two cases. The first is the search for your African ancestor. The second is a much more unusual case. One of threatening behaviour and criminal damage.'

'I don't understand,' said Rachel.

'Since I took your case, Rachel, I have received a threatening phone call, my car was nearly run off the road, I have been spied on and, finally, last night, my house was broken into.'

'You were burgled, Mrs Sinclair?' asked David.

'No. Nothing was stolen, except Rachel's necklace.'

'My necklace was stolen? But I asked you to take good care of it, Jayne, it was given to me by my mother!'

Jayne held her hand up. 'Don't worry, I know where it is.' She turned towards David. 'Mr Marlowe, you made the threatening phone call as soon as you heard I had been commissioned to work on this case. Why?'

David laughed. 'I would hardly classify the call as threatening, Mrs Sinclair. I can't remember what I said, but I'm sure I didn't threaten you.'

'You actually said, "I'm very proud of my family and its history, Ms Sinclair. I wouldn't want it to be sullied in any way."'

'Don't be such a snowflake, Mrs Sinclair. I wouldn't call that a threat, more a statement of my feelings towards my family.'

'Normally those words would not be classified as a threat, but given the incidents that followed, the threat is implied.'

'All I meant is that I take my reputation and that of my family seriously. I didn't mean to threaten you at all. I know nothing about your other problems, I swear on my honour.'

'And yet you have lied to me and to Rachel regarding your family and the family tree, haven't you?'

For a moment, David looked sheepish. 'I don't know what you mean.'

'Three years ago, you started to investigate your family's genealogy. You discovered there were missing records from the church, or you removed them yourself—'

'I did not,' he shouted.

Jayne carried on undaunted. 'So you followed up as we did, visiting the archives in Chester and discovering the true ancestry of Henry Marlowe; he married into the family and was originally a Roylance from Liverpool. I checked with the Cheshire archivist this morning. They went through their visitors book. She even remembered you. I think her exact description was "an obnoxious, rude man".'

'What of it? I did find out about Henry, but that doesn't change anything. He became the adopted son of Sir Philip Marlowe and as such was his rightful heir.'

'True, but it does make your claim to a family tree stretching back in an unbroken line to a soldier of William the Conqueror untenable, doesn't it?' Before David could answer, Jayne carried on. 'But one matter troubles me. Why three years ago? What happened then that suddenly made you decide to investigate your family history?'

David's face reddened. 'I found something.'

'You found what?'

'I don't have to tell you.'

'But you do have to tell the other members of your family.' She pointed to his father and sister. 'And I don't think you have.'

'What is it, David? What did you find?' Rachel asked.

David Marlowe's head sunk down. 'I found a notebook,' he whispered.

'What notebook, whose was it?'

His head came up again. 'It belonged to Emily Roylance.'

'The sister of Henry? The woman who was living here at the time of the 1841 census?' said Jayne.

He nodded. 'I found it in there.' He pointed at the glass-covered bookcase. 'Hidden in another book. I don't think it had been touched since she placed it there before she died.'

'Where is it now?'

David stood and strode over to the bookcase. Pulling a key from his pocket, he inserted it in the lock and turned. The door squeaked open. He reached up to the top shelf and pulled out the book *Pickwick Papers* by Charles Dickens. He opened it up and hidden inside was a small notebook. 'I was looking for first editions. They can be extremely valuable these days.'

'You've been selling our books?' Rachel asked.

'He's been doing that for a long time, haven't you, David? It covers his gambling debts, you see.' Sir Harold Marlowe spoke for the first time.

'You know, Father?'

'I've always known, David, ever since you stopped asking me for money. I worked out you must be getting an income from somewhere. Your sudden interest in spending time in the library intrigued me.'

Jayne held out her hand. 'Can I see the notebook?'

David Marlowe handed it to her.

Together with Rachel, she sat down at the library table and opened it to the first page and the first entry.

An Account of the Life of Emily Roylance

My name is Emily Roylance and I was born on March 4, 1806; the daughter of Jeremiah Roylance, merchant, and Dolores Sharpe, spinster, on the Perseverance Estate in the island of Barbados.

CHAPTER FIFTY-FIVE

October 12, 1842
Wickham Hall, Cheshire

1842 – Cheshire

I know the end is near.

I can barely leave my bed now, my body is so weak. I spend much of the time sleeping, crossing between the worlds of the conscious and unconscious as if the barrier no longer existed.

Yesterday, I dreamt Charles visited me and sat by my bed. He asked me to join him, holding out those strong hands that had once gripped a bible or a lectern.

I hesitated.

Not because I was unwilling to be with him. On the contrary, the prospect of spending the rest of eternity with the man I love is so appealing.

But I knew I still had one thing left to do. So tonight, after everyone had gone to bed, I summoned all that remained of my strength and tumbled from my bed.

My legs were so weak and shrivelled from lack of use that I barely managed to stagger to the desk. I took out my notebook and began to write these words.

I have long planned for this day. I took a pair of scissors I had hidden in my drawer and began to remove the pages from Mr Dickens' book to create a hole where my notebook could fit snugly.

It amused me to secrete my book within another book. It was as if my memoirs had been published within these pages. And, knowing my brother, it will be the last place he would ever look. The maid has been instructed to take it down with all the other books and place them all in the library where it will lie hidden in plain sight.

Perhaps one day, in the fullness of time, somebody will eventually discover the story within. I hope my future kin – for I believe it will be one of my family – read the words and understand my life.

I have left a note in my will for Liberty; I cannot bear to call him Royston. I do hope he understands, but I cannot be certain. He is eight years old now but already bears the signs of Henry's influence. I have left him my mother's necklace with instructions that he is to add to it and pass it on to a daughter, if he has one.

I pray he discovers the world has more to it than the acquisition of money and power.

I am finished now and must return to my bed to die.

I have made many mistakes in my life, but I believe all have come from love and passion rather than fear and hate.

I am ready to spend the rest of time with Charles.

Remember this, dear reader, if you are one of my kinsmen or women. Love conquers all, even death.

CHAPTER FIFTY-SIX

Thursday, August 22, 2019
Wickham Hall, Cheshire

'"Remember this, dear reader, if you are one of my kinsmen or women. Love conquers all, even death."'

Jayne spoke the last words out loud and closed the notebook.

'What an amazing woman,' said Rachel, 'and what a story.'

'You see now that I had to hide it, to protect our family's reputation,' David said.

'But there was no need to attack Jayne, or destroy her house. What did you mean to gain by that?' Rachel thrust her face towards her brother.

'He didn't,' said Jayne.

'What? What do you mean? You just said he knew about the Roylances.'

'I thought about it last night. Your brother did know the family secret, and would have gone to any legal lengths to keep it quiet, wouldn't you, David?'

'I told you as much, Mrs Sinclair.'

'But he wouldn't have been able to order one of the estate's gamekeepers to attack me, would he, Sir Harold? Only you could do that.'

All eyes turned to look at Sir Harold, sitting upright in his armchair.

'And why would I do that, Mrs Sinclair?'

'Because you've known about this family secret for a long time, haven't you? Well, before David ever did his research.'

'I may have done.'

'My ex-colleagues checked the Police National Computer. Your man – John Goddard is his name – has form, doesn't he? Theft, assault and battery, GBH. He has an impressive rap sheet. Has he always done your dirty work, Sir Harold?'

The man smiled. 'We have known each other a long time and John is very good at his job. But you can never prove anything, Mrs Sinclair, he's always very careful. A true professional.'

'Father, why?' cried David.

'You don't understand, David. You've been so wrapped up in your political ambitions, you forgot that politics is a dirty game where people will stop at nothing to humiliate you, and that's just the ones on your own side.'

He turned to his daughter. 'As for you, Rachel, with your lovey-dovey actor friends and political beliefs gained from the pages of the *Guardian*, I begged you not to take part in that programme but you insisted. "It would be good for my career" you whined. What career? Playing damsels-in-distress rescued by knights in shining armour from Islington?' He paused for breath and pointed at himself. 'It was I who guarded this family and its reputation whilst you two frittered it away. Yes, we have black ancestors – we were slave merchants, for God's sake. Look around you, what do think paid for all this? Half the aristocratic families received money to free the slaves; the Camerons, the Gladstones, the Earl of Harewood, the banking Barings, two Lord Chancellors, even that champion of socialism, George Orwell – his family received money. And now you want to find out who your black ancestor was? What a waste of time. You have many black cousins, most of whom are still alive in the West Indies.'

'And it was you who visited the Liverpool archives last week?' Jayne asked.

The old man nodded. 'Once I had seen what the Carruthers box contained, I asked the archivist to restrict access to the records, but she refused. "They are in the public domain," she said pompously, as if the public ever had a "domain".'

David spoke. 'You said we have cousins in the West Indies, but how could that be? I have no African ancestry, Father. Remember, my DNA was tested.'

Jayne stared across at Sir Harold Marlowe. 'Are you going to tell him or shall I?'

The owner of Wickham Hall stared open-mouthed at her.

She turned back to face David. 'There can only be one answer for your lack of African DNA if everybody else in the family possesses it.'

'What? What is it?'

'You have had your DNA tested, haven't you, Sir Harold?'

The old man slowly nodded his head. 'I did it as soon as I heard Rachel was definitely going to appear on that damn-fool programme.'

'And you have African ancestry?'

'From the same region of Africa as Rachel, apparently.'

'I don't understand. If Father has it and so does Rachel, why don't I?'

'How did you know?' Sir Harold asked of Jayne.

'It was the only logical conclusion. It's true there are a few cases where children inherit all their DNA from one parent, but I don't think it happened in this case, so there can only be one answer.'

'What's going on? What answer?'

'Are you going to tell him?' Jayne asked once more.

The old man took a deep breath. 'David, you are adopted.'

CHAPTER FIFTY-SEVEN

Thursday, August 22, 2019
Wickham Hall, Cheshire

'What?'

'You have to understand, your mother and I had been trying for so long. We married late and became desperate. The family line had to continue. I found the notebook in the library and it gave me the idea. I went to one of the orphanages in Liverpool. They were always happy to arrange adoptions, especially with an esteemed family like mine. I met all the children and chose you.'

'Like picking a prize bull at a market. You were looking for good breeding stock. Sorry to have disappointed you.'

'You never disappointed me. You were always the son I wanted. A little wild in your youth, but that was to be expected, and gambling has always run in this family. What do you think I've been doing all my life? Except in my circles it's known politely as stock-market investing. It's simply gambling, that's all.'

'But that means we aren't brother and sister?' David pointed at Rachel.

'Not blood relatives, but you are both my kin just as much as anybody else.'

There was a loud knock on the front door that could be heard even in the library.

A few moments later, two plainclothes policemen entered the room. The taller and fatter of the two approached Sir Harold and said. 'Sir, I am arresting you for conspiracy to commit burglary and grievous bodily harm. You are not required to say anything, but anything you do say will be taken down and may be used in evidence against you.'

'What about John Goddard?' asked Sir Harold.

'He has already been taken into custody and admitted all the charges.'

'How did you know?'

The detective placed a blue plastic glove on this right hand and walked over to where Jayne was still sitting. 'We could hear everything loud and clear, but I'm afraid we have to take this as evidence.'

'Don't worry, I have another,' said Jayne.

He picked up her phone and placed it in an evidence bag, signing and sealing it. 'Now, sir, if you wouldn't mind coming with us.'

'John had nothing to do with this, it was all my idea.'

'Be quiet, Father,' David shouted, 'don't say a word. I'll get on to our solicitors and we'll have you out this afternoon. And detective, the Chief Constable will hear of this outrage.'

'I'm afraid he already knows, sir. Who do you think approved the investigation?'

CHAPTER FIFTY-EIGHT

Thursday, August 22, 2019
Wickham Hall, Cheshire

As David rushed out after the policemen and his father, Jayne was left alone with Rachel.

They both stayed silent for a moment before Rachel spoke. 'I wish I'd never started this bloody thing.'

'Sometimes it's best to leave family secrets buried. I did warn you.'

'It's too bloody late now. We've destroyed the family and we're still no closer to knowing the truth.'

'If it's any consolation, because of his age your father will probably receive a suspended sentence. However, John Goddard has a record and he'll undoubtedly be sentenced to prison.'

'You don't get it, do you? You've destroyed my family's reputation and my brother will probably have to resign from his party.'

'These days, breaking the law doesn't seem to disqualify anybody from being an MP.'

Rachel heaved a long sigh. 'All this and we still haven't found who my African ancestor was.'

Jayne stood up and pointed to the computer sitting on its table in the corner of the library. 'May I? There's a possibility I know who it is.'

Jayne walked over to the desk, followed by Rachel. 'There are some Caribbean records at Familysearch.' She entered the website and began typing. 'If we search for Emily Roylance's birth certificate in 1806, it will give us details of her parentage.'

Rachel leaned in closer to the screen.

'There is a hit for a Dolores Sharpe.' She clicked the page and an image began to form with beautiful copperplate handwriting for St Joseph's parish church, March 1806. It was a register page divided into three columns for Births, Marriages and Burials.

Jayne scanned down the page, reading the entries for births aloud.

'March first. Alexander Hagan, slave of Mr John G. Eastmouth.'

'But this is a birth. Does that mean as soon as they were born these people became slaves?'

'And the property of their owner.' Jayne carried on reading. 'March second. Phoebe, Jane and Rachel, mulatto slaves of Mary Dowding.'

'Three children owned by a woman?'

'Slave ownership was gender neutral. March third. Mary Jane, daughter of Sarah Simpson, a free negro.'

'They seem to be pointing out the racial status of each of the births.'

'Remember, it was a society based on race and social status. This woman was free. Hold on. March fourth. Emily Roylance, daughter of Jeremiah and Dolores Roylance, Perseverance Estate.'

'That's them. It's the same names as in the notebook. But there's no race attached to the name.'

Jayne sighed. 'Strange. I was certain this was your African ancestor.'

'Who, Dolores Sharpe? Emily's mother?'

Jayne nodded. 'But there is no racial status for the child. If Dolores had been black, it would have been stated on the register. The child would have been named as a mulatto. We can check Henry's birth records too.'

She typed in the name, and the same information appeared in the same copperplate writing.

July 18. Henry Roylance, son of Jeremiah and Dolores (nee Sharpe) of Perseverance Estate.

'The clerk even gives her maiden name on this record.'

'She definitely was Emily and Henry's mother.'

'Finally, we can check the marriage.' Jayne typed in a new address for Select Caribbean Marriages, 1591 to 1905. Again, one hit was recorded.

January 2, 1804. Jeremiah Roylance, Merchant, to Dolores Sharpe, Housekeeper.

'It seems Jeremiah married one of his servants.'

'And that's probably why she didn't return with them to England. An ambitious family like yours had to be accepted in polite society, but if your wife was a former servant then that would have been difficult.'

'So we still don't know who my African ancestor was?'

'I'm afraid not.'

'So I'll have to face the red-tops this weekend with nothing to say except "I'm going to find out who it was"?'

'I'm sorry once again. I tried my best, but the timing was just too short.'

Rachel took a cheque out of her pocket and looked at it. 'I believe we had an agreement, Jayne. No results, no payment.'

'That's right.'

Rachel tore the cheque into little pieces, letting them drift down slowly to the Persian carpet. 'I'll thank you to leave my house immediately. I do not want to see or hear from you ever again.'

CHAPTER FIFTY-NINE

Thursday, August 22, 2019
Wickham Hall, Cheshire

Outside in her BMW, Jayne banged the rim of the steering wheel in frustration. She didn't care about the money, but she hated letting her clients down. Sir Harold Marlowe deserved whatever he got, but ultimately she had failed.

A wave of anger spread through her body and the words of her mother came whispering in her ear.

'You'll never be a success, Jayne, you're too weak ever to do well.'

She knew it was stupid to think like this. Her mother had many problems, most of which she laid at Jayne's door. She recognised her mother's constant demeaning of her had driven her on to succeed at whatever she did. Failure wasn't something she experienced often and, when she did, she hated the feeling it gave her.

All the police vehicles had already left, just leaving their tyre traces in the gravel of the drive.

She sat for five minutes, alone in the car and alone in her world.

She couldn't face going home to an empty house, not with that graffiti daubed on her kitchen walls. She switched on the engine and listened as it purred over, like a cat waiting to pounce.

It was time to go and see Robert and Vera. Time to be around people who cared for her, and to be as far away from here as she could.

Putting the car in gear, she glanced back at Wickham Hall. It no longer looked beautiful to her.

All she could see was the sweat, blood and tears of thousands of slaves whose hard graft and sad lives had helped to create it.

CHAPTER SIXTY

Thursday, August 22, 2019
Buxton Residential Home, Derbyshire.

When Jayne arrived, Robert and Vera were sitting in their usual places out in the garden, a completed crossword lying between them. They weren't talking, just enjoying the silence and each other's company.

'Hi there,' said Jayne.

'Hello, lass, we weren't expecting you till tomorrow.'

'I just thought I'd come to visit you early.'

Robert's eyes narrowed and he looked her up and down. 'Is everything okay?'

'I'm fine, Robert.'

'I've known you since you were five years old, Jayne Sinclair. When you say "I'm fine," it means you're not. What's up, lass?'

There was no hiding anything from Robert. She told him everything that had happened that morning and her research into the family history of the Marlowes.

It was Vera who spoke first. 'You did the right thing, Jayne. I don't care who they are, these people should be ashamed of trying to frighten you. All for their family honour! Pah, they have no family honour.'

She gave her stepmother a big hug. 'Thanks, Vera, I knew I could rely on you.'

'But it's not about them, is it, Jayne?' Robert asked shrewdly.

She shook her head.

'It's about the feeling you failed, isn't it? You let down a client, didn't solve the problem?'

'How did you know?'

'I know you, lass. You've always been the same. Like your mother – driven, unhappy with second best. It's one of the things I love about you.'

She bent down and gave Robert a hug too until he said, 'Now, don't go all soppy on me, Jayne Sinclair.' When she had stood up, he continued speaking. 'Let me have a look at the research? I have a couple of thoughts that may help.'

She opened up her laptop and clicked on the case file. While she chatted with Vera, Robert pored over the notes, checking them against the family tree. He couldn't read Emily Roylance's notebook, so Jayne explained the contents to him.

'Well, lass, I think you were right to look at the mother, she was the obvious choice. But there's one other possibility you should check.'

'Who's that?'

'Charles Carruthers. If there were no children from the Marlowe family, and none from Henry Roylance either, then it strikes me that the African ancestor must have come from somewhere else. And

273

the one obvious location is the union between Emily and Charles, which produced the child Royston Marlowe – or to give him his real name, Liberty Carruthers.'

Jayne thought for a moment. 'I think you're right, Dad.' She took the laptop and checked the Wikipedia entry for the Carruthers family of Liverpool. 'Listen to this.' She began reading the article out loud.

'"James Carruthers was a prominent Liverpool clergyman who, along with his two sons, Charles and Ebenezer, was at the heart of the anti-slavery movement in Liverpool. James was born into a Quaker family and at the age of 22 was sent overseas to Barbados in the Caribbean to spread the word of God, particularly amongst the African slaves in that area. He clashed repeatedly with the estate owners and managers, criticising their inhumanity and the treatment of the slaves under their control repeatedly in three pamphlets published after 1807. After the Bussa's rebellion of 1816, many of the planters ostracised him, banning their workers and slaves from attending his church. He returned to Liverpool in 1817, rapidly making contact with William Wilberforce and becoming one of his right-hand men in the north of England."

'"Little is known about his personal life. He married once in 1798 in Barbados, to one Madeleine Clay. His two sons were active in the anti-slavery movement. Charles, a fine orator, was based in Manchester and died in 1834 before realising his dream of freeing the slaves. Ebenezer moved to Africa, becoming one of the first missionaries to that continent. He died in 1843 from beriberi. James Carruthers died in his bed in Liverpool in 1850, leaving his estate and his collection of pamphlets, speeches and notes to his daughter. These were passed to Liverpool Council in 1903 and can now be found in the International Slavery Museum on the waterfront."'

She paused for a moment. 'Those are the records we saw, Robert. I think you're on to something.'

She quickly opened up the Barbados birth records again. 'I wonder if Charles was born in Barbados?' she wondered aloud.

She typed 'James Carruthers' into the search field. There were two hits in different handwriting.

September 18, 1801. Charles Carruthers, son of James and Madeleine (nee Clay), Negro, of St George's Parish.

April 1, 1803. Ebenezer Carruthers, son of James and Madeleine (African) of this parish.

Jayne sat back. 'It was staring me in the face all the time. The African ancestor came from Charles Carruthers' line when he married Emily and she gave birth to Liberty.'

'It's always there in the documents, lass, you just have to look in the right place.'

'What are you going to do, Jayne?' asked Vera.

'Do? With the information, you mean?'

Vera nodded. 'You owe your client nothing. They haven't paid you for your work and asked you never to get in touch with them again.'

'I don't care about the money, Vera, you know that.'

Jayne thought for a moment. What was the *right* thing to do?

After a few minutes she opened up her laptop and composed an email.

Dear Rachel,

Please find attached the following birth certificates. As you can see, Charles Carruthers' mother was listed as being Negro in the birth registry. As Liberty Carruthers was adopted by Henry Roylance as his son and renamed Royston Marlowe, he is most likely your African ancestor.

Please use this information as and when you wish.

I do not want any payment from you for my work, nor do I want to be involved with your family in any way at all. In my opinion, you all deserve each other.

If you are so inclined, I would donate the money to the charity of your choice.

Best regards,

Jayne Sinclair

She clicked the send button and sat back. 'You know what, I won't be unhappy if I never see that client again.'

Robert held up his newspaper. 'I think that's going to be hard, Jayne, she's just signed a Hollywood contract to play Superwoman.'

The picture was of Rachel Marlowe dressed in a tight blue leotard and red cape.

'Well, that's one picture I won't be going to see.'

Vera announced, 'The tea round's due any minute. I'll get the packet of chocolate digestives from my room.'

As Vera left, Robert said, 'You can't win them all, you know. Sometimes you just have to accept that some problems can't be solved.'

'I know, Robert. I'm learning.' In the back of her mind, she was thinking about the divorce. 'Sometimes we just have to accept that things can't be perfect, but they work out in the end.'

'Aye, lass, now here's Violet with the trolley. Can you get me a tea with three sugars and a milky coffee for Vera?'

She stood up and bent over to kiss the top of his head. 'You're so sweet, Robert.'

'I know, it's the sugar in the tea.'

THE END

HISTORICAL NOTE

As ever with the Jayne Sinclair novels, the subject matter came along by chance. I was visiting Liverpool one day to research something else and found time to pop in to the International Slavery Museum at the waterfront. It's a fascinating and unique place to visit, dealing as it does with the slave trade and Britain's unique place in it.

At the same time I became aware of the work of University College London on the Legacies of British Slave Ownership and its searchable database. I typed in the area where I live and immediately three names came up of a family who were slave owners and received money from the British government to free their slaves in 1834.

Additionally, I had recently received an updated version of my DNA results from Ancestry and a story began to form.

Further researches in Hansard, the transcript of Parliamentary debates, led me to some fascinating exchanges regarding the Emancipation Act, which came into force in 1834. As ever, the two sides of the argument talked at odds with each other. One argued about the moral inequity of slavery, and the other for an economic imperative and property rights. In the middle of the debates from 1832 to 1833, the attitude of the British government changed. From advancing a loan of fifteen million pounds to assist the planters in freeing their slaves, this became an outright purchase of their freedom with a fund of twenty million – the equivalent of seventeen billion pounds in today's money. It was then nearly 40 per cent of the government's yearly budget and, amazingly, the UK only finished paying the loan back in 2015!

Almost 6,000 people from all over the British Isles received the money from a special department created to disburse it. Politicians, churchmen, businessmen, factory owners, traders, ship owners and countless ordinary people were paid a sum for freeing their slaves. Many small families, sometimes owning only one or two slaves, received funds. Larger amounts were paid out too; the Gladstones of Liverpool and of prime ministerial fame, received over 93,000 pounds for 2,039 slaves, the equivalent of twelve million pounds today.

The government department responsible for disbursing the money kept meticulous records. To check if your family were slave owners or received money, it is possible to search the database at https://www.ucl.ac.uk/lbs.

The documents here are incredibly detailed, recording who received the money, why they received it and how many slaves they received it for. Each slave having a particular price dependent on their age, sex, and skills. They were property and were priced as one would price a wagon or a plot of land.

The slaves themselves, of course, received nothing. Instead, they had to work for the next five years as apprentices and were then freed with no land, no work and no money. Most stayed on their estates to work for a pittance, or migrated to the uncolonised interior of the island of Barbados to farm poor land.

There were also the physical results of slavery, seen throughout the United Kingdom. Some of the most important buildings built at the time came about through being funded from the profits of slavery.

Even after slavery was abolished in 1834, the money received for the freeing of the slaves often went into constructing the railways, canals, factories, banks and insurance companies that created the Industrial Revolution and the great Victorian age.

The precise impact of this huge disbursement of money has still to be assessed. Did it finance the second stage of the Industrial revolution? The jury is still out.

The speeches in this book come from research into the pamphlets of the time and the various meetings held by both pro- and anti-slavery groups.

The anti-slavery societies were particularly effective at creating a mass movement against slavery through a series of petitions, which effectively forced the British government to revise its position.

But in my opinion, there was also a realisation by the large planters that the system was no longer economically viable when the source of slaves was cut off by the banning of their capture and trade in 1807. When this was combined with revolts by the slaves themselves in Barbados in 1816, Guyana in 1824 and Jamaica in 1833, the end of slavery in the British colonies was unstoppable, if not inevitable.

One last thank you to Peter Calver, founder of LostCousins, www.lostcousins.com, for his advice, especially on the DNA aspects of the novel. The science and possibilities of this new technology are changing constantly. I am very grateful to Peter for taking the time to explain the latest developments to me. Any errors in the history or the science, however, are my own.

Finally, the last word must go to a former slave. In this case, an American – Frederick Douglas – writing in 1845.

'No man can put a chain about the ankle of his fellow man without at last finding the other end fastened about his own neck.'

The impact of slavery is still being felt on British society today as it was in the eighteenth and nineteenth centuries. We have yet to come to terms with it.

If you enjoyed reading this Jayne Sinclair Genealogical Mystery, please consider leaving a short review on Amazon. It will help other readers know how much you enjoyed the book.

If you would like to get in touch, I can be reached at www.writermjlee.com. I look forward to hearing from you.

Other books in the Jayne Sinclair Series:

The Irish Inheritance

When an adopted American businessman who is dying of cancer asks her to investigate his background, it opens up a world of intrigue and forgotten secrets for Jayne Sinclair, genealogical investigator.

She only has two clues: a book and an old photograph. Can she find out the truth before her client dies?

The Somme Legacy

Who is the real heir to the Lappiter millions? This is the problem facing genealogical investigator Jayne Sinclair.

Her quest leads to a secret that has been buried in the trenches of World War One for over a hundred years – and a race against time to discover the truth of the Somme Legacy.

The American Candidate

Jayne Sinclair, genealogical investigator, is tasked to research the family history of a potential candidate for the Presidency of the United States of America. A man whose grandfather had emigrated to the country seventy years before.

When the politician who commissioned the genealogical research is shot dead in front of her, Jayne is forced to flee for her life. Why was he killed? And who is trying to stop the details of the American Candidate's family past from being revealed?

The Vanished Child

What would you do if you discovered you had a brother you never knew existed?

On her deathbed, Freda Duckworth confesses to giving birth to an illegitimate child in 1944 and placing him in a children's home. Seven years later she returned for him, but he had vanished. What happened to the child? Why did he disappear? Where did he go?

Jayne Sinclair, genealogical investigator, is faced with lies, secrets and one of the most shameful episodes in recent history as she attempts to uncover the truth.

Can she find the vanished child?

The Silent Christmas

In a time of war, they discovered peace.

When David Wright finds a label, a silver button and a lump of old leather in a chest in the attic, it opens up a window onto the true of joy of Christmas.

Jayne Sinclair, genealogical investigator, has just a few days to unravel the mystery and discover the truth of what happened on December 25, 1914.

Why did her client's great grandfather keep these objects hidden for so long? What did they mean to him? And will they help bring the joy of Christmas to a young boy stuck in hospital?

The Sinclair Betrayal

In the middle of a war, the first casualty is truth.

Jayne Sinclair is back and this time she's investigating her own family history.

For years, Jayne has avoided researching the past of her own family. There are just too many secrets she would prefer to stay hidden. Then she is forced to face up to the biggest secret of all; her father is still alive. Even worse, he is in prison for the cold-blooded killing of an old civil servant. A killing supposedly motivated by the betrayal and death of his mother decades before.

Was he guilty or innocent?

Was her grandmother really a spy?

And who betrayed her to the Germans?

Jayne uses all her genealogical and police skills to investigate the world of the SOE and of secrets hidden in the dark days of World War 2.

A world that leads her into a battle with herself, her conscience and her own family.

Printed in Great Britain
by Amazon